UNDER THE ASHES
MURDER AND MORELS

A BURR LAFAYETTE MYSTERY

UNDER THE ASHES

MURDER AND MORELS

A BURR LAFAYETTE MYSTERY

Charles Cutter

MISSION POINT PRESS

Published by Mission Point Press
2554 Chandler Rd.
Traverse City, MI 49696
(231) 421-9513
www.MissionPointPress.com

ISBN: 978-1-958363-63-8
Library of Congress Control Number: 2023900496

Manufactured in the United States of America
First Edition/First Printing

For
Cash and Topper

"Hell hath no fury like a woman scorned."

—William Congreve,
The Mourning Bride

CHAPTER ONE

Nick sent the soup back, not that there was anything wrong with it.

"You are so fussy," Molly said.

He swirled his wine. The thin, red pinot noir ran up and down the glass.

"Please don't send the wine back," she said.

He took a sip, set his glass down and stood. "I'll be right back."

Molly looked at him. "You don't have to go. They'll do just fine if you leave them alone."

"Maybe it will be hot enough when I get back." He pushed back his chair and left.

The waitress, a tan college-age woman in the green and white uniform of the Arboretum, rushed back to their table. "Is everything all right, Mrs. Fagan?"

Molly smiled at her. "Everything's fine. Nick had to go to the car for a minute. He'll be right back."

The waitress started off.

"When you bring it back, make sure it's too hot to eat."

The waitress nodded.

"Ask Rudy to make me a martini," Molly said. She set her glass down. "Never mind, I'll ask him myself."

Molly made her way through the tables to the bar in the back of the Arboretum, every table full on the Saturday night of Memorial Day weekend. She had long legs that looked longer in her heels, maybe a little too fancy for Harbor Springs, but she liked the way she looked with bare legs, cream heels and a belted sapphire dress that ended nicely above her knees. It was barely spring here, fifty degrees and a northwest wind, but it was sunny, and Molly didn't care if she was hurrying summer.

She sat on a stool at the oak bar and looked over at the lounge full of resorters waiting for their tables. There was a black baby grand across the room.

The Arboretum was nothing fancy on the outside, just a yellow, single-story block building with a flat, tar-paper roof covered with gravel, which was only important because killdeer nested there every spring. The patrons insisted the birds be protected, which annoyed Sammy Fairley, the owner, but was probably good for business. The walls were covered in floral wallpaper with big, gaudy, orange and yellow and pink flowers. There were potted trees and shrubs everywhere.

One of the trees had a string of Christmas tree lights, the old-fashioned kind. Big bulbs — red, blue, green, yellow, orange, and white. The kind that didn't blink.

Rudy stood in front of her and smiled. A big smile full of the biggest, yellowest teeth Molly had ever seen. She found a cigarette in her purse. Rudy lit it for her.

"Did Mr. Fagan go out to the car again?"

Molly nodded.

"He just won't let it rest."

"No, he won't," Molly said.

"That's why it's such a great radio station."

Molly thought there were other ways to make it a great radio station, but she didn't say anything.

"The usual?" he said.

She looked over at the baby grand. "Is Hoagy playing tonight?"

Rudy nodded.

"Do you think he'll take requests?"

"As long as it's not *Stardust*."

"Would you ask him to play *Heart and Soul*?"

"He's in the kitchen with Cat."

Molly took a twenty out of her purse and set in on the bar in front of Rudy.

"I don't think it's easy being Hoagy Carmichael, Jr." Rudy picked up the twenty and disappeared through the double doors to the kitchen.

Molly Fagan was tall, all of five ten, over six feet in heels and looked like a dancer. She had shoulder-length black hair, green eyes, a thin nose and full lips. She liked pink lipstick, and if her teeth were a little crooked, no one cared.

Rudy came back smiling his yellow-toothed smile.

It was all she could do not to turn away again.

"A very dry, very dirty gin martini on the rocks. With Bombay Sapphire. Like your dress," he said.

She nodded.

Rudy filled a rocks glass with ice. "There's a guy that comes in here, drinks exactly the same thing. Big-shot lawyer. Or at least he was. He's got an old sailboat in the harbor."

"Really," Molly said, not really interested.

"Supposed to be a great trial lawyer. Or at least he was," Rudy said again. He poured two generous shots in the glass then he picked up the vermouth.

"Half a capful," she said.

Rudy poured half of the capful in the glass and threw the rest in the sink. He filled the rest of the glass with olive juice then speared four big cocktail olives with a toothpick and stirred the drink. He set the martini in front of her.

Molly took a sip.

"Nick sent the morel bisque back again, didn't he," Rudy said, not asking.

Molly took a big swallow, then nodded.

"Was there anything wrong with it?"

She shook her head.

"I hope Cat doesn't find out." He smiled at her again.

Molly wished Rudy would leave. She could go back to their table, but she didn't want to sit by herself, and there was no way to know how long Nicky would be gone.

"I hope he isn't here for the veal morel. Cat used the rest of the morels in the bisque."

"Nicky brought his own morels."

"One of these days, he's going to push her too far."

The Arboretum was a fine restaurant, maybe the finest in northern Michigan, for one reason. Cat Garrity, the seventy-year-old chef. No one could get along with her, but she knew how to cook. Busboys, waiters, waitresses, dishwashers, prep cooks all lived in fear. Somebody got fired at least once a week. She had freckles, fiery red hair, and a wicked smile. Sammy had to give her a piece of the restaurant to keep her, and she acted like she owned all of it.

Cat was famous for her morel bisque. It had a cream and sherry base and a hint of something that made it tangy. No one really knew what it was, and Cat wasn't telling. She was the diva of the kitchen, and it was all Sammy could do to keep the peace, which meant keeping Cat happy, which was a full-time job.

Rudy started to say something just as Hoagy Carmichael, Jr. made his entrance from the kitchen. He had on a blue blazer and gray linen pants. The diners clapped. Hoagy sat at the grand piano and lit a cigarette.

Rudy took him a scotch. He smiled at Molly and played *Heart and Soul*.

* * *

Earlier that day, Nick had walked down the two-track with a mesh bag. He'd taken 131 south, past Boyne Mountain, and turned on a dirt road, then another and another, each one narrower and more rutted than the one before. He ended up on No Grouse Road and parked in a patch of ferns next to a two-track. He had listened to the radio for ten minutes, switching from station to station. It had been all he could do to turn off the radio. He had to go to the station, even if was Saturday, but he was going to get away even if it was only for an hour.

Nick took his mesh bag and started off into the woods. The woods smelled green, like new leaves and wet soil. There were a few hemlocks, but mostly tall, old maples, oaks, beeches, and ash. They were just starting to leaf. They'd keep the woods in the shadows until October, but today the sun crept past the leaves and lit the woods. There were a few spring beauties, adder's tongues, and bloodroots still blooming where there had been early sun, but the forest floor was covered with trillium: bright-white, three-petaled flowers.

But he wasn't there for the trillium. He was there for the morels, but he usually found them where the trillium grew, especially under the ashes.

The black morels were long since gone and it was late for the whites, but it had been a cold and rainy spring, and he thought he might find some here. He hadn't told anyone about this place, not even Molly, and he'd made sure no one had followed him. He knew it was silly to be so secretive, but morels were morels.

He wandered through the woods scuffing up last year's leaves, brown and rotting. It would be another month before there was enough green to cover them up. He found a few whites under a beech tree, a few more near a towering white ash, but not enough for a meal. Cat had told him she'd make him veal morel tonight if he brought his own morels. Nick loved Cat's morel bisque but there was nothing like her veal morel.

It had been a bad season for morels. Too dry, too cold, then too wet, but it had warmed up two days ago and rained last night. Nick thought that, if there were ever going to be morels this year, it would be today.

He found a few more at the edge of a clearing, but he didn't have anywhere near enough. He found a patch of morels, but he thought they looked like false morels, poisonous but not fatal. He picked one of the mushrooms and broke off a stem. It came off cleanly at the cap. The stem of an edible mushroom ran up under the cap, covering the stem like a hood.

The edible morels — the black, white, and caps — had a light, nutty flavor that made them the most sought-after mushroom on the forest floor. They were only found in old forests in the north and not very often there. They couldn't be commercially grown. A once-a-year delicacy with snob appeal. And scarce. Especially this year.

Nick kept going. He was half a mile off the two-track when he found what he was looking for. The ash grove was where he'd remembered it, down in a small valley with ferns in a clearing to the north.

And there they were. White morels. A few clumps of spongy, light-brown mushrooms. Some almost six inches. He pinched them off at the base and put them in his bag, careful not to pack them tightly.

After he filled the bag, he walked back and forth through the patch, swinging the mesh bag ever so slowly. Just enough to release the spores so that, weather permitting, he could harvest them again next year, if no one else found this place.

Nick left the patch, found the two-track and hurried back to the car. He had a few stops to make before dinner.

* * *

Nick came back into the Arboretum. He said something to Sammy at the maître d's station who handed Nick the phone and stepped away. Nick made a call, then sat down at their table. He looked over at Molly, still at the bar. She tried to ignore him, which was impossible, then took herself and her martini back to their table. He stood and pulled out her chair for her.

Nick was almost a head shorter than Molly, even with his lifts. He had a full head of black hair, styled every week, dark eyes, square jaw, and a dazzling smile. He was short, very short, and he liked tall women.

"Sorry, baby," he said.

Molly wiped the lipstick off the rim of her glass but didn't say anything.

"I had to hear what Jack was saying in and out of the stop set."

"Did you have to do it now?"

"It's what I do."

She put her drink down. "It's Saturday night. You just had the biggest month in the history of the station. Can't you just leave it for a couple of hours?"

"Jack can't keep his mouth shut."

"He is a disc jockey."

"No one wants to hear about Bayview's production of *Fiddler on the Roof.*"

She brushed a stray hair off her face. "It's what's important here." Sometimes it was hard to be with Nick.

"Not to our audience."

Nick had signed on WKHQ-FM two years ago. It had the biggest signal in northern Michigan – Traverse City to the Bridge to Cheboygan to Grayling and back. No one here had ever heard anything like it. It was far and away number one in audience and billing, but his competitors hated him, his employees were terrified of him, and some days Molly didn't like him much either.

She put her drink down. "You fired him, didn't you?"

Nick didn't say anything.

"That's why you were on the phone."

Nick started to say something, but Molly cut him off. "If you have something to say that our listeners would rather hear than Michael Jackson or Mick Jagger, say it. Otherwise, shut up and play the music." She lit another cigarette.

"Do you have to smoke?"

Molly put her cigarette in the ashtray and took a sip of her martini. "Who's coming in?

"Tommy." Nick waved at the smoke.

"Who else did you call?"

Nick started to say something, but the bisque came, steaming, and too hot to eat.

They each ordered a Caesar. Molly ordered the planked whitefish and another martini.

"I'd like the veal morel," Nick said.

"I'm sorry, Mr. Fagan, but we don't have any more morels," the waitress said. Molly dug into her purse and took out a plastic bag. "Nick found these this morning."

"I'll take them to Cat and see if she'll make it," the waitress said. She reached for the bag.

"I'll take them to her," Molly said.

The waitress left.

Molly turned to Nick. "Did you have to fire him on a Saturday night?"

"Baby, you know I love you."

"You love KHQ more."

"No, I don't."

"Who else did you call?"

"No one."

Molly didn't believe him, but Nick's bisque had cooled enough to eat, and he started in on it.

It was creamy, with pieces of chopped morels, butter, sweet vermouth, salt and a pinch of nutmeg.

"This is spectacular," Nick said.

"I'll be right back." Molly got up and took the bag of morels into the kitchen. She found Cat looking over the shoulder of one of the prep cooks, a terrified young man who couldn't have been more than eighteen.

"That's not how you do it." Cat yanked the knife out of the cook's hand and started chopping. "Like this." She tossed the knife at him. He missed it, and the knife fell to the floor. Cat turned to Molly. "There's no customers allowed in here."

Molly smiled at her. "I was hoping you'd make veal morel." She tried to hand the bag to Cat, but she turned her back on her and walked away.

Molly caught up with Cat at the salad station. "Please, Cat. Just this once."

"It's not just this once, and you know it. And I'm sure it's a trade. The answer is 'no.'" She turned her back on Molly again.

"I'll take care of it, Mrs. Fagan," Sammy said. Fairley was a thin, sallow man, short with a black comb-over. His smile took up most of his face. He was always smiling, which annoyed Molly, but she thought it was probably helpful for the owner — who was also the maître d' — to have a smile that wouldn't quit. He took the bag from her and shooed her out of the kitchen. She walked back to their table.

The waitress brought their salads.

Molly drank her martini and picked at her salad. "Who else did you call?"

Nick looked up from his salad. "No one."

She still didn't believe him. The waitress cleared their salads. Molly ordered a glass of Chardonnay then took something out of her purse. "I'm going to check on the veal morel." She disappeared into the kitchen then came back to their table. The waitress brought Molly's whitefish and Nick's veal morel.

Cat served the whitefish on a maple plank, topped with thick lemon slices, dusted with paprika and served inside a ring of Duchess potatoes.

She cut off a piece. It flaked on her fork.

"How is it, baby?"

"It's almost too pretty to eat."

Nick cut a slice of the veal medallion and soaked it in the morel sauce. Cabernet, cream, flour, butter, and morels, mostly morels. The Cabernet gave the morels more bite than the bisque and added a touch of cherry and vanilla.

"This is heaven," Nick said.

"If you cut me a slice of your beloved veal, I'll know you really love me."

It was all he could do to cut a slice for her. He passed her a fork full of veal.

She shook her head "no."

"I thought you wanted some."

"I was testing you."

Nick ordered the Baked Alaska for dessert. Baked Alaska wasn't his favorite, but he thought fire always made things taste better.

Molly ordered a glass of sauvignon blanc. She thought it was probably too early in the season for it, but it was Memorial Day weekend, and it was a short season.

The waitress poured the brandy on the Baked Alaska and lit it. Nick took a deep breath and blew out the flames. His face turned red, and he fell face first into the Baked Alaska.

CHAPTER TWO

Burr woke up when his sunglasses slipped down his nose and the sun got in his eyes. He sat up and pushed the glasses back up his nose. Zeke woke up, wagged his tail and tipped over Burr's beer.

"Damn it all."

The beer ran around the radio, down onto the cockpit sole, down the drain, and into the harbor.

"Zeke, that's a waste of a perfectly good Labatt. But it was a little warm."

The aging yellow Lab looked up, then put his head back down.

Burr went down below, took another Labatt from the icebox and climbed the companionway stairs back to the cockpit. He propped himself back up and opened the beer. He took a swallow and looked past the Spindrift's stern toward the boats tied up at the main dock.

It was the Fourth of July in Harbor Springs, the biggest holiday of the year. The city was packed and the marina was full. Burr had a buoy in the harbor, but he'd managed to get a slip for Spindrift at the Harbor Springs Marina for the weekend.

A smile and a hundred-dollar bill go a long way. Mostly the hundred-dollar bill.

A soft wind drifted in from the southwest. It was seventy-five and mostly clear. A cloud covered up the sun every now and then. Burr smelled the lake, the sand, and the cedars on Harbor Point.

He ran his hand along the top of the gunwale in the cockpit — silky, varnished mahogany with four coats of Valspar. It would need a light sanding and another coat before the summer was over. He looked over at the teak deck, nicely oiled, which gave it a wet look, then past the tiller and the boom crutch to the stern.

"Smooth as silk."

Spindrift was a 1940 wooden, thirty-four-foot cutter-rigged sloop. The cabin leaked when it rained, and the hull leaked all the time, which is why he had two bilge pumps. Spindrift had a main salon, forward cabin and a midships galley. She was no *Kismet*, his last boat, but then *Kismet* was about five miles due west, on the bottom of Lake Michigan in two hundred feet of water, more or less.

He looked up at the mast, all forty-seven feet of it. Spindly pine held up by more rigging than on a clipper. He took a swallow of his Labatt then laid back down.

"Mr. Lafayette?"

She has a pretty voice, but it's never good when someone calls me 'Mr. Lafayette' when I'm on a boat.

Burr hid behind his sunglasses and pretended he hadn't heard her.

"Mr. Lafayette?" she said again.

Burr ignored her.

This never works.

"Mr. Lafayette?"

Burr thought it might be worth a try to pretend he wasn't Burr Lafayette, but he hadn't had much luck with that either.

I give up.

"Yes?" he said, not turning his head.

"Did I wake you up?"

"No, I was just enjoying the day by myself."

"My name is Molly Fagan. I'm sorry to bother you, but the harbormaster said I'd find you at slip 62."

A hundred dollars should buy a little privacy.

"Could we talk for just a minute?"

Her voice was clear and musical, maybe a bit husky. Burr still hadn't turned his head, but he did like her voice.

She must be an alto.

"Please, Mr. Lafayette. It's important."

"It's a holiday weekend. Can't it wait until next week? Or the week after?"

"No, it can't."

Burr looked at her. She was a vision of beauty. Black hair tied back in a ponytail. Green eyes with a hint of pink lipstick. Tan legs in a khaki skirt that didn't leave much to the imagination.

If I'd known she looked like this, I'd have looked at her right away.

"Yes?" he said.

"Mr. Lafayette, I need your help."

"I'm on vacation."

"My husband is dead, and I need your help."

Burr ran his hands through his hair, front to back.

"Mrs. Fagan, I'm very sorry for your loss, but I'm afraid I can't help you." He took a swallow of his Labatt.

Burr wasn't a criminal lawyer, but he'd been dragged into more than one murder trial, and he had no intention of being dragged into another one.

"He wasn't murdered. He had a heart attack."

"That's something," Burr turned down the radio.

"I beg your pardon?"

"Mrs. Fagan, I'm sorry for your loss," he said again, "but I'm afraid I can't help you."

"You don't even know what I want."

He looked back up at her. "That's right, but if it involves someone who's dead, I can't help."

"It's about life insurance."

At least it's not about murder.

"I really do need your help." She grabbed a piling, climbed aboard and sat down next to Zeke. She scratched behind his ear. He put his head in her lap.

Traitor.

"Who's this?" she said.

"Zeke," Burr said. "His name is Zeke."

"He's a handsome fellow." She scratched behind his ear again.

He'd purr if he could.

Molly looked at Burr. "My husband and I were at the Arboretum over Memorial Day. He had a heart attack there and died a week later."

"Did he fall into the Baked Alaska face first?"

I shouldn't have said that.

"It's one thing to not want to help me. It's quite another to make fun of me."

"I'm sorry, Mrs. Fagan. I eat there all the time. I couldn't help but know."

She sat up straight and put her hands in her lap.

That diamond is as big as a cocktail olive.

"We had life insurance, but the insurance company is refusing to pay. That's all the money I have. The rest is tied up in the business."

Burr turned down the radio.

"We got him to the hospital in time, but Nicky had high blood pressure." She looked at Burr looking at her diamond and put her hand over it. "From all the stress. He had a massive heart attack a week later and died in the hospital."

"Mrs. Fagan, in addition to all the other things I don't know anything about, I also don't know anything about life insurance. There's a library somewhere full of what I don't know about life insurance."

"Sammy told me you were the best lawyer he knew."

Thanks, Sammy.

"And he told you I had a boat here."

Burr had helped Sammy with a food poisoning case and a liquor commission violation. Sammy was always short on cash and let Burr eat and drink for free.

Molly ran her hand along the smooth-as-silk gunwale. "I thought it would be …" she looked around "… newer."

"I'm sorry, I don't do insurance work."

"Just what kind of work do you do?"

"I'm an appellate lawyer." Burr took another swallow of his beer. "Now."

Burr had been the head of the litigation department at Fisher and Allen, one of Detroit's best firms. He had been, perhaps, Detroit's best commercial litigator but had given it up, as well as his marriage — but not his son — over a client. A provocative client. A striking woman almost young enough to be his daughter. Over an affair that hadn't turned out. He'd been a fool and he knew it. After the year it had taken to ruin the prior twenty, he moved to East Lansing and started an appellate practice. Complicated, esoteric litigation punctuated with oral arguments that had made him famous in select legal circles. It had gone swimmingly except for the money part, which, of course, was the most important part.

Molly leaned back against the gunwale. "An appellate lawyer." She scratched Zeke's ear again. He yelped.

"I'm so sorry, Zeke," she said.

"I'm sure I can help you find someone who can help you."

Molly looked at her hands but didn't say anything.

With a diamond like that, there must be some money somewhere.

Burr picked up his beer, thought better of it and put it back down. He looked across to the other dock. Boaters, resorters and tourists everywhere.

Molly didn't say a word. Neither did Burr. They sat there, the two of them.

Molly cracked her knuckles.

That's attractive.

"Can I get you something to drink?"

She looked up at him. "I'll have a Labatt."

She has good taste.

Burr went below and brought her a beer.

The widow Fagan sipped her beer. "Thank you."

"Sure."

"It's very nice sitting here."

"It is."

Molly reached past Zeke and turned up the radio. *No One is to Blame* was playing. "What station is this?"

"106 FM."

"What do they play?"

"Top 40."

She smiled. "Aren't you a little old for Top 40?"

"I love Top 40."

Burr had grown up on Top 40 when CKLW was king. Now in his late forties, he was six feet tall, or at least he had been, and still lean. He had sky-blue eyes, straight white teeth, and a hawk nose, sunburned and peeling from Memorial Day to Labor Day. His hair was still the color of an acorn in autumn. He had a few gray hairs, but he pulled them out as soon as he found them. His eyebrows arched when he spoke.

Molly turned the radio down. "That was my husband's station."

"He owned KHQ?" Burr ran his hands through his hair, front to back.

"Do you do that when you're nervous?"

Only when I'm flummoxed.

He turned the radio back up. KHQ played *Beat It.*

CHAPTER THREE

"Your Honor, I object," Burr said, standing.

"Of course you do," Judge Nickels said. "Please sit down."

"Your Honor, this is —"

The judge cut him off. "Please sit down," he said again.

"Your Honor, I have —"

"Mr. Lafayette, sit down."

Burr stayed on his feet.

"Sit down this instant or I will have Mr. Drum remove you."

The bailiff, a beefy man in a Charlevoix County deputy's uniform — dark brown shirt, tan slacks and a sidearm — smiled at Burr. He had a gap between his front teeth, big enough to drive a truck through.

Burr sat slowly, his new client to his left. Burr had told her to dress in black like the widow she was, but the touch of pink lipstick took it all back.

"That wasn't so bad, was it?" Judge Nickels said.

Burr didn't say anything. He tapped his pencil, then stopped and looked at it. It needed sharpening, and he'd worn the eraser down to nothing.

If Eve were here, I'd have a brand-new Number 2 yellow pencil. Fortunately, she's not here.

"I asked you a question, Mr. Lafayette."

"I didn't think it called for an answer." Burr tapped his pencil again.

"Stop that blasted tapping and answer my question."

"Would you please repeat the question, Your Honor?" Burr smiled sweetly at Judge Nickels.

The judge took off his bifocals. He rubbed his eyes, opened them, and looked at the woman in the witness stand. "Would you please excuse us a moment, Miss Watson?" The judge turned to Burr.

"Mr. Lafayette, I have been a judge in Charlevoix County for the past thirty-seven years. I am about to retire. I don't feel any need to go out in a blaze of glory." He tapped his glasses on his desk. "I had hoped to leave quietly. This is my last case … which I had hoped would settle. It's life insurance. Life insurance cases always settle." He tapped his glasses again. "But you don't seem to be a man willing to compromise." He put his bifocals back on and lined his eyes up so he could look down at Burr. "Are you willing to compromise?"

Burr stood. "Your Honor, I have an objection."

Judge Nickels shut his eyes again.

Perry Nickels, a slight man of sixty-nine, had a pale, narrow face and a nose barely big enough to hold up his glasses. His hair had retreated halfway back on his head, but it was still black, which made him look younger than he was. He looked like his robe was about to swallow him. He spoke softly.

Judge Nickels opened his eyes. "Can we settle this? Right here and now?"

Julian Flintoff stood. "Your Honor, I have no interest in settling this whatsoever."

"God help me." Nickels looked over at Julian Flintoff, counsel for the Dearborn Life Insurance Company. Flintoff was tall, thin and severe. He had a thin face to go along with his thin nose and thinning hair. His eyes were too close together and he scowled when he spoke. Actually, all he did was scowl, ranging from a simple frown to a look of pure hatred.

"Your Honor, I have an objection," Burr said again.

"For mercy's sake, sit down. Both of you."

Burr and Flintoff sat.

They were in the courtroom of the Honorable Perry Nickels, judge of the Charlevoix County Circuit Court. Nickels was the only circuit judge in Charlevoix County, so sparsely populated that it barely warranted a circuit court.

The county building that housed the courthouse was between Lake Michigan and Round Lake, two blocks up from the Villager, which had Labatt on tap. Burr found that bars were useful landmarks in figuring out where things were, especially courthouses.

The county building was a two-story building with a flat roof except for the entrance, which was two stories fronted by four white Roman pillars that looked like they had come from the set of *Ben-Hur*. Judge Nickels' courtroom was strictly "modern bureaucrat." Beige walls, dull linoleum, tired

18

varnish on the tables and the pews. And windowless. Judge Nickels' raised desk gleamed in the fluorescent lights.

Burr was here with his new client trying to collect on her late husband's life insurance policy, which the Dearborn Life Insurance Company had no intention of paying.

Molly had persuaded Burr to help her collect on the policy. It wasn't because she was so pretty or because Burr loved Top 40 radio. It was because Molly had said she'd pay him out of the proceeds of the policy. Her husband had life insurance, and he had died.

What could be easier?

Except that it wasn't.

"Your Honor," Burr said.

Judge Nickels shrank into his robe. "All right, what is it?"

Burr stood again. "Your Honor, the witness has no firsthand knowledge of when the life insurance premium check was received."

Flintoff shot to his feet. "That's not true. Miss Watson just testified that the check was received after Mr. Fagan died."

"Your Honor," Burr said, "the witness testified that she was told that the check was received after Mr. Fagan died. 'She was told.' That, Your Honor, is hearsay and is inadmissible."

"That is exactly what happened, Your Honor," Flintoff said.

"Your Honor, if that is, in fact, what happened, Mr. Flintoff should produce someone from the Dearborn Life Insurance Company who knows what happened firsthand."

"Nonsense," Flintoff said. "This is an evidentiary hearing."

"Your Honor, it doesn't matter when Mr. Fagan died. All that matters is that the check was received during the grace period."

Burr walked up to Nickels, pulled down the cuffs of his baby blue pinpoint oxford shirt, which didn't need pulling down, then straightened his red tie with the little black diamonds that didn't need straightening. He put his hands in the pockets of his thousand-dollar, tropical-wool charcoal suit with the chalk stripe, now a little threadbare. He looked down at his cordovan loafers with the tassels, perennially in need of polishing. He rocked back and forth, heel to toe. All was as it should be.

"Your Honor, this is indeed an evidentiary hearing, which is precisely why any evidence Mr. Flintoff wants to offer must follow the rules of evidence."

"We can easily have someone from the company testify," Flintoff said, scowling.

Burr turned to Flintoff. "Then I suggest you do it. Because Miss Watsons' testimony is hearsay."

Nickels banged his gavel. "Stop it, both of you. In the interest of time, I'm going to allow the testimony of Miss Watson."

Burr walked back to his table. "In the interest of justice, her testimony is inadmissible," he said, more or less to himself.

"I heard that," the judge said.

Burr sat and looked at the judge. "I beg your pardon."

"We've only just met," Nickels said, "but you are already the most contentious lawyer I've ever had the misfortune to have in my courtroom. Thank God my time here is almost over."

"Amen to that," Burr said, *sotto voce*.

Nickels ignored him. "Mr. Flintoff, where were we? From the beginning, please."

It was Flintoff's turn to approach the bench, his scowl not quite so severe.

That's probably as close to a smile as he gets.

"Your Honor, as you know, we are here in the matter of a certain life insurance policy issued by my client, the Dearborn Life Insurance Company. Nick Fagan was the insured. Molly Fagan, his wife, was the beneficiary. The premium was due on the first of May of this year and was unpaid. Mr. Fagan died on the second of June. His wife applied for his death benefit on the fifth of June, which, unfortunately, the company cannot pay because the policy was no longer in force."

It was Burr's turn to leap to his feet. "Your Honor, that is patently untrue." Burr glared at Flintoff. "And you know it." Burr turned back to the judge. "Your Honor, all life insurance policies have a thirty-day grace period. If the premium is paid during the grace period, the policy is in full force and effect. The policy never lapsed. It is a matter of state law."

"That's not what happened," Flintoff said.

"That is exactly what happened," Burr said. "The premium was paid on the twenty-first of May. Her unfortunate husband died twelve days later. The policy was in force. The Dearborn Life Insurance Company is trying to welch on its obligations. After all, the company was paid its premium, one of many paid over the life of the policy."

Judge Nickels smiled weakly at Burr. "I think that's why we're here, Mr. Lafayette." Then to Flintoff, "You may continue."

Flintoff stood to the right of Pearl Watson, a tiny woman who could barely see over the railing of the witness stand. Her feet barely touched the floor. She had ivory skin, big brown eyes, and full, round lips framed by a black bob with bangs.

She looks like a doe.

Flintoff looked at his witness. "Miss Watson, you are the employee of the Dearborn Life Insurance Company in charge of this file? Is that right?"

"I am in charge of disputed claims."

Flintoff nodded. "Did Mr. Fagan's policy lapse on May 1?"

"Objection," Burr said. "There is a grace period, a thirty-day grace period in Michigan."

Flintoff gave Burr a withering look. "I withdraw the question."

He looks so much more like himself when he's scowling.

Flintoff started over. He tried smiling at Miss Watson, but it came off as a sneer. She cringed. "Miss Watson, assuming for the sake of argument that Mr. Fagan's policy was in force on the day he died, the second of June, when did the company receive the check?"

"June third."

"What happened to the check?"

"We kept it."

"Did you deposit it?"

"No."

"Why not?"

"The check was received after the policy had lapsed and after the grace period had ended. In these situations, we keep the check, but we don't cash it. There's no reason to cash a check on a lapsed policy."

Flintoff scowled.

A smile was too much to hope for.

Flintoff walked to his table and returned with a file. He took out a light blue check. "Your Honor, I'd like to introduce this check into evidence. It's the check that supposedly paid the life insurance premium."

"Let me see it," Judge Nickels said.

Flintoff passed him the check. Nickels looked at the front, then the back. "Mr. Lafayette, would you like to examine this?"

This isn't going to be good.

"Yes, Your Honor." Burr walked up to the aging judge and took the check. It was dated May 21. Burr turned it over. There was no endorsement on the back and no marks showing that it had been deposited. He turned it back over.

There was a date stamp on the front of the check that read *"Received June 3."*

Damn it all.

Burr held the check in both hands. "Your Honor, I object to the introduction of this document into evidence."

Judge Nickels rolled his eyes. "What on earth for? It's just a check."

"Your Honor, there is a date stamp on this check that I believe is fraudulent."

"How could you possibly know that," the judge said.

"Because this check was mailed on the twenty-first of May. It doesn't take two weeks for the post office to deliver a check from Charlevoix to Dearborn, no matter how slow they are."

"I'm going to admit this into evidence as Plaintiff's Exhibit One. You can fight about the date stamp on your own." Nickels held his hand out to Burr. "Hand me the check."

Burr looked at the check.

If I rip this thing up, we'll be done with this fiasco.

"Don't even think about ripping up that check. Hand it to me, Mr. Lafayette."

They've probably got a copy.

Burr handed the check to the judge, who handed it to Flintoff, who handed it to the tiny witness.

"Miss Watson, is this the premium check received by the Dearborn Life Insurance Company?" Flintoff said.

"Yes."

"Thank you, Miss Watson. A few minutes ago, you testified that the check was received on the third of June. How do you know that?"

"Because of the date stamp on the check."

"Would you please show us the date stamp?"

She looked at the check, then put the tip of her tiny index finger on the date stamp. "Here it is."

"And just to be sure, please read the date."

"June third."

Flintoff took the check and set it on the railing in front of the witness. "Thank you, Miss Watson."

Flintoff took a step toward the judge. "Your Honor, Dearborn Life Insurance Company clearly received the premium check after the policy lapsed." Flintoff looked back at Burr. "And, after the grace period expired."

Flintoff took a step toward Judge Nickels. "Your Honor, while it is unfortunate that the check wasn't received in time, the law is clear and the date stamp on the check is clear. This policy lapsed, and there is no death benefit due. Nothing could be clearer."

"Persuasive, Mr. Flintoff. Very persuasive." Nickels rubbed his nose. "Anything further?"

"No, Your Honor." Flintoff walked back to his table and sat.

"Mr. Lafayette, is there anything else you could possibly say?"

Burr walked up to the witness and picked the check up from the railing. He made a point of studying it, then showed it to her. "Miss Watson, did you put the date stamp on the check yourself?"

She sat back in the chair, which almost swallowed her. "I beg your pardon?" Her doe eyes fluttered.

Burr put his finger on the date stamp. "I said, did you mark this date yourself?"

"No."

"Who did?"

"Someone in the mailroom."

"Someone in the mailroom," Burr said. "Who in the mailroom?"

Pearl Watson cleared her throat. "I don't know."

"You don't know," Burr said. "Then how do you know someone in the mailroom stamped the check?"

"That's how we do it."

"But you don't know who."

"No."

Flintoff stood. "I object, Your Honor. Counsel is harassing the witness."

"Your Honor, I am merely trying to establish the evidentiary chain, which is nothing if not broken. There is no way to know when the check was received, which is exactly why I made my hearsay objection."

Nickels put a hand to his forehead. "If I had only retired before you got here," he said, muttering.

"I beg your pardon?" Burr said.

"Nothing," Nickels said. "Mr. Flintoff, your objection is overruled. But you," Nickels said, pointing at Burr, "you mind your manners."

Burr smiled insincerely. "Yes, Your Honor." He turned back to Miss Watson.

"How much was the life insurance policy on Mr. Fagan?"

Pearl Watson turned another shade of red.

She doesn't look like a pearl now.

"Miss Watson, do you know how much Mr. Fagan's life insurance policy was for?"

"No. No, I don't think so."

"I think you do."

"Objection," Flintoff snarled.

"Mr. Lafayette, what did I tell you about your manners?"

Burr sighed, for effect. "Your Honor, Miss Watson testified that she had been assigned this file. She knows the questionable policies of the Dearborn Life Insurance Company when it comes to honoring its obligations. She knows the date of the check, the date stamp of the check, and what the mailroom does when a check comes in." Burr put his hands in his pockets. "But she doesn't know how much the policy was for. How can that be?"

The judge shut his eyes again. He opened them and shooed his hands at Burr.

Burr turned back to the witness. "Miss Watson, Mr. Fagan was insured for one million dollars. Surely you knew that," Burr said, not asking.

She didn't say anything.

"Surely you'd agree that's a lot of money."

She still didn't say anything.

"Miss Watson, did you know Mr. Fagan?"

"No."

"Good. You do know something." He went on before Flintoff could object or Nickels could scold him. "Have you ever heard of Mr. Fagan?"

She didn't say anything. Again.

"Miss Watson?"

She nodded.

"How had you heard of him?"

"He is … was … a famous disc jockey."

"Really? Where?"

"In Detroit."

"In Detroit. In fact, before Mr. Fagan started WKHQ, he was the biggest name in Detroit, wasn't he?"

"Objection. Calls for an opinion. And it's irrelevant."

"Sustained."

Thank you for that.

"Your Honor, nothing could be more relevant. I submit that Mr. Fagan was so well known and his policy was for such a large amount that someone or someones purposely held the premium check to avoid having to pay off the policy."

"This is preposterous." Flintoff wrung his hands.

"Your Honor," Burr said. "The Dearborn Life Insurance Company has been accused of far worse. And convicted of it."

"I won't hear of this." Flintoff stomped his feet.

"Your Honor, the Dearborn Life Insurance Company is a privately held, for-profit company. What they don't pay out in claims, they keep."

"Your Honor, I insist that this be stricken from the record."

I think there's steam coming out of his ears.

"That's enough, Mr. Lafayette. Do you have any further questions for Miss Watson?"

"No, Your Honor." Burr walked back to his table and sat. Molly leaned over. "Thank you, I think," she said, whispering.

Nickels looked down at the witness. "You're excused."

Pearl Watson climbed down from her chair, her pearl complexion restored.

Nickels found his wrist in the folds of his robe and looked at his watch. "It's almost lunchtime." The judge looked at Flintoff. "Do you have any more witnesses?"

"No, Your Honor."

"Delightful." Then to Burr, "Do you have anything further, Mr. Lafayette?"

"Yes, Your Honor."

"That's what I was afraid of." The judge stuck out a hand, palm up, and curled his forefinger like a mother calling her disobedient children. "Approach the bench. Both of you." Burr and Flintoff lined up in front of the hungry judge. Burr brought a black three-ring checkbook with him. Flintoff brought his disagreeable disposition. Nickels looked down at Burr and the checkbook. "Do I dare ask what that is?"

"Your Honor, this is the WKHQ checkbook. I'm going to introduce it into evidence and have the business manager testify that she wrote the check and mailed it."

"That won't prove a thing," Flintoff said.

Burr set the checkbook in front of Nickels. He opened it to a paper-clipped page, with three check stubs, then turned it to Nickels so he could read it.

"Your Honor, this is the checkbook of the radio station. There are three checks to a page and three matching stubs."

Burr cringed. The Lafayette and Wertheim checkbook looked just like this, and that checkbook caused him nothing but trouble, mostly because there was never any money in it.

I have to get through this.

"Your Honor, here is the check stub for the life insurance check. Number 1989. There are checks before this one and checks after. They were all cashed on a timely basis." Burr turned and pointed to a pretty young woman in the back of the courtroom. "Melissa Warren, the business manager, is going to so testify."

"That won't prove a thing," Flintoff said.

"Your Honor, in Michigan, there is a presumption that when a check is mailed via the post office, it is presumed to be received on a timely basis. That legal presumption, together with Miss Warren's testimony, and the prior bad corporate behavior of the Dearborn Life Insurance Company and its principal shareholder, Max Tallman, will carry the day."

"This is hogwash," Flintoff sputtered.

"This is lunchtime," Nickels said.

"Your Honor, I would like to submit my proofs." Burr pulled his cuffs down again.

"I can't believe my ears," Flintoff said.

Molly cracked her knuckles, then leaned toward Burr. "Do you think you're pushing him too far?"

"No."

You haven't seen anything yet.

Nickels sat. And sat. And sat.

Finally, he took off his glasses. "Mr. Lafayette, none of your statements or your evidence are a matter of record." He slammed the checkbook shut.

Flintoff lost a little of his scowl.

"But if I live past lunch, you have the right to introduce them. However, the two of you, particularly you, Mr. Lafayette, have worn me out."

Burr straightened his tie.

"Please, Mr. Lafayette, I beg you, stop with your personal grooming."

Burr put his hands in his pockets.

"Thank you." Nickels looked at Flintoff, matching his scowl. "As for you, if Mr. Lafayette can prove what he says, and I think he just might be able to, I am not going to grant your motion to dismiss the case. There will then be a trial, with a jury no doubt. And you may well lose."

Flintoff started to say something, but Nickels raised his hand. "Don't say another word."

Burr started to say something, but Nickels waved him off and folded his hands. "This is what we're going to do. I'm going to have my lunch. Then I'm going to take a nap. I don't care what the two of you do this afternoon, but we're not going to do it here. Is that clear?"

Burr nodded.

"Mr. Flintoff?"

Flintoff didn't say a word.

"I'll take that as a 'yes.' Sometime in the next thirty days, the two of you are going to settle this case. And if you don't, you're not going to like what happens. Either of you."

Nickels took off his glasses and glared at Flintoff. "Especially you."

CHAPTER FOUR

"I can't believe you just said that," Eve said.

"It's time," Burr said.

"Say it again. Just to make sure I heard you right."

"You know what I said."

"I can't believe my ears." Eve tugged at her earring.

I must have really gotten to her this time.

Eve McGinty sat in one of the navy-blue leather wing chairs facing Burr. Eve McGinty had been his longtime, long-suffering legal assistant at Fisher and Allen. When he'd resigned, he'd begged her to stay at the firm, but she insisted on following him to East Lansing. She said she wanted a house with full sun so she could have a perennial garden. Burr thought there must be full sun somewhere in the Detroit area.

She was short with chin-length brown hair, a pretty smile, and a mouthful of white teeth. She had a few wrinkles around the corners of her mouth and a hint of crow's feet. She favored gold hoop earrings, big ones, which she tugged at when she was nervous, which was now.

Eve was the brains of the operation, and they both knew it. Burr knew that she didn't like being a year older than him and, no matter how old he was, she was always going to be a year older.

"Come on, say it."

Burr shook his head, then reached into his desk for a brand new, extra sharp No. 2 Yellow Pencil. He tapped it on his desk and put it down, then ran his hands through his hair, front to back.

"You must really be nervous about this," Eve said.

"I beg your pardon?"

"You only do that when you don't know what to do."

"Like your earring?"

"I deserved that," she said.

Burr looked over at Zeke, snoring softly, on the matching navy-blue leather couch on the other side of his office. Burr didn't care much about things, but he loved his boat, his Jeep and his office. It had oriental rugs, over hardwood floors, oak paneling, and cherry furniture. There were cars smaller than his desk, and he'd made sure his couch was long enough for him to stretch out and take a nap, when Zeke wasn't using it. But what he liked most was the walk-in cedar closet. He could never find anything, but he liked to step inside and smell the cedar.

"I'm sorry," Eve said. "Let's start over."

Burr swiveled his swiveling chair and looked out at downtown East Lansing, six stories below, the campus to his left, fraternity and sorority houses to his right, bars and restaurants in front of him. He liked it here. It just hadn't quite turned out, so far.

"It's fine if you don't want to look at me. Just tell me."

Burr turned back around.

"Don't do that thing with your hair and I won't tug my earring."

Burr put his hands on his desk, then picked up his pencil.

"Don't do that either."

Burr looked up at the painting of ducks landing in Walpole Marsh on a cold fall day. It was all browns, grays, and blacks except for green heads on the drake mallards.

I wish I was there.

He looked back at Eve. "We need to fix the elevator," Burr said.

"What did you say?"

"You heard me."

"One more time, please."

"We need to fix the elevator."

Eve jumped to her feet and twirled around. Her skirt came up to her thighs.

"Stop looking at my legs."

Burr stood and started out. "That's it."

"I'm sorry. I was celebrating," Eve said. "I can't believe you're finally going to get the elevator fixed."

Burr sat. "It's time." Burr tapped his pencil.

"Why now?"

"Because it doesn't work right."

"It hasn't worked right since we moved in."

Burr had bought the six-story Masonic Temple building when he'd moved to East Lansing from Detroit. It was beat up and nothing like his office in the Renaissance Center. He had the building redone when he was still flush with cash. He'd put his office and living quarters on the top floor. It was a narrow, brown brick building with no parking. The bottom floors were to be a restaurant and shops, offices above, but it hadn't quite worked out that way. Redoing his building had almost broken him, especially the elevator. Burr hated elevators. He didn't trust them. He didn't like being shut in a box and not being able to do anything about it. He didn't like pushing the buttons. The doors never closed when he wanted them to or opened when he wanted them to. And they were slow.

The elevators at the Renaissance Center had been too fast, and they were in glass tubes that ran up and down on the outside of the building, which made him nervous.

He and Zeke took the stairs, which was fine by him.

"Why now?" Eve said again.

"Because we don't have any tenants except Scooter and the bookstore."

"Scooter is on the first floor, and the bookstore is on the mezzanine. They don't need an elevator."

"I'm going to lose this building if we don't get some tenants. No one is going to move in here if the elevator doesn't work right. At least most of the time."

Burr took an envelope out of his top desk drawer and handed it to Eve.

"Certified. Return receipt requested." Eve scrunched her nose. "You never accept these."

"The mailman tricked me."

Eve studied the envelope. "East Lansing State Bank. Do they mean it this time?"

Burr nodded.

"They're finally foreclosing?"

Burr nodded again.

"How late are you?"

Burr tapped his pencil.

"How late?"

"Six months."

Eve scrunched her nose again. "That's nothing for you."

"Please call the elevator guy and have him come fix it once and for all."

"How are you going to pay him?"

"I'm just about to settle Molly's case."

"You said Flintoff never settles."

"He's going to this time."

"Just because the judge told him to doesn't mean he will."

"This time he will. Burr has him." Jacob Wertheim, the Wertheim in Lafayette and Wertheim, stood in the doorway with perhaps the fattest file Burr had ever seen. Jacob was in his mid-forties, shortish but not short, medium build, prominent nose, olive complexion and hair like steel wool with a touch of gray.

Jacob sneezed.

Here we go.

"You know I'm allergic to dogs." Jacob looked over at Zeke, who woke up from his nap and wagged his tail.

"You're not allergic to dogs," Burr said for the umpteenth time.

"I'm allergic to that one." Jacob sneezed again.

Burr walked to the wing chair reserved for Jacob and brushed it off.

"Sit down and tell me what you found."

"Not while he's here." Jacob pointed at Zeke.

"Zeke is taking a nap. Come over here and sit down."

Jacob sighed, made a show of how put upon he was, then sat in his wing chair.

When Jacob sat down, Eve got up from hers. "I think I'll leave you two to settle the case with the man who never settles." She walked out.

It's a miracle anything ever gets done around here.

"Where are we with the research?" Burr said.

"Don't you mean where am I with the research?" Jacob said.

Jacob had also been a partner at Fisher and Allen, and despite Burr's objection, he had insisted on following Burr to East Lansing. When it came to legal research and appellate briefs, Jacob was without peer, which was exactly why Burr needed him. But Jacob had two of the worst qualities a litigator could have. He abhorred conflict and was deathly afraid of public speaking.

Jacob picked a dog hair off his slacks. "The real question is, where are you with Flintoff?"

How could he possibly see a dog hair of a yellow Lab on khaki slacks?

Jacob had on a khaki summer suit, a starched white shirt, and a blue, green and pink striped pastel tie. Jacob was nothing if not natty. He dressed to the nines but spent almost all his time in the Lafayette and Wertheim law library but rarely saw anyone other than Burr, Eve, and, unfortunately, Zeke.

"Where are you with Flintoff?" Jacob said.

"Six seventy-five," Burr said.

"As in, six hundred and seventy-five thousand?"

Burr nodded.

"Good God, man. Take it."

"Take it before something goes wrong," Eve said from her desk in the reception area.

"How many violations has the Dearborn Life Insurance Company had with the Insurance Commission in the last two years?"

Jacob rummaged through his file and took out a piece of paper. "Nineteen."

"I can get more out of Flintoff," Burr said.

"You told me Flintoff said that was his final offer," Eve said.

"Why don't you just come back in here?" Burr said.

"Take the offer, Burr." Jacob twirled one of his steel wool curls.

Now he's nervous.

"Are you tugging at your earring?"

Eve ignored him. "I really think you should take this."

"Don't press your luck." Jacob said, twirling.

Burr tapped his pencil.

I've got to stop doing this.

"The Dearborn Life Insurance Company has a history of welching on their policies. You know it. I know it. The insurance commissioner knows it and, most importantly, Flintoff knows it. We don't have to get all of it, but there's more there."

"Are you doing this for Molly or for your massive ego?" Eve said.

Burr dialed Flintoff's number.

CHAPTER FIVE

Burr sat by himself at the defense table in Judge Clyde Striker's courtroom. He was the only one here, so far. As much as he liked courtrooms, he didn't like being in Charlevoix District Court. It was a step down from the Circuit Court, a bit on the dingy side and not nearly as up-to-date as Nickels'.

It could use a few white columns.

The big problem was his chair. It wouldn't stop wobbling, and the other two chairs at the defense table were worse.

Burr switched the chairs with the chairs at the prosecutor's table.

This is much better.

Not that Burr thought it was going to matter very much. Burr had gotten a collect call from inmate Molly Fagan last night, and this was going to be terrible.

Ten minutes later, a big man lumbered in. He was all of six-five and at least two hundred and seventy-five pounds. He had bushy brown hair to go with bushy brown eyebrows and a bushy brown mustache. His head was two sizes too big for the rest of him, which was something for a man of his size. His nostrils flared when he breathed. He sat across from Burr.

He must be the prosecutor.

The big man sat. His chair creaked, then wobbled. He wiggled in it. It wobbled again. He tried the other chairs. They both wobbled. He heaved himself back to the first chair, then looked over at Burr.

"You have my chair."

"I beg your pardon."

My guess is he makes sure all the defense chairs wobble.

The big man stood and pointed a thick, stubby finger at Burr's chair. "That's my chair." He started toward Burr.

"I have no idea what you're talking about," Burr said, who knew exactly what the prosecutor was talking about.

He started toward Burr just when Molly Fagan walked down the aisle, dressed in an orange jumpsuit, a woman jailer at her side. The big man backed up and sat. His chair wobbled.

Burr pulled out a chair for Molly. "I got here as soon as I could," he said.

She looked right through him to the big man. "You bastard."

"I am but a humble public servant doing my duty," he said.

She started toward him, but Burr took her arm. "Not now."

He still hadn't heard back from Flintoff, and now they were back in court.

"You have no idea what I've been through." She started at the prosecutor again when the bailiff said, "All rise. The court of the Honorable Clyde Striker is now in session."

We're already standing.

"Be seated."

The prosecutor glared at Burr. "I want my chair back."

Burr smiled at him and sat. Molly sat, but she didn't smile.

"You'll regret crossing the Great Oz." The big man sat.

The Great Oz?

"Mr. Oswald, I think we're here at your request," the judge said.

The prosecutor stood back up.

He's spry for his size.

"Phillip Oswald for the state, Your Honor."

"I know who you are, Oz. This had better be good."

Oswald ran a fat finger between his neck and collar. "Your Honor, we are here today in the matter of the murder of Nick Fagan."

"I thought he had a heart attack."

"He did, Your Honor. But he had food poisoning. That's what caused the heart attack."

Oswald looked at the judge as if he were talking to a child. "Your Honor, on the night of May 26 of this year, the defendant ..."

Burr stood. "Mrs. Fagan is not a defendant."

Judge Striker was about fifty. He had a goatee and looked like he hadn't missed too many meals. "Mr. Lafayette, do you have to start like this?"

"Your Honor ..."

The judge rubbed his goatee. "Mr. Oswald, please address Mrs. Fagan by her given name."

The prosecutor looked down at his puffy hands. "She'll be a defendant when I'm done with her."

"I heard that," the judge said.

Oswald started over. "Your Honor, my suspicions were raised after the untimely death of Mr. Fagan. He was in such good health, I couldn't fathom how he could die of a massive heart attack."

Fathom?

"My suspicions were raised, so I ordered an autopsy."

Burr turned toward Molly. "Did you know anything about this?"

"Nicky had high blood pressure but no heart problems. Not until that night."

Burr stood. "Your Honor, I object. The next of kin must be notified before an autopsy can occur."

"Not in the case of murder," Oswald said.

"Nick Fagan wasn't murdered."

Judge Striker looked up at the ceiling. "What's done is done. Continue Mr. Oswald."

"Your Honor …"

"Mr. Lafayette, I have noted your objection."

"Your Honor," Burr said, "there was absolutely no reason to arrest Mrs. Fagan. Mr. Fagan had high blood pressure. Mrs. Fagan hasn't been charged with a crime, and she's certainly not a flight risk."

Judge Striker looked at Burr. "Perry warned me about you." Then to Oswald, "you may continue."

"Your Honor, the autopsy showed that Mr. Fagan had eaten poisonous mushrooms. The mushrooms reacted with his system and caused him to have a heart attack."

Burr stood again. "Your Honor, it's well known that Mr. Fagan was an expert when it came to morels. He gathered them himself and gave them to the cook at the Arboretum, who prepared them. If he was poisoned, he poisoned himself. Which I highly doubt."

"Your Honor, may I please finish?" Oswald said.

"Sit down, Mr. Lafayette."

"Your Honor, the defendant, Mrs. Fagan, was seen in the kitchen tampering with the morels."

"She was most certainly not tampering," Burr said.

"Quiet," the judge said.

"Your Honor, Mrs. Fagan was seen in the kitchen of the Arboretum adding something to Mr. Fagan's meal."

"Even if all this is true, why in heaven's name would she want to poison her husband?" the judge said.

The Great Oz looked at the judge with an *I thought you'd never ask* look. "Your Honor despite the outward appearances, it seems as though there was trouble in paradise."

Judge Striker cocked his head.

"Mr. Fagan was about to divorce his wife. She murdered him so she could get the life insurance before he changed the beneficiary."

"How do you know all this?"

"I have been ably assisted by an able insurance investigator and an able insurance attorney." Oswald looked to the back of the courtroom.

Burr turned around. Pearl Watson and Julian Flintoff sat in the back row.

"I never settle," Flintoff mouthed at Burr.

* * *

Burr pulled a noodle from his clam linguine with red sauce. It was long, thin and freshly made in the kitchen at Michelangelo's. He held the noodle over the side of the table. Zeke sucked it in.

"Well done, old friend."

Burr twirled a forkful of the linguine and dipped it in the clam sauce.

He sat at his favorite table, the one with a view of downtown East Lansing and where he could see the door. Burr didn't like to sit with his back to the door. It made him nervous. He could have any table he wanted at Michelangelo's, and he wanted this one. Michelangelo's, his first-floor tenant, and just about his only tenant, was a better-than-average northern Italian restaurant, but it was deserted in August. The white tablecloths were crisp and the hardwood floor gleamed. The walls were white stucco above a chair rail, paneling below. It was hot and humid outside but just right in here.

Judge Striker had charged Molly with murder. Burr had gotten her out on bail, and Flintoff, true to form, had refused to settle and had no intention of settling. Ever. He was going to let Oswald try Molly for murder.

Burr poured himself another glass of Chianti, swirled his glass, and took a sip. "Zeke, it's opening up nicely." He fed Zeke another noodle.

"Damn it all, Zeke. Flintoff played me for a fool. And it worked."

"Mr. Lafayette, there are no dogs allowed in Michelangelo's."

Burr looked up at Scooter, the pasty, slightly round owner of Michelangelo's, not a drop of Italian blood in him and one of Burr's two tenants.

"Zeke and I are the only ones in here."

Scooter put his puffy hands on his hips. "The health department will close me down if they find out."

"Zeke is a seeing eye …"

Scooter raised his hand. "Please, Mr. Lafayette, we go through this every time you're here."

I want him to say it.

"Zeke …"

Scooter stood and put his hands on his hips. He didn't say a word. Finally, "All right. Zeke isn't a seeing eye dog and you're not blind."

Thank you.

"And that's my best bottle of Chianti."

Burr finished his wine and poured himself another glass.

"You're eating me out of house and home."

"Scooter, old friend, if I ate breakfast, lunch and dinner here from now until Christmas, you'd still be behind on the rent."

"I simply can't afford this."

"It was your idea to trade food and drink for rent."

"I didn't think it would go this far."

"Far? You're six months behind on the rent."

Burr fed Zeke another noodle. Zeke sucked it in, gracefully.

Scooter looked around to see if he could find someone who was equally horrified by the noodle-sucking dog.

"Scooter, you've got to actually pay your rent. In cash."

The tardy tenant cringed.

"Mr. Lafayette, there's no one in East Lansing right now." Scooter swept his hands around the empty restaurant, triumphant in his failure.

"If you don't pay me, I'm going to evict you."

"Then how will I pay you?"

Touché.

Burr drank half the wine in his glass. "You're in default."

The restaurateur turned pink over his pastiness. "Mr. Lafayette, you're the one who's in default."

"Me?"

"The elevator doesn't work."

Burr rolled his eyes. "You're on the first floor."

"This building has no tenants except for me and the bookstore."

"My office is here and so is my apartment."

"If you had more tenants, if you had *any* tenants, I'd have more customers. And you won't get any tenants until you fix the elevator."

* * *

When they reached Grayling, Burr tuned in KHQ. *What's Love Got To Do With It* came on, then *Man in the Mirror*. He listened to it all the way to Boyne City. Zeke, riding shotgun, slept all the way.

"The signal goes forever."

Zeke woke up when they started up the east side of Lake Charlevoix. He pawed at the window. Burr put the passenger window down and the aging Lab stuck his head out, ears flapping in the wind.

Five miles out of Boyne City, Burr turned into a paved driveway that wound through the woods, ending on a circle drive in front of a two-story cedar-shake house with a chimney at each end.

"Zeke, old friend, it's subtly overstated."

Molly met them at the door. She wore a black sleeveless top, jeans and sandals. She led them through a grand kitchen with a hardwood floor and granite counters. A calico cat on the counter eyed Zeke, who did his best to ignore it. Molly led Burr through a living room with a cathedral ceiling and floor-to-ceiling windows and out to a covered porch with white railings and a baby-blue beadboard ceiling.

They sat across from each other in white wicker chairs. There was a turret at the end of the north end of the house.

I love turrets.

"Can I get you something to drink?" Molly said.

I could really use a beer.

"I'm fine, thanks."

"I have Labatt."

"Thank you."

"I'll be right back."

If she lives in this house, she can definitely write a check.

Burr heard *Higher Love*. He looked up at the ceiling and found the speakers.

It was all Zeke could do to lay at Burr's feet. There were two cats in the kitchen, and Lake Charlevoix was only a hundred feet off, a sloping lawn away.

A light wind drifted in from the west, waves to match, not a cloud in the sky. Much better than August in East Lansing just north of Horton Bay, Hemingway Point off in the distance. A white plank dock ran out into the lake, a Boston Whaler rested on a lift alongside the dock.

"I know you want to go in, but we have important business."

Molly came back with Burr's Labatt and an iced tea.

Zeke walked to the edge of the porch and looked down at the lake.

"What does he want?" Molly said.

"He wants me to throw a stick in the lake. It's his second favorite thing."

"Second favorite?"

"He'd rather bring back a duck."

"This isn't about ducks and sticks." She grabbed the edge of the table with her hands. "This is just so terrible. Nicky's gone and now this. I could never murder anyone. Especially Nicky."

Another cat appeared, this one orange. It jumped up on the table and rubbed against Burr's beer.

Zeke sat up.

"This is Sweet Potato." Molly sneezed.

"Bless you."

"Nicky loved cats. I'm allergic, but I can't seem to get rid of them." She pushed the cat off the table. She sneezed again. "You've got to help me. First Nicky. Now this."

"I'm sorry."

"You're sorry? That's it. You're sorry? What do we do now?"

"We wait for the preliminary exam. You haven't been formally charged. We need to see if Oswald has anything other than allegations."

"They're lies."

This isn't getting us anywhere.

Burr took a swallow of his beer. "Was there any trouble between you and Nick. Was he filing for divorce?"

"No. We were trying to get pregnant."

"Nothing about a divorce?"

"Whose side are you on?" The cat jumped back up on the table. Molly pushed it off and sneezed again.

"Bless you."

"We had some money trouble."

Money trouble?

"We were always a little short. I couldn't understand how, with the station so successful."

"And?"

"We argued about that. Now, it's worse."

Burr stared at his Labatt. "Worse?"

"With Nicky gone, there's no money from the station."

"I thought he owned the station."

"He did. Part of it. The other owners paid his salary for two months after he died. Then they stopped."

Burr scratched Zeke's ear. The dog yelped.

"I have to figure out how to get some money," Molly said.

So do I.

* * *

Burr lay in bed. Zeke was next to him, his head on a pillow, snoring softly.

"Zeke, if I ever have another girlfriend, this will have to stop."

Zeke snored on.

"Not that there's anyone on the horizon."

With his living quarters right next to his office, Burr thought he must have the shortest commute in the universe. One door down. He quite liked his apartment. No lawn to mow or snow to shovel. A bedroom for him and one for Zeke-the-boy. A galley kitchen, a breakfast room, a living room with big windows, a dinette, and a partly covered balcony. Burr liked to sit under the canopy when it rained. Zeke liked to sit next to Burr, in the rain.

The rent from his tenants would easily pay for his office and apartment. If he had any tenants.

He lay in bed and listened. And listened. He heard his office door open and close. Ten minutes later, again. He made himself a cup of coffee, took a shower, and went next door.

He sat at his desk. He'd counted to nineteen when Jacob came in waving his check. He'd made it to thirty-one when Eve came in with her check. They sat across from him in their assigned seats, Zeke on the couch.

"Thank you for the check," she said, "but there's no money in the checkbook."

Burr swiveled to the window.

"Would you please stop swiveling," Jacob said.

Burr looked out the window.

"You know you're not to go near the checkbook," Eve said.

It's nicer out there than it is in here.

"We've got about another day of float before the other checks clear."

Jacob twirled his hair.

He needs to stop doing that.

Jacob stood. "I'm going to the bank."

"How much did you borrow?" Eve said.

Burr swiveled back around and looked at Eve. "I beg your pardon."

"You borrowed against your Jeep again."

Burr loved his Jeep, and he hated borrowing against it.

It was a black Grand Wagoneer with fake wood sides, the kind they didn't make anymore. He could get twelve miles a gallon if he drove forty-five, and he only had to add one quart of oil when he filled up. The rear window didn't work right, and he'd broken off the rear windshield wiper before it could break. The four-wheel drive worked. It had leather seats, and it always started.

"The payment book will be here in a few days. You might as well confess now."

How does she always know everything?

"Molly didn't pay you, and we're off to the races again with a client who hasn't paid us."

Burr swiveled back to the window.

CHAPTER SIX

Burr sat at the defense table, Molly to his left. Jacob beside her, Eve behind them in the first row of the gallery. Oswald across the aisle. Burr's chair wobbled. He'd gotten here as soon as he could, but Oswald had beaten him.

Damn it all.

It was a beautiful August day, partly cloudy, crisp north wind. It was the last of summer, and it smelled like freshly cut grass. That was all about to change. The first of the aspen had turned yellow.

Burr had left all that outside, and as much as he loved courtrooms, this one was stuffy by anyone's standards. He'd already started to sweat, the air-conditioning working in fits and starts.

Judge Striker sat at his raised desk. He rubbed his goatee. "We are here today in the matter of State of Michigan versus Molly Fagan. To determine if there is sufficient evidence to charge the defendant with murder."

The Great Oz stood, his belly hanging over his belt. "Thank you, Your Honor. I will show that the defendant, Molly Fagan, must be charged with open murder. At the trial, I will prove that she committed first-degree murder, and that she murdered her husband with malice aforethought."

Oswald pointed at Molly. "She killed her husband with poisonous mushrooms. She killed him. She intended to kill him, and she had a plan to kill him."

That just about sums up first-degree murder.

Oz beamed. "I will show —"

Judge Striker rubbed his goatee again. "Mr. Oswald this is a preliminary exam. Rather than tell us what you're going to do, why don't you just do it."

"Your Honor?"

"There's no jury." He pointed a pudgy finger at the empty jury box. "It's just me, Miss Meecher and Mr. Drum," he said, pointing at the court reporter, a slim young, world-weary woman who looked like she'd already seen everything twice, and the beefy bailiff. "And whoever you brought to testify."

Burr looked behind him at the prosecutor's witnesses, including Julian Flintoff.

We're only here because that slimeball doesn't want to pay the policy.

"Call your first witness."

The prosecutor nodded. "The state calls Rory Nettles."

What kind of a name is Rory?

A slight young man in a sincere blue suit at least two sizes too big stood in the witness stand. He had thinning blond hair, a long face, and not much of a jaw. The bailiff swore him in.

Oswald stood in front of Nettles. The prosecutor was so wide and Nettles so thin that Burr couldn't see him.

"Your Honor," Burr said, standing.

"Mr. Lafayette, how could you possibly have an objection. We haven't even started."

"Your Honor, I can't see the witness when Mr. Oswald stands there."

Judge Striker pointed to his left. "Mr. Oswald, stand over there. You're big enough to block the sun."

The Great Oz scowled but moved over. He still dwarfed the witness.

Laurel and Hardy.

Oz introduced the witness as the Charlevoix County coroner ran through his qualifications.

"Thank you, doctor. Would you please tell us the cause of death?"

"Mr. Fagan died of a heart attack, but the cause of the heart attack was food poisoning."

"And how do you know that?"

"I did an autopsy."

"And what did you find?"

As if you don't know.

"Mr. Fagan's liver cells were dissolved, and he had lyses."

"Lyses?"

"His blood cells were all white. The hemoglobin had been destroyed."

"What does that mean?" Oswald said.

The skinny coroner cleared his throat. "That's what happens with food poisoning. It eats away the body from the inside out. Gruesome, really."

"Thank you, Doctor Nettles. I have no further questions." The prosecutor lumbered back to his chair, which didn't wobble.

Burr approached the witness. He pulled his cuffs down, which didn't need pulling down then he reached for his tie.

Striker struck his gavel. "Mr. Lafayette, stop that silly preening. If you have any questions, ask them. Otherwise, sit down."

"Your Honor …"

"And don't start with Dr. Nettles' qualifications. I take judicial notice that Dr. Nettles is qualified."

Burr reached for his tie again, then stopped. He looked down at his shoes. His cordovan loafers with the tassels still needed polishing.

Maybe I really should stop this silly preening.

"Are you with us, Mr. Lafayette?" the judge said.

"Quite, Your Honor. I'd like to introduce the autopsy report of Nick Fagan as Defense Exhibit One." He walked back to the evidence table and came back with Nettles' autopsy. Burr turned to the coroner. "Dr. Nettles, you wrote this autopsy. Is that right?"

"I did."

"And what did you determine was the cause of Mr. Fagan's death?"

"Food poisoning."

Burr flipped through the report until he found what he was looking for. "Dr. Nettles, on page thirteen, you said that Mr. Fagan died of a heart attack."

"A heart attack caused by food poisoning."

"I object, Your Honor. We've been through this," the Great Oz said, sitting.

"Mr. Oswald, it is customary to stand when addressing the court," Judge Striker said.

"My knees, Your Honor."

Burr looked back at the prosecutor. "If you pushed yourself away from the dinner table sooner, you wouldn't look quite so much like a hippopotamus."

That brought Oz to his feet.

"What did you say, Mr. Lafayette?" the judge said.

Burr looked at the judge. "I said, 'I'm sorry his knees hurt so much.'"

"That is not what he said," Oswald said, turning red.

Striker rapped his gavel. "You may sit, Mr. Oswald. Continue, Mr. Lafayette."

"Your Honor, Dr. Nettles' autopsy said that Mr. Fagan suffered an apparent heart attack at the Arboretum. He was transported by ambulance to the hospital in Petoskey, then transferred to the hospital in Traverse City, where he had another heart attack. That one proved fatal." Burr held the autopsy in front of the coroner. "How did you come up with food poisoning as a cause of death."

The coroner turned a whiter shade of pale. "I got a phone call."

"A phone call?" Burr said. "From whom?"

"Him." Dr. Nettles pointed to the back of the courtroom.

"Dr. Nettles, please identify who you are pointing at."

"Him," the coroner said again, still pointing. "Mr. Flintoff."

I should have known.

"Did Mr. Flintoff, general counsel for the Dearborn Life Insurance Company, call and tell you to check for food poisoning."

"Not exactly."

"What exactly?"

"He suggested I check further."

"He suggested you check further."

The coroner's color was coming back, which Burr didn't think was a good sign.

"He said to check the organs and the contents of the stomach, which I did. And I found that ..."

Burr waved him off.

"You may finish answering, Dr. Nettles," Judge Striker said.

Nettles smiled at Burr. "I found that the heart attack was caused by food poisoning."

Nuts.

"I have no further questions," Burr said.

"You may call your next witness," the judge said.

"The state calls Paula Caruso," he said.

A short, plump woman in her sixties limped slowly up the aisle. She had jet black hair and a nose that covered most of her face.

She must dye her hair, but that nose is all hers.

Oswald helped her into the witness chair.

The bailiff swore her in and the prosecutor started in. "Ms. Caruso, would you please tell the court your occupation."

"I'm a mycologist," she said in a strong, clear voice.

"And what is a mycologist?"

"I study fungi, a group of organisms that includes mushrooms."

"Are you trained in this field?"

"I have a doctorate in mycology."

As if he didn't know.

Oswald beamed. "I take it you're familiar with morels, Dr. Caruso."

"I am."

"Are morels edible?"

It was Caruso's turn to beam. "They have an incredible flavor and texture. Smooth and supple. A little nutty."

"Dr. Caruso, I take it that morels are edible."

"Oh, yes."

"Are all morels edible?"

"Actually, no."

Oswald tapped his foot. "Dr. Caruso, would you please tell the court which morels are edible and which are not."

She took a deep breath. "White morels, black morels and caps … they're all edible. The false caps are poisonous."

"Is it difficult to tell them apart?"

"Not to the trained eye, but people are poisoned by false caps and beef-steak mushrooms every year."

Burr leaned over to Molly. She'd dressed just as he'd told her, a knee-length black dress, two-inch black heels, and no lipstick. Perfect for the widow *du jour*. "Could Nick tell the difference?"

"I don't know. We never talked about mushrooms."

"In your opinion, was Mr. Fagan poisoned by false caps or beefsteak mushrooms?"

The witness shook her head. "Based on the report I read, Mr. Fagan died of monomethyl hydrazine poisoning, which is found in high concentrations in Amanita mushrooms, but not in morels or beefsteaks. It dissolves liver cells and the hemoglobin in red blood cells."

"Excuse me, Dr. Caruso. In your opinion, what killed Mr. Fagan?"

"In my opinion, he died from eating Amanita mushrooms."

"I see." Oswald paced back and forth, as well as a 275-pound man could.

"Is there any significance to the fact that you believe he was poisoned by Amanita mushrooms?"

Dr. Caruso nodded knowingly. "It's highly unusual because Amanita mushrooms don't grow at the same time as morels or beefsteaks. They grow later in the year, well after the morels have come and gone."

"And what does that mean?"

"It means that Mr. Fagan could not have picked Amanita mushrooms when he picked the morels."

"So, his death could not have been an accident?"

Burr stood. "I object, Your Honor. The witness can't know if Mr. Fagan's death was accidental or not."

"Sustained."

"Your Honor," Oswald said, "Dr. Caruso has testified that morels and Amanitas don't grow at the same time. It follows that someone must have put Amanita mushrooms, picked last year, in Mr. Fagan's veal morel. It could not have been accident."

"Your Honor," Burr said, still standing, "if, in fact, Mr. Fagan was killed by poisonous mushrooms, it could have been an accident."

Oswald stamped his foot. "No, it couldn't."

Striker rapped his gavel. "The court notes that, for purposes of today's proceedings, Mr. Fagan died from ingesting Amanita mushrooms. It has no opinion as to whether his death was accidental or intentional."

Oswald scowled. "I have no further questions." He walked back to his table. "How's your chair?" he said, beaming at Burr.

Burr ignored the prosecutor and sat at his table, flummoxed again. He had no idea what to do. He started to tap his pencil. Eve reached over the railing and tapped him on the shoulder.

Judge Striker peered down at Burr. "Do you have any questions for the witness, Mr. Lafayette?"

I hate science.

Burr stood, not sure where to start or what to ask. He didn't trust anything he couldn't see or touch.

If I'm not careful, I'm going to make things worse.

He walked up to the witness. "Dr. Caruso, you have a Ph.D. in …"

Judge Striker cut him off again. "Mr. Lafayette, the court also takes judicial notice of Dr. Caruso's qualifications. There will be no questions attacking her qualifications or her credibility."

"Your Honor …"

"You heard me."

"What we have here is voodoo science," Burr said, not too quietly.

"I didn't hear that, Mr. Lafayette."

"There is nothing more relevant than voodoo science," Burr said, quietly this time.

"One more comment like that and you will find yourself out in the hall," Judge Striker said.

It wouldn't be the first time.

"Yes, Your Honor." Burr looked at the witness. "Dr. Caruso, you said that Mr. Fagan was poisoned by Amanita mushrooms. Is that right?"

"Yes."

"Isn't it possible that because Mr. Fagan picked the mushrooms himself, he, in fact, poisoned himself?"

The old mycologist scrunched her nose but didn't say anything.

"Dr. Caruso?" Burr said.

"I don't think so."

"You don't think so? How could you possibly know? Were you at the restaurant that night?"

Oswald stood. "I object, Your Honor. Counsel is taunting the witness."

"Watch your manners, Mr. Lafayette," Judge Striker said.

"Your Honor, I would like an answer to my question."

The judge looked down at the witness.

"It is my understanding that Mr. Fagan was an experienced mushroomer."

Mushroomer? Is that even a word?

"Your Honor," Burr said, "this is hearsay at its worst. The fact of the matter is that the witness has no idea who, if anyone, poisoned Mr. Fagan. He may have picked the mushrooms himself or got whatever he got from bad spinach."

"That would be impossible," Dr. Caruso said. "Amanitas don't grow at the same time of year that morels do."

Burr glared at her. "I didn't ask you a question."

"Yes, you did," Oswald said.

"Stop it, both of you," the judge said. "The court notes that the witness believes the victim died from eating poisonous mushrooms, source unknown at this point. Anything further, Mr. Lafayette?"

"No, Your Honor."

I'm going to have to find someone who knows something about this.

Oswald called Cynthia Showalter, a long-legged young woman who was working in the kitchen at the Arboretum that fateful night.

"Miss Showalter, did you see Mrs. Fagan at the Arboretum on the night of May 26?"

"Yes."

"And what was she doing?"

"I saw her put something in one of the entrées."

"Do you know which entrée it was?"

"It was the veal morel."

"And how do you know that?"

"We were out of morels so we didn't have veal morel on the menu that night. The only veal morel that night was one order made from morels brought in by a customer."

"So, Miss Showalter, you saw Mrs. Fagan put something in the veal morel."

"Yes."

"Just to repeat, you saw Mrs. Fagan put something in Mr. Fagan's entrée."

"I did."

"How did she seem when she was doing it?"

"She looked like she didn't want anyone to see her do it."

Burr stood. "I object, Your Honor. The witness can't know what Mrs. Fagan was thinking, and we certainly don't know that she put anything in anything."

Oswald sucked up his stomach. "Your Honor, I asked Ms. Showalter how Mrs. Fagan seemed?"

"That is my point precisely. Calls for an opinion."

Judge Striker rubbed his goatee.

I wish he'd quit doing that.

"Mr. Oswald, I agree with Mr. Lafayette."

Oswald turned a full circle toward the witness stand. "Miss Showalter, how could Mrs. Fagan possibly have access to the kitchen?"

"She came into the kitchen and said something to Cat, the chef. I saw her take a salt shaker out of her purse. Cat pointed at the entrée. It was still on the stove. I saw Mrs. Fagan lift the cover off. She made a show of salting it, but she had her back to everyone, and I saw her put something else in."

"Did she see you?"

"No, I don't think so."

"Thank you, Miss Showalter." The prosecutor turned to the judge. "Your Honor, this is clear evidence that Mrs. Fagan poisoned Mr. Fagan."

Burr jumped up. "It's not clear at all. If, in fact, Mrs. Fagan was in the kitchen, and if, in fact, she wanted to poison her husband, she would never do it for all the world to see."

"It's not your turn," Oswald said. The prosecutor threw out his chest as best as a man with a stomach like Oswald's could.

"It certainly is," Burr said. "I object."

Striker slammed his gavel. "I'm in charge here. Although you'd never know it." He looked at the prosecutor. "Mr. Oswald, while I appreciate your rhetoric, I'll decide what is or isn't clear. Is that clear?"

The Great Oz grumbled. "Yes, Your Honor."

To Burr, "As for you, Mr. Lafayette, you seem to lack the basic notion of turn-taking. Whoever raised you failed miserably in that regard."

It never took.

"Your Honor, it's not at all clear —"

Striker's gavel thundered. "Did you hear what I said?"

I think it comes from being an only child.

Burr nodded.

"Mr. Oswald, do you have anything further for the witness?"

"No, Your Honor." He walked back to his table and sat.

"Your witness."

Burr leaned over to Molly. "Did you go into the kitchen?"

She nodded.

"Why?"

"The first time, I took the mushrooms in, I had to convince Cat to make the veal morel."

"You went in twice?"

Molly nodded.

This is terrible.

"The second time was to check on his food and add the spices he liked. Nicky was so particular. I always checked his food."

"What on earth for?"

"It was easier than having him send it back."

"I wish you'd told me."

"I always checked his food and brought his favorite spices." She brushed a stray hair off her face. "You're supposed to be on my side."

The judge tapped his gavel. "Mr. Lafayette, it's your turn."

Burr ignored him. "What did you put in Nick's veal morel?"

"Salt."

"Salt?"

"And rosemary. Nicky liked rosemary."

Striker rapped his gavel again.

Burr stood and walked up to the witness. He had no idea who had done what in the kitchen, and he didn't want to make it worse than it already was.

"Miss Showalter, did you see Mrs. Fagan put Amanita mushrooms in Mr. Fagan's veal morel?"

Oswald bolted from his chair. "Objection, Your Honor. Asked and answered."

Now I've got him.

"Your Honor, Miss Showalter testified that she saw Mrs. Fagan put something in addition to salt in Mr. Fagan's veal morel. She didn't say what it was."

Striker looked up at the ceiling and pulled on his goatee, then looked at Oswald. "Mr. Oswald, I agree with Mr. Lafayette. Overruled."

Oswald sunk back into his chair.

Burr smiled at Oswald, then at Oswald's witness. "Miss Showalter, did you see Mrs. Fagan put Amanita mushrooms in Mr. Fagan's veal morel?"

"I saw her put something in. They could have been."

"You don't know what Mrs. Fagan put in her husband's food, do you?"

Cynthia Showalter didn't say anything.

"Do you?"

"No," she said quietly.

"No, what?"

Oswald lumbered to his feet. "Asked and answered."

"Sustained," Judge Striker said. "Mr. Lafayette, the witness said she didn't know if Mrs. Fagan put Amanita mushrooms in Mr. Fagan's veal morel."

"I have no further questions, Your Honor."

It's almost lunchtime.

"Call your next witness," Judge Striker said.

I've never known a judge to work through lunch. This can't be good.

"The state calls Matthew Tomlinson."

A fortyish man glided down the aisle. Medium height, medium build, tan face, straight nose, blond hair. He walked like an athlete.

He looks like a golf pro.

Tomlinson took the witness stand and flashed a brilliant smile.

And the homecoming king.

The bailiff swore him in.

Oswald got right to the point. "Mr. Tomlinson, you were Mr. Fagan's insurance agent. Is that right?"

"Yes."

"And you sold him the million-dollar insurance policy issued by the Dearborn Life Insurance Company."

"I did."

"And who was the first beneficiary?" Oswald looked back at Molly.

"Molly Fagan," Tomlinson said.

Oswald hitched up his pants. "Mr. Tomlinson, did Mr. Fagan come to see you about changing the beneficiary on his life insurance policy?"

"He did."

"Do you remember when?"

"In March of this year."

"I see," Oswald said, knowingly. "Do you know why he wanted to change his beneficiary?"

Tomlinson cleared his throat. "Nick told me he was going to get a divorce, and he didn't want Molly on the policy."

Burr cringed. "Is that true?"

Molly shook her head.

"So, Mr. Fagan was going to divorce his wife, and he didn't want her to be the beneficiary on his life insurance policy."

"That's what he told me."

The prosecutor looked at Judge Striker. "This is the motive, Your Honor,

Molly Fagan murdered her husband so she could collect on his million-dollar life insurance policy before he took her off it." Oswald hitched up his pants again. "I have no further questions, Your Honor."

"Mr. Lafayette?" Judge Striker said.

Burr walked up to the athlete. "Mr. Tomlinson, did Mr. Fagan give you a signed change of beneficiary form?"

The smile faded a bit. "He was murdered before he could give it to me."

"Answer the question, please."

Tomlinson looked at Oswald, then at Burr. "No," he said.

"So, for all you know, he changed his mind. Or maybe he never intended to change his beneficiary in the first place."

"I know what happened."

"But he never brought it back to you."

"No."

"Did Mr. Fagan tell you who he was going to change the beneficiary to?"

Tomlinson squirmed in his chair.

"Mr. Tomlinson?"

"No."

Burr took a step toward Striker. "Your Honor, this is mere speculation. Just like the rest of the prosecutor's silly claims. Mr. Fagan may have died from poisonous mushrooms. Mrs. Fagan may have put something other than salt in her husband's veal morel." Burr looked at Tomlinson, then back at the judge. "And now we're told that Mr. Fagan wanted to change the beneficiary on his life insurance policy, but he didn't do it." Burr put his hands in his pockets and looked down at his shoes. He rocked back and forth, heel to toe, then looked up at Judge Striker. "Gossamer and whimsy. That's all this is. Gossamer and whimsy."

The judge cocked his head. "What did you say?"

"Gossamer and whimsy," Burr said.

Judge Striker started to rub his goatee but stopped. "Do you have anything further?"

"No, Your Honor."

"Thank heaven for small favors," the judge said to no one in particular. He turned to the prosecutor. "Do you have any more witnesses?"

Oswald struggled to his feet. "No, Your Honor, but I'd like to address the court."

The judge tapped his watch. "It's almost lunchtime."

I knew he'd be hungry.

"Your Honor, the state has shown that there is probable cause that Molly Fagan murdered her husband, Nick Fagan." Oswald lumbered up to the judge. "It's clear that he was poisoned by Amanita mushrooms. Mrs. Fagan was seen in the kitchen of the Arboretum, putting the poisonous mushrooms in Mr. Fagan's veal morel. Finally, we know why she murdered him." Oswald looked back at Molly and sneered. Molly looked away. "Because he was taking her off his life insurance policy."

"Gossamer and whimsy," Burr said.

Striker banged his gavel.

Oswald cleared his throat. "Your Honor, the standard for charging a defendant in a criminal case is probable cause. Is it more likely than not that Molly Fagan murdered her husband?

"I ... the state, has clearly met that standard. The standard for conviction is 'beyond a reasonable doubt.' Let the jury decide that at trial. I ask that you charge Molly Fagan with murder. At trial, I'll prove it beyond a reasonable doubt."

"Stand up, Mrs. Fagan," Judge Striker said. Molly didn't move.

"Your Honor ..."

"Quiet, Mr. Lafayette. You've said quite enough."

"Your Honor...."

"I said, be quiet. Go stand next to your client and be whatever help you can be."

Burr opened his mouth.

"Not a word."

Burr walked slowly to Molly. He pulled out her chair and helped her up. "I'm sorry," he said.

She looked at him but didn't say anything.

Judge Striker looked down at her. "Mrs. Fagan, you have been arraigned on the charge of murdering your husband. Today, Mr. Oswald seeks to formally charge you with murder."

Striker looked at the Great Oz, who was beaming again.

"I find some of his arguments compelling," he continued. "But on the whole, I find them ephemeral. Case dismissed."

Oz lost his beam. "Ephemeral?"

"Gossamer and whimsy," Burr said.

The judge looked at Molly again. "Mrs. Fagan, I'm sorry for your loss, and I'm sorry you were put through this." He looked at the bailiff. "Please see to it that Mrs. Fagan's bail is returned to her. Forthwith."

Now I can get paid.

Molly stood where she was.

"You're free to go, Mrs. Fagan," Judge Striker said. He tapped his gavel. "We are adjourned."

The Great Oz stood there with his mouth open. Burr picked up his papers and led Molly out, followed by Eve and Jacob. Burr stopped in front of a seething Julian Flintoff and a not-too-happy Pearl Watson. "I expect the insurance check," Burr said. "Forthwith."

Burr looked back at Oswald on his way out of the courtroom. Flintoff was talking to Oswald, poking him where his chest should have been.

CHAPTER SEVEN

"I still can't believe this happened. It's just so horrible."

"I'm sorry, Molly, but it's over."

I hope.

"It's so awful. Losing Nicky and now this."

"I'm sorry," Burr said, again. He desperately wanted to order another Labatt, but he was pretty sure his timing would be bad.

Burr and Molly were sitting in the late afternoon sun on the deck of the Weathervane. It was seventy-five and sunny. Much better than Judge Striker's stuffy courtroom.

After Jacob and Eve had left for East Lansing, Burr insisted on buying Molly lunch. He thought he had a little room on the Lafayette and Wertheim credit card.

I'll pay it off as soon as Molly pays me.

The Weathervane was full of tourists, cottagers, and a few locals. Molly and Burr were decidedly out of place, Molly in her black dress and Burr in his suit. At the table next to them, a man in khaki shorts and a blue polo, the woman in a Lilly Pulitzer flowered skirt, a lemon top and rope sandals.

Burr didn't care if he was out of place. He was always happy when he won.

The Weathervane, a two-story stone and stucco building, had once been a four-story flour mill on the banks of the Pine River in Charlevoix. The river was right in front of them, but now it was a concrete channel from Lake Charlevoix to Lake Michigan. The drawbridge opened, and the *Emerald Isle*, the car ferry to Beaver Island steamed by. Burr smelled the diesel, the green and white ferry passing so close Burr thought he could reach out and touch it.

The waitress delivered lunch, Great Lakes chowder and a whitefish sandwich for Burr, a chicken Caesar for Molly, dressing on the side.

Of course.

Burr nodded at his glass and the waitress went to get him another Labatt. *Couldn't help myself.*

"Why would that awful man accuse me of murder and get the prosecutor involved?" Molly said.

"It's about the money."

"It's always about the money."

It always is.

"Now what do we do?" Molly said.

"Now we get the Dearborn Life Insurance Company to pay on the policy."

"Do you think they will?"

"I don't think Flintoff has any more arrows in his quiver."

I hope.

Molly picked at her salad. Burr was starving, and he had to make himself slow down. Molly didn't have anything more to say and he was beginning to think lunch, except for the Labatt, had been a bad idea. He called for the check, then Molly said, "I can't thank you enough. I don't know where I'd be without you." She smiled at him. "Actually, I do. I'd be in jail. Is there anything I can do for you?"

Just pay me.

He shook his head no.

The waitress came back with the check. Burr gave her his card.

"There must be something."

Burr finished his beer. "There is one thing."

* * *

Burr and Molly walked across the drawbridge to downtown Charlevoix, such as it was, two blocks of two-story buildings, all of them at least fifty years old. The sidewalk was littered with the same clientele that was at the Weathervane. A block and a half later, Molly took a key from her purse and unlocked an oak door with a small brass sign that said *Private.* The door opened on a stairway. Burr followed her up to a landing on the second floor and another locked door on the first floor. She unlocked it with a different key. Burr followed her in.

The radio station played *Big Love.* A desk the size of a Cadillac to the left, side chairs the size of motorcycles in front of the desk. A conference table big enough for shuffleboard. A sitting area in one of the corners with two chairs and a coffee table. A bar on the other side with a refrigerator. A trophy case and pictures of Nick with the governor, both senators and Barry Sanders. On one wall, a floor to ceiling window that looked out at Main Street, Round Lake beyond. Two of the walls had floor to ceiling curtains.

I thought I was going to get a tour of KHQ.

"This is, was, Nicky's office."

Burr ran his finger across the desk and dragged dust along the varnish. The office smelled like no one had been in it in months. Burr pulled out the desk chair.

This is like a throne.

He sat and bumped his feet against a stool.

"Ouch."

"That's where Nicky put his feet. He didn't like to look up to anyone."

"Can I see the radio station?"

Molly walked over to one of the curtains and pulled it part way open. A waist to ceiling window ran along the wall. Burr saw a young man with headphones sitting at a console. Reel to reel tape players behind him, two turntables and black machines that looked like shoeboxes with eight tracks in them.

Burr stood and banged his foot on the stool again.

"Damn it all."

He walked over to the window.

"That's the control room," Molly said.

"The control room?"

"The main studio. That's Doctor Records, the afternoon jock."

"I thought he'd be older." He was fat, bald and had yellow teeth, but he looked like he was eighteen. He looked at them and Burr waved. The jock picked up a clipboard, changed the eight tracks in the black machines.

Burr waved again.

"This is a one-way window. He can't see you."

"What?"

"Nicky wanted to know what was going on all the time. He was crazy about quality."

Maybe just crazy.

The disc jockey pushed a yellow button on one of the machines and a commercial for Brown Motors came on.

"That's a cart machine," Molly said. "That's how the commercials are played."

It ended and Olson's Market started.

"That's a triple stack. It plays three in a row. The music is on the reel to reels. It's all programmed."

"Doesn't the DJ pick the music?"

"Not here. It's an art form turned science. The turntables collect dust."

A commercial for the Bahnoff sport shop played, then Dr. Records was on. "It's clear and sunny over at the Irish Boat Shop and sunny and seventy-four at KHQ, northern Michigan's hit radio station."

Doctor Records looked at them again. He yawned, then lit a cigarette.

"He's got a voice for radio. And a face for it, too."

Burr looked at her.

"Old joke," she said.

Doctor Records punched a button. One of the reel-to-reels started and *Take Me Home Tonight* came on.

Molly opened the curtain the rest of the way. "This is the news studio. It's empty now, and the jock and the newsperson can see each other through the window between the studios, but they're soundproof." She pointed to the right side of the window. "These are the two production studios where we make commercials, the promos. Anything that's prerecorded."

"I thought this was all live."

"Nicky never left anything to chance. He said that a radio station is all in your mind. All of the elements have to fit. It was an art form to him." Molly looked away. "He loved everything about it."

Molly opened the other curtain.

"This is the main office area. Those cubicles are for the salespeople. Offices for the sales manager and business manager, and a conference room. Engineering is through that door."

A short, not quite petite woman walked out of one of the offices. Burr thought he recognized her from the courtroom. "Who's that?"

"That's Missy. She's the business manager."

"Missy?"

"Melissa. Melissa Warren."

Another woman — a tall blonde — walked in from a door on the far side of the room.

She's taller than Molly.

She said something to an even taller redhead.

"Nicky liked to hire women for sales. Most of the people who buy advertising are men. He said it worked better."

"And tall, too," Burr said.

Molly didn't say anything.

* * *

Jacob paced back and forth in front of Burr's desk.

"Would you please stop pacing and sit down," Burr said. "Better yet, why don't you pace somewhere else."

"There's something wrong. I know there is." Jacob sat in his side chair. "I'm sure Flintoff hasn't paid Molly, and I know Molly hasn't paid us."

"Eve, would you please come in here for just a minute."

Burr reached into a desk drawer and took out his stapler. He slid two pieces of paper in and thwacked it. He took the papers out, but they weren't stapled. He tried again. Still no staple.

"I'm sure Flintoff hasn't paid Molly, and I know Molly hasn't paid us." Jacob said again. He stopped pacing and looked at Burr. "Would you stop fooling around with that blasted stapler and find out what's going on."

"I'll call Molly as soon as I get the stapler fixed." He raised his voice a little. "Eve, would you please come in here?" Burr thwacked the stapler again.

Jacob grabbed the stapler from Burr. He sat down and set it in front of him, safely out of Burr's reach.

Eve came in and sat in the other side chair.

"We're all in our places," Burr said.

"We haven't been paid," Jacob said.

"I had a tour of KHQ."

"We haven't been paid," Jacob said again.

"It's nothing more than an illusion."

"What are you talking about?" Jacob said.

"A radio station." Burr turned around and looked out the window. "It's an illusion. It was nothing like I thought it would be. People and machines. Mostly machines. A bunch of machines I don't understand. They're all cobbled together, and that's a radio station."

"What does this have to do with us getting paid?" Jacob said.

"It's theater of the mind," Burr said, his back still to Jacob and Eve.

"You asked me to come in here for this?" Eve said.

Burr ignored her. "It's an illusion,"

"It's a delusion, and you're delusional," Jacob said.

He doesn't get it.

Burr turned back to Jacob and Eve and reached for his stapler, but Jacob jerked it out of Burr's reach. "My stapler doesn't work."

"What does that have to do with anything?" Jacob said.

"This is the third one in two months," Eve picked up the stapler and clicked it twice. Nothing.

"See what I mean?"

Jacob grabbed it from her. "Stop it, both of you."

Eve opened the stapler. "It's not broken. It's empty."

"Really?" Burr said.

"Burr, please," Jacob said.

Burr looked at Eve. "Get me Molly's number and I'll call her."

"What if the insurance company hasn't paid her?" Jacob said.

Burr drummed his fingers. "You may as well get me the insurance company's number while you're at it."

Eve showed Burr the stapler. "It's empty."

Burr took it from her. "If it won't staple, then it's not working. If it's not working, it's broken."

"I can't babysit everything."

"I'm sure the two staplers you threw away weren't broken. They were just empty, weren't they?"

"They wouldn't staple."

Burr heard the door open. Eve got up and left.

"Now you've done it," Jacob said.

Burr looked at Jacob. "It's just the mail."

Eve came back in with a box of staples and an envelope. She took the stapler from Burr and loaded it. Then she opened the envelope and took out two loose pieces of paper. She lined them up and stapled them together.

"You're a genius," Burr said.

"And you're too lazy to learn how to load a stapler."

"I am not lazy. I am untrained."

"How many perfectly good staplers have you gone through?"

I think the best thing for me to do is not say anything.

"Before we have the stapler training session, you should look at this."
Eve handed him the newly stapled sheets of paper.

"Damn it all."

"What is it?" Jacob said.

"It's another warrant for Molly's arrest."

* * *

For the first time he could remember, Burr didn't want to be in a courtroom.
Molly sat to his left, Oswald to his right. Judge Striker peered down from
his perch.

*I'm sure Flintoff is sitting in the back with that Pearl what's-her-name,
but I'll be damned if I'll give him the satisfaction of looking at him.*

Burr tapped his pencil. His chair wobbled.

Damn that Oswald.

"We are here in the matter of the People versus Fagan. Again," Judge
Striker said. "Mr. Oswald?"

"Thank you, Your Honor. As I'm sure you recall, the last time we were
here, you dismissed the murder charge against Mrs. Fagan for lack of probable cause." Oswald hitched up his pants. "Your Honor, as you may recall …"

"Stop with the 'as you may recall.' I may be old, but I have a perfectly
good memory."

Oswald nodded. "Your Honor, one of the primary reasons you dismissed
the case was because the prosecution couldn't produce a change of beneficiary form. You ruled there was no showing of motive without it."

Striker nodded back.

"Your Honor, the state would like to introduce a change of beneficiary
form signed by the deceased, Nick Fagan, and dated May 17 of this year."
Oswald looked over at Molly. "A little over two weeks before Molly Fagan
murdered him."

Burr stood. "Objection, Your Honor. Nothing whatsoever has been introduced so far that has the slightest probative value."

Striker raised his eyebrows. "Probative?"

"It means...."

"I know what it means, Mr. Lafayette." Striker turned to the prosecutor. "You may continue, Mr. Oswald."

Oswald opened a file and took out a single piece of paper. He held it reverently. "Your Honor. The people would like to introduce this change of beneficiary form."

"Let me see that," Striker said.

Oswald handed Striker the piece of paper.

Burr walked up to Striker, who handed him the form. It was a Dearborn Life Insurance Company change of beneficiary form. Nick's name was on it as was the $1 million dollar policy amount. There was a signature at the bottom. It was dated May 17th of this year. Burr started to hand the form back to Striker but pulled it back.

He ran his finger down the form. The new beneficiary was Alexandra McCall.

Who is she?

Burr handed the form back to Judge Striker. "I object, Your Honor."

"On what grounds?"

"Your Honor, there is no proof that this is genuine. Who's to say that this is Nick Fagan's signature?" Burr poked at Nick's signature. "This may well be a forgery." Burr ran his fingers down the form and stopped near the bottom and tapped the form once, twice, three times, then looked at it closely.

"Mr. Lafayette, do you have anything to say or are you trying to memorize the form?"

Burr looked up at the judge. "Your Honor, this form calls for a witness, and there's no witness signature here."

"That doesn't matter," Oswald said.

"Your Honor, this change of beneficiary form wouldn't be valid for the Dearborn Life Insurance Company. Yet you'd admit it for purposes of charging my client with murder?"

Oswald took a deep breath and puffed himself up where his chest should have been. He exhaled and his chest sagged back to his belly.

"Your Honor, we are not here today to determine the validity of a life insurance claim. We're here to determine if there is probable cause that Molly Fagan murdered her husband. When we were last here, you said that there was no probable cause. I have produced a signed change of beneficiary form. I ask that you admit it into evidence and find that there is probable cause to charge Molly Fagan with murder."

Striker rubbed his goatee.

I wish he'd quit doing that.

The judge looked down at Burr. "Mr. Lafayette, hand me that form." Burr handed it to him. "Admit this into evidence." He cleared his throat. "The court finds that—"

"Your Honor," Burr said.

Judge Striker waved his arms at Burr. "Don't interrupt me, young man."

He's going to fly away if he keeps waving his arms like that.

"Your Honor, we have no idea where or how the prosecutor came into possession of this form. For all we know, he found it in a box of Cracker Jack."

"Don't be smart with me."

Judge Striker looked at the prosecutor.

"Mr. Oswald, how did you get this form?"

"I got it from the Dearborn Life Insurance Company."

"That in itself makes it highly suspect," Burr said.

"For the love of Mike, be quiet, Mr. Lafayette."

Burr leaned toward Molly. "Did you know about this?"

"No," she said.

"Who is Alexandra McCall?"

"I don't know." Molly cracked her knuckles.

"Did you go through Nick's desk after he died?"

She nodded.

"Did you find this?"

"I told you I didn't."

If she'd found it, she'd have gotten rid of it.

Judge Striker rapped his gavel. "Mr. Lafayette, you may confer with your client later." Striker looked at the prosecutor. "Mr. Oswald, we need to hear from the Dearborn Life Insurance Company."

"Yes, Your Honor." Oswald grinned at Burr. "The state calls Pearl Watson."

I knew she'd be here.

The tiny, pale investigator from the Dearborn Life Insurance Company took the witness stand and was sworn in.

"Ms. Watson, would you please tell us how this form came into your possession."

The prim witness folded her hands in her lap. "I contacted Robert Davies, one of the owners of the radio station and asked him if he had any of Mr. Fagan's papers. He said he'd gone through Mr. Fagan's office after he died, and I was welcome to come look at them. I did just that and found the change of beneficiary form."

Burr stood. "Your Honor, I object. Not only is part of Mrs. Watson's testimony hearsay, there is no control of the chain of evidence."

"I beg your pardon."

"Tinker to Evers to Chance."

"Of course. Sit down, Mr. Lafayette," Judge Striker said.

Burr sat.

"Anything further, Mr. Oswald?"

The prosecutor huffed himself up again, then, "Ms. Watson, just to be clear, Mr. Davies found this form in Mr. Fagan's papers and gave it to you. Is that right?"

Burr started to stand.

"Mr. Lafayette," Judge Striker said, "sit back down. Answer the question, Ms. Watson."

"Yes."

"Thank you," Judge Striker said. "Please stand, Mrs. Fagan."

Molly and Burr stood.

"Molly Fagan, I find that there is probable cause that you murdered your husband, Nick Fagan. You are charged with open murder. Bail will be set at the same amount as before. This case is now going to circuit court. Judge Nickels' clerk will contact you with scheduling dates." He raised his gavel. "We are—"

"Your Honor—" Burr said.

"Whatever it is, the answer is no. We are adjourned." Judge Striker tapped his gavel and glided out.

CHAPTER EIGHT

Jacob creased his slacks again. One leg, then the other. And back again.

"You bounce back and forth between East Lansing and the judge's courtroom like a ping-pong ball."

He creased his slacks again.

"Would you please stop whatever it is you're doing," Burr said. "There is a lot of back and forth, but I have to represent our client."

Jacob looked up from his slacks. "Our client who hasn't paid us."

"The insurance company hasn't paid her."

"Because she's been charged with murder. She must have some money. Her husband owned the biggest radio station in northern Michigan."

Burr ignored his partner. "So, this is what we must do."

"I'm sure you mean the 'royal we,' as in me."

Jacob has seen this movie.

"Whatever it is, I won't do it."

Burr took the stapler *du jour* out of his desk and crunched two pieces of paper between its jaws. "It's not broken yet."

"No one, even you, could have lived this long without knowing how to load a stapler."

"They did all that for us at Fisher and Allen."

Burr opened the bottom right drawer of his desk. Jacob peered over Burr's desk. "There must be half a dozen staplers in there."

"I like to keep Eve on her toes." Burr shut the drawer. "I need you to find out where Robert Davies is and what he does."

"Who is Robert Davies?"

"Nick Fagan's partner. The one who found the signed change of beneficiary form signed."

* * *

Burr sat in yet another Adirondack chair. This one, forest green, on yet another covered porch at yet another white Victorian cottage overlooking yet another perfectly lovely blue water lake in northern Michigan.

Burr thought it was all so perfect. The chairs matched. The shutters matched the chairs, and the chairs matched the trim.

And of course, the sky blue beadboard ceiling on the porch matched the sky. Lake Charlevoix right in front of him, two shades darker than the sky, soft waves washing in from the south.

It was all so perfect. Except it wasn't.

He was sitting next to Robert Davies, the one who'd found the signed form in Nick's desk, that had gotten Molly charged with murder.

How did I get mixed up in this?

"Thank you for having me," Burr said, who wasn't particularly glad to be here.

"You're quite welcome."

"I wish it were under different circumstances."

"So do I."

Robert Davies was in his sixties. He had long legs and long arms. The best that could be said was that he was lanky. He had a round face on a round head with steely hair. He wore round glasses with black frames.

He looks like a spider missing four legs.

"I'm here to learn a little more about how you came to find the beneficiary form in Nick Fagan's desk."

Davies sat straight up. "I'm not sure I like your tone."

Burr smiled at the spider. "Bob ..."

"Robert," said Robert.

I knew he wouldn't like that.

"Mr. Davies, as you know, I'm representing Molly Fagan on a murder charge. The case was first dismissed, but this new piece of evidence got her charged again."

Just then the maid brought out two glasses with ice and a pitcher. She set the glasses down on the cocktail table between them and poured each of them a glass.

Sun-brewed iced tea. With fresh mint.

Damn it all.

Davies pointed to a creek at the edge of the yard. "We get the mint over there."

I hate iced tea.

"There are certain amenities we don't have at the Belvedere Club, but other things help compensate." He picked up his glass and clinked Burr's. "Cheers."

Burr took a swallow. "Delicious," he said, lying.

Burr didn't think the Belvedere Club was exactly slumming. It was on the north shore of Lake Charlevoix. The best of the best cottages, like Robert's, sat just off the beach and looked south toward Hemingway Point. *Northease* was an early twentieth century three-story Victorian with a turret, three fireplaces and no insulation, livable from Memorial Day to Labor Day, but cold on either side of the season.

Burr put his iced tea back on the table. "May I ask you a few questions?"

"I suppose so."

This guy thinks he's really top drawer.

Burr turned his chair toward Davies, not so they were face to face but enough so he could look at him.

"Mr. Davies, I thought Nick owned KHQ."

Davies looked at Burr. "That's what he wanted everyone to think."

"Was it true?"

"It was good for business."

"I beg your pardon."

"Nick had an ego as big as a barn. As long as the world thought KHQ was his radio station, he was on top of the world. Nick put everything he had into the station. He was KHQ. He did mornings. There was a sales manager and salespeople, but Nicky was the top biller."

"Did he own the station?"

"Yes." Davies walked his spidery fingers to his glass and took a swallow of his iced tea. "And, no."

Burr turned his chair toward Davies. "Did Nick own the radio station?"

"Harvey Wall and I own the station."

"You have a partner?"

Davies nodded. "A difficult but prosperous man."

I know less about this than I did before I got here.

"What about Nick?"

"Nick was our shill."

That's flattering.

"The FCC made a license for a Class C FM signal available to Charlevoix." Robert looked down his nose at Burr. "Do you know what a Class C FM is?"

Burr shook his head.

"It's a hundred-thousand watts. The most powerful FM allowed. The signal goes forever."

That's for sure.

"Of course, you have to put the tower in the right place."

Burr cocked his head. Just like Zeke.

"If you put the tower in Charlevoix, most of the signal is wasted on Lake Michigan. But if you put the tower to the southeast, off toward Mancelona, you can cover all of northern Michigan." Davies took another drink. "Which is what we did."

"Mr. Davies, I still don't know if Nick owned any of KHQ."

"I'm getting to that. The FCC has very complicated and arcane rules about who can get a license. Nick was almost a perfect owner in the eyes of the FCC, so we had him apply for the license. There were other applicants, but we either litigated them out or bought them out. Nick had all of the common stock, but Harvey and I controlled the station with the preferred stock."

"So, Nick did own the station."

"Technically, yes. For all the world to see."

"So, now his estate owns his share, which means Molly owns all of the common stock."

"Technically."

"Mr. Davies, why do I have the feeling that you don't want anyone to know anything about Nick's ownership of KHQ."

Davies leaned toward Burr. "Because it's none of your business."

We'll see about that.

"Mr. Davies, how was it that you found the signed change of beneficiary form?"

Davies slid Burr's glass toward him. "Drink up, Mr. Lafayette. Before all the ice melts."

Burr and Zeke-the-Boy had a list of foods that taste like dirt. Iced tea was at the top of the list.

Burr picked up the glass but didn't drink any of it.

Davies looked at Burr's glass, then at Burr. "When we found out that Nick died, we needed to make sure the station kept going. I went to his office to see where things were."

"And you found the form."

Davies nodded.

"Where was it?"

"In an envelope. In his desk."

"Was his desk locked?"

"I have a key."

"What did you think about the form?"

"The form? Nothing. I didn't think about it. I didn't think about it until Molly was arrested."

Burr set the iced tea back on the table. "You didn't think about it?"

"Why would I think about it? I put it in a folder and forgot about it until Molly was arrested."

"Why then?"

"If there was any truth to what what's-his-name, the prosecutor, said, I thought it might be important."

"Did you look at it when you found it?"

"I don't remember."

"But then you did look."

Davies cleared his throat. "I guess I did."

"Who is Alexandra McCall?"

Davies crushed a mint leaf in his iced tea. "I haven't the faintest idea."

"And then you felt you had to tell the prosecutor."

"I was fond of Molly."

"Mr. Davies, did it occur to you that the only reason Molly has been charged with murder is because you gave that form to Oswald?"

"I hardly think so."

"For all I know you filled out that form yourself."

Davies took Burr's glass from him. "It's time for you to leave."

Burr handed his iced tea to Davies. "It tastes like dirt."

* * *

Burr sat at the bar at *Tonight Tonight* next to Harvey Wall, the owner of the strip club and Robert Davies' partner at KHQ. It was so dark that he could barely see Wall, and he couldn't see who was sitting at any of the tables. But the stage and the stripper's pole were lit up like a Christmas tree. The young woman swaying on the pole wore a big smile and not much else.

Burr had another iced tea in his hand, and he was going to drink this one.

"Shame about Nick," Wall said. "It's killing us."

Burr cocked his head, but he wasn't sure that Wall could see him.

"He was the radio station. It's hell without him." Wall banged on the wall.

Burr took another swallow.

Tonight Tonight was just outside the Cadillac city limits. Harvey owned this one and a dozen other *Tonight Tonight*s in northern Michigan, strip clubs, adult bookstores, and X-rated theaters. Wherever zoning or a fistful of money could shoehorn them in. He was medium height and build, with dirty blond hair that fell on his face, and glasses that covered up his lazy eye. He only took off his glasses when it was dark, which it always was at *Tonight Tonight*.

"The real problem with a radio station is accounts receivable." Wall took off his glasses. Burr took another drink, making a point not to look Wall in the eye.

"Get him another," Wall said to the topless bartender.

"I'm fine."

"I insist. Get me another club soda and lime." He looked at Burr. "It's the accounts receivable. They're killing us."

I know something about trying to collect accounts receivable.

"Listening to the radio is free. Right. We make money selling ads. We get a contract, run the ads, send the bill. Once in a while we get paid in thirty days. More like ninety or one-twenty. Our bills are payroll and utilities, so we have to pay them when they're due. It's terrible. If I'd known that, I'd never have let Davies talk me into this deal."

The waitress brought Burr's tea. He finished the one he had and handed her his glass.

"What I got here is a cash business. All cash. A few credit cards, but that's like cash. Almost all cash, but cash has its own problems." Wall banged on the wall again.

"How did you get involved?"

"The license came up. Seemed like a good idea. Davies is one of my better customers here. Don't tell him I told you. He thinks it's a big secret." Wall smiled at Burr in the dark.

"The real story, though, is Davies has got this big station in Detroit. Big Top 40 FM. He's killing it. Got it from his father. Anyway, Nick comes to town to work at a tired old 'beautiful music' station. The first thing he does is flip it to Top 40. He's a brilliant programmer and starts giving Davies his lunch. Nick has an affair with one of the salespeople at the station. He divorces his wife and marries her. Turns out to be Molly. But that's another story." Wall shook his head.

"Davies hires a new program director, advertises like hell. He gives thousands of dollars away on the air. None of it works. Nick Fagan is killing him. Davies tries to hire him, but Nick has a covenant not to compete in Detroit that is airtight. Airtight. You get it?"

"I do," Burr said, who didn't.

"You don't get it, do you?"

I have no idea where this is headed, but the more tea I drink, the less I care.

Burr took a big gulp of his iced tea.

"This is what happened. Nick is killing the ratings on Davies' station. He's taking all his audience. Davies can't hire him away because Nick has a covenant not to compete. Davies gets his pals in other cities to offer Nick a better job, but Nick loves Michigan so much he won't leave. The only thing to do is have Nick killed."

Burr knocked his drink over. The waitress came over and cleaned it up.

Harvey grinned. "That was a joke." He pounded the wall again.

That's getting annoying.

"So, here's what Davies does. He hears about this new radio license up here. He tells Nick he'll make him an owner and let him run the whole show if they get the license. Nick goes for it. Davies brings me in. Turns out, none of these radio guys have any cash." Harvey shook his head. "I should've known better."

That's a Richard Marx song.

The bartender brought Burr another iced tea. He felt a pleasant fog settling over him.

"Are you listening to me?"

Burr nodded.

"Anyway, we get the license. Nick is the king of Up North radio until he died. And now Davies and I are screwed."

Burr took a drink of his new drink.

"Why didn't you have key-man life insurance on him?"

"I told Davies we needed it. I told him over and over. He was too cheap. Said KHQ was so big nothing could tip it over. He was wrong about that."

"It didn't happen right away. Davies gave me the 'I told you so' treatment, but now it's happening. The other stations all hate us because we upset their apple cart, and now they're all coming after us. A nick here, a nick there. No pun intended."

Harvey smiled at Burr. He waved over the bartender. It was all Burr could do to keep his eyes off her.

"One more for the nice man."

"I couldn't possibly drink another one."

"It's on me."

She took his glass and turned away.

She looks good in both directions.

"This wouldn't be such a problem if we'd had life insurance on Nicky. But then we'd probably be the ones accused of murder."

Burr sat straight up.

"Bad joke," Harvey said.

The new iced tea arrived, along with the bartender.

"Easy on the eye," Harvey said. "For somebody who came to see me, you don't have too many questions."

"I've been listening."

"I guess that's what a good lawyer does. The IRS tried that, but I didn't say much. Just 'I don't know,' 'I forgot,' 'I don't remember,' Maybe a 'yes' or 'no.' That's what my lawyer told me to do. They always think I cheat. Because this is a cash business." Wall took off his glasses again.

Burr looked away.

"Mr. Wall, why do you think Nick wanted to change his beneficiary?"

"Damned if I know."

"There must be a reason."

Wall shook his head.

"What about the new beneficiary, Alexandra McCall?"

"What about her?"

"Who is she?"

Wall shook his head. "No idea."

"Was she his girlfriend?"

"No idea."

"Did Nick have girlfriends?"

"We were partners. Not friends. Nick was a damn good radio guy. That's all I know." Wall looked at Burr's glass. "You want another tea?"

Burr looked at his mostly empty glass. "I don't think so."

Wall waved at the waitress. "Get the curious man another one." She took Burr's glass and left.

"Mr. Wall, I'm trying to figure out who murdered Nick."

"Maybe it was an accident."

"Maybe it was."

The waitress brought Burr a fresh tea. He took a swallow.

This is the best iced tea I've ever had.

"Who might want him dead?"

"I can think of at least a dozen people," Harvey said.

"What?"

"Maybe more."

"Who are they?"

Wall studied Burr with his good eye. "Just about everybody who owns a radio station north of Cadillac."

Burr looked at his drink. There's something special about this tea.

"We, Nick, gave 'em their lunch. Absolutely killed them. Took their listeners and their advertisers. Ruined a couple of 'em."

"Is that a reason to kill Nick?"

"Best one I can think of." Wall looked at Burr with his lazy eye.

Burr's stool came up on two legs. He almost tipped over.

"Watch yourself." Wall grabbed Burr by the shoulder and steadied him. "Now we're gettin' our lunch."

"I beg your pardon."

"We can't keep it going without Nick. I knew we should've had life insurance. I could strangle that idiot Davies."

Burr stood and knocked over his stool.

"Be careful there, big fella. You all right?"

Burr nodded. But he was a little dizzy.

"Looks like you can't hold your tea."

Burr put his hands on the bar. "What kind of tea is that?"

"Yeah. That's right. Long Island Iced Tea." Wall slapped the wall.

* * *

Burr rescued Zeke and walked him around the parking lot. It wasn't clear who was walking whom.

"Zeke, old friend, that was the best iced tea I've ever had." Zeke looked up at him. "Because it wasn't iced tea."

Zeke stopped at a red Honda, sniffed one of the tires and lifted his leg.

"So that's what Long Island Iced Tea is. I should stick to gin."

Zeke led them back to the Jeep. Burr managed to open the door. Zeke climbed in and took shotgun. Burr saw a Cadillac sheriff's car drive by, stop for a minute, back up, and pull next to the Jeep.

A grim-faced deputy got out. "Give me your keys," he said.

Burr leaned against the Jeep. "What?"

"I said, give me your keys." He held his hand out, palm out.

"Why would I do that?"

"Because if you don't, I'm going to arrest you for public intoxication."

Burr stood up as straight as he could. "I'm not intoxicated." Burr fell back against the Jeep.

The deputy put his hands on his hips. "You can barely stand up."

"There's nothing wrong with me."

"There's nothing wrong with you that sleeping it off in your car won't fix." He put his hand out again. "Give me your keys."

"No."

The deputy took out his cuffs. "Come with me."

Burr gave the deputy his keys and climbed in his Jeep and fell asleep.

Four hours and a pounding headache later, the deputy came back and woke Burr up. He lectured Burr who pretended to listen. The deputy handed

Burr his keys. Burr and Zeke drove to Harbor Springs and rowed out to *Spindrift*. She rocked in time with the waves. Burr lit the alcohol stove and made his signature dinner, Koegel's Vienna Sausages and Bush's baked beans. He shared it with Zeke, washed the rest down with a Labatt, and went to bed.

CHAPTER NINE

"Molly doesn't know?" Jacob said.

Burr nodded.

"That's impossible."

Burr tapped his pencil. Zeke snored softly on the couch. Jacob ran his thumb and finger along the crease in his linen slacks. Then he sneezed. "Damn that dog." Jacob looked at Zeke then back at Burr. "What exactly did she say?"

Burr stopped tapping. "She said 'I don't know who Alexandra McCall is.' Unquote."

"I don't believe it," Eve said, out of sight but not out of earshot.

"That's what she said," Burr said, softly.

"I don't believe it," Eve said, again.

Burr leaned toward Jacob and whispered. "I went to see her the day after I saw Robert Davies and Harvey Wall. She swore she didn't know who Alexandra McCall was."

"You went to see Harvey Wall?" Eve said.

How could she possibly hear that?

Eve stood in the door. "I also know what you're thinking."

I don't think I'm going to bring up what happened in the parking lot.

She sat down next to Jacob.

Now everything is as it should be. "I can't believe you saw the porn king," Eve said.

"Why not?"

"He's a known criminal."

Jacob looked at her. "It's not as if we don't deal with criminals."

"Your esoteric appellate practice has gotten away from you," Eve said. "Again."

"We simply aren't doing business with a porn ... whatever he is." Jacob twirled a curl in his steel wool hair.

Now he's nervous.

"Harvey Wall is one of the owners of KHQ. He said he didn't know who Alexandra McCall was either. We have to deal with him."

"I'm sure you can't believe a word he says." Eve smiled at Burr. "I hope he didn't get you drunk."

How could she possibly know that.

"I never drink while I'm working."

"Of course not," Eve said.

"Robert Davies said he didn't know who she was either," Burr said.

"What about Molly?" Eve said.

"Burr said she told him she didn't know who what's-her-name is," Jacob said.

"Lawyers lie. Witnesses lie. Clients lie. Mostly clients." Burr said.

Burr swiveled his chair and looked out the window. Rain tapped against the window.

Like my pencil.

It ran down the pane, puddled in the sill and leaked through.

I never should have bought this building.

"I still think this could have been an accident. People die of mushroom poisoning every year," Burr said. He turned back to Jacob and Eve. "Sometimes what looks like what happened is what really happened."

"I beg your pardon," Eve said.

"Eve, I need you to find us our own mushroom expert."

She tugged at her earring.

Now they're both going at it.

"That was pretty special iced tea he was pouring down your throat." Eve smiled at him. "I think you need to find the mystery woman."

Burr ran his hands through his hair, front to back.

We've all got our tics going.

He turned back around and looked at the rain. It was pounding on the window, leaking through the window, and dripping on the floor.

If it's raining this hard in Harbor Springs, Spindrift will be really wet down below.

"You know what they call Harvey Wall, don't you?"

"No," Burr said.

"Harvey Wall Banger."

* * *

"Would you like another beer, Mr. Lafayette?"

Burr looked longingly at his empty glass, then up at the waitress. "Thanks, Norma, I don't think so." She nodded, then left.

Burr was two beers in, and he knew he needed to stop.

"Come on, Dad. Let's go."

Burr could barely hear Zeke-the-Boy over the crashing and rumbling. They were tucked away in the basement of the Grosse Pointe Yacht Club at Lane 2 of the three-lane bowling alley. Burr hated bowling, especially in the summer, but his eleven-year-old son loved it, especially with the bumpers set up in the alley. It was all Burr could do to bring Zeke down here, but Grace, his ex, had offered to watch the other Zeke, and Burr still paid for the membership at the yacht club.

They must think we're still married.

Zeke was on his third Cherry Coke and was climbing the walls. Burr desperately wanted a third beer but thought better of it.

We're not married, but we're still a family.

"Come on, Dad. It's your turn."

"Mr. Lafayette?"

There was Molly.

What's she doing here?

"Mr. Lafayette."

And why is she calling me 'Mister'?

"You are Burr Lafayette, aren't you?"

"Molly," Burr said, flummoxed.

"I'm Kelly Fagan."

"Molly's sister?"

"Come on, Dad."

"Excuse me, I'll be right back." Burr followed Zeke to the alley. Zeke pushed the start button. The pins racked.

"You go first this time," Zeke said.

Burr picked up a dark blue ball with gold flecks. He split the pins.

"That's tough, Dad."

"Take my turn. I'll be right back."

Burr walked back to the table where a slightly shorter, slightly older version of the fetching Molly Fagan stood.

She's almost as good looking as her sister.

"Kelly Fagan." She stuck her hand out at Burr, who shook it.

"I'm Nicky's first wife." She looked down her nose at him.

If looks could kill.

"Please sit down."

Kelly Fagan had the same black hair that Molly had, maybe a bit shorter, and the same pink lipstick, maybe a shade darker than Molly's. She had on jeans and a black top that didn't leave much to the imagination.

"Your assistant told me it was your day with your son and he loved bowling. I didn't think you'd be at a regular bowling alley."

Burr smiled at her.

"Nicky pays for my membership here, at least he did until he was murdered. It was in the divorce decree."

I'm still paying for Grace's membership here.

"Can I get you something to drink?" Burr said.

"Stoli on the rocks."

Burr waved at the waitress.

"Would you like something, Mr. Lafayette?"

"A Stoli on the rocks, and I'll have my usual."

"With him here?" She nodded at Zeke-the-Boy, who was sending ball after ball down the lane.

"Yes."

"I won't tell Grace," Norma said as she left.

Everyone knows what's best for me.

Burr looked back at Kelly. "Where were we?"

"We were at the place where you thought I was Molly's sister."

"You did take me by surprise."

"Surprise? I'll tell you about surprise. I was married to that son-of-a-bitch for seven years when she came along and stole him from me. Nicky couldn't keep it in his pants. She's taller and younger, but she's not prettier."

No, she's not.

"You think I'm pretty, don't you?" Kelly pushed her hair off her face. "I'm prettier than that bitch, but she's taller. And younger. There's nothing I can do about that. Nicky hired her for sales at the station here in Detroit.

She was good at it. I didn't find out about it until it was too late. He loves tall women and young ones. I'm younger than Nicky. But it wasn't enough." She brushed her hair out of her eyes. "He was a good father. Good enough. We live on Rivard. In the Farms. Zack is devastated. I don't know what I'm going to do."

I have no idea why you're here.

"What do you think I should do? You're that bitch's lawyer. I'm sure you don't care."

"Her name is Molly."

"I know what her name is."

Mercifully, Norma came back with Kelly's Stoli on the rocks and Burr's *usual*, a very dry, very dirty Bombay gin martini on the rocks with four olives.

Kelly sipped her drink and left pink lipstick on the rim. Burr took a big swallow of his martini. Then two more.

"You're probably wondering why I'm here."

"The thought crossed my mind."

She took another sip. She reached into her purse and took out about twenty sheets of paper folded in two, and nicely stapled.

Someone knows how to work a stapler.

She unfolded the papers.

Zeke-the-Boy appeared. "Come on, Dad. It's your turn."

"I'll be right there."

"What's that?" Zeke-the-boy pointed at Burr's martini.

"Ice water."

"I never saw olives in ice water. Those are big olives."

"Sometimes parents put olives in their ice water," Kelly said.

Thank you for that.

"Come on, Dad. It's your turn."

"You take my turn."

"I did. I'm killing you. Come on."

"I'll be right there."

"When?"

"In a few minutes."

"Can I have another Cherry Coke?"

"No."

"You're probably going to keep losing." Zeke-the-Boy turned and left.

Burr studied his martini.

"It's tough being divorced," Kelly said. "Which is why I'm here. I've got a son to raise. And now I've got to do it by myself."

"Nick had a son?"

"Yes. Zack. He's about the same age as your son. Except your son has a father." The former Mrs. Fagan flipped through her papers. She found what she was looking for, read it to herself, lips moving. Then she looked up at Burr. "That bitch had a life insurance policy on Nicky. That's why she killed him.

"But the insurance company doesn't want to pay," Kelly said.

They certainly don't.

Kelly pushed her vodka away. "It's too early for me." She handed the papers to Burr. "Nicky was a good enough father. He's gone, but this little paragraph trumps everything.

Burr flipped back to the first page. At the top of the first page, in big, bold letters, '*Divorce Decree.*' Burr turned to the paragraph Kelly had pointed out.

This isn't good.

"You get it, right?"

Burr didn't say anything.

"It doesn't matter which of those two is on the policy because this trumps everything."

It just might.

"That's why I'm here. I don't care who the policy names. Nicky agreed I'd have a million dollars of life insurance, and that's what I want." She picked up her Stoli and took a swallow. "And I didn't kill Nick. Zack and I were at my mother's that day."

I knew she'd have an alibi.

"Mrs. Fagan, I'm not sure that your rights take precedence over my client's."

"Your client poisoned Nicky, so she can't collect on the policy, and the new beneficiary isn't valid because there was no witness. So, I win."

CHAPTER TEN

Zeke trotted up to Burr and sat in front of him. He held the stick in his mouth until Burr took it from him. Burr threw it. Zeke didn't move. Burr gave Zeke a line with his arm, then said, "Zeke." The dog ran off. Zeke came back with the stick.

"I didn't come out here for a dog training exhibition," Gretchen Freeman said.

This is all I've gotten out of it so far.

"Throw the stick away," she said.

"He'll bring it back."

"Throw it where he can't see it."

"He'll find it. That's what Labs do."

"Your assistant said you needed an expert. I'm an expert if there ever was one, but you don't seem to have any interest in what I'm trying to show you."

Gretchen Freeman was another one of Eve's ideas. Burr thought it was a pretty good idea, but he hated science, and Gretchen Freeman was nothing if not a scientist.

Burr had lost every game to Zeke-the-boy at the Yacht Club, not all of them on purpose, mostly because he'd been stewing about what Molly either hadn't told him or had lied about. He wanted to find out what was really going on with Molly, but Eve had made this appointment, and she'd told him to keep it.

Here he was in the forest primeval, somewhere south of Charlevoix, on the same two-track where Nick picked the poisonous mushrooms. Or did he?

The two-track wound through the bottom of a valley, great, tall trees on either side. Maples, oaks, beech, and ash. Ferns underneath the trees. Blue sky peeked through the leaves, streaky sunlight slanting through the trees. The forest was still but the leaves shook at the treetops, the air clear in the late August afternoon. The woods smelled like dirt and green, a fading green, but green.

Gretchen took off ahead of him, then stopped under a cluster of trees with big trunks. She pushed the ferns out of the way and scratched through the leaves. "Come over here," she said. "And keep that dog away from me."

She's not to be trifled with.

"Zeke, stay," Burr said.

Gretchen Freeman, Ph.D., was eighty if she was a day, but she had blond hair in a long braid. She had a strong jaw, smooth, almost wrinkle-free skin, and fierce blue eyes that flashed when she spoke. She walked fast and talked faster.

"This is where the morels like to be. Here in the woods. Under the ashes." She patted the trunk of the tree closest to her. Then she rubbed the bark. "See these ridges and these furrows? They're deep. That's how you can tell it's an ash. And the leaves, there's six or seven on a twig." She pointed up. "But you can't see them from here. Morels like elms, too, but they're all dead."

"Who's dead?"

"The elms. From Dutch elm disease."

Do I need to know this?

"Kneel down next to me."

She scratched the soil again. Burr smelled the dead leaves, the dirt and the green of the ferns.

"Morels like dry, well-drained soil, like this. They like to be around the roots of ashes, beeches a little, and elms."

"But they're all dead."

Gretchen looked sideways at him.

"Where are the morels?"

"They're out season."

Of course they are.

"That's why we're here. If you want to know where Nick picked the poisonous mushrooms, you need to know the places where they grow." She crouched and scratched at the soil with her hand. "But Nick didn't die from poisonous morels."

Gretchen scraped the leaves away with her boot. The leaves underneath were wet. A nightcrawler shrunk back in its hole.

"This is where they grow. Usually in May. There won't be any until next year."

Burr nodded.

The aged mycologist stood and looked at Burr. "Morels aren't poisonous. You can't die from eating morels, even if they're spoiled."

I was better off with Zeke and his stick.

"Why exactly are we here?"

"I'm sure I don't know why." She scuffed the dirt with her boot. "Because your assistant asked me to help you. And you really need the help."

Do I ever.

"Mr. Lafayette, I'm a mycologist. I have a Ph.D. in mycology. I'm attached to the University of Michigan Biological Station at Douglas Lake."

"Isn't that where Paula Caruso works?"

"Why do you ask?"

"She testified at the preliminary exam."

"She doesn't know a thing."

Testy.

"If it wasn't morels, what did kill Nick?"

The professor started down the two-track, then turned back toward him.

"Beefsteak mushrooms are edible. They can make you sick, but they're hardly ever fatal."

She got down on her knees again and brushed away some leaves.

"This is a beefsteak."

The mushroom was brown and looked like raw beef.

"A beefsteak doesn't look a bit like a morel. You do know what a morel looks like?"

Burr nodded but didn't.

"They're spongy, with holes, and the caps flow into the stems, like an umbrella."

Burr nodded again.

"But this one." She scratched at the leaves. "This one will kill you." She pointed down at a mushroom with a red cap and a white stalk. "This is an Amanita. They're very common and very poisonous."

Burr bent down and ran his hand across the cap, then started to put his hands on his mouth.

"Stop that."

Burr jumped.

"Don't touch your mouth."

Burr wiped his hand on his pants.

"If I were going to poison someone, this is what I would use," she said.

"It doesn't look a bit like a morel."

"If you cut it up in small pieces and mixed it in with the morels, no one would ever know."

Burr looked for Zeke but couldn't see him.

"He went that way." Gretchen pointed to her left. "Shouldn't you go find him?"

"He'll be back."

With a stick.

"Do you think that's what happened?" Burr said.

"I wasn't there."

"Could it have been an accident?"

"Anything is possible." She pointed to her right. "Here he comes. With a stick."

Zeke ran up to Gretchen and dropped the stick at her feet. Her braid fell over the front of her shirt. She swung it over her shoulder and picked up the stick.

Damn it all.

"Dr. Freeman, do you think it was an accident?"

She threw the stick. Zeke ran after it. "It could have been an accident, but I doubt it."

"Why not?"

The aged mycologist picked the Amanita and held it in her hand. She broke off the cap. "Because these grow in the summer and fall. Morels grow in the spring."

"And?"

She shook her head.

Patience isn't her strong suit.

"As I just said, Amanitas grow in the summer and fall. They don't grow at the same time morels do."

"So, if Nick was poisoned by these things, someone had to plan months ahead."

"If it was intentional, whoever did it knew exactly what they were doing." She crushed the mushroom in her hand.

It could have been Molly.

Zeke came back with the stick and dropped it at her feet. She threw it, and he brought it back again.

She looked down at the stick.

"He'll bring it back until your arm falls off."

"I can see that."

* * *

The next afternoon Burr sat in the cockpit of *Spindrift*. He and Zeke had driven to Harbor Springs after leaving Gretchen Freeman. It was midweek and he'd managed to find a slip at the city docks, without having to bribe anyone.

The sun wasn't quite over the yardarm, but Burr was nursing his second Labatt. The sun was at his back and the wind, what there was of it, drifted in his face. KHQ played *Brilliant Disguise*.

Burr looked at Zeke.

"Who is Alexandra McCall?"

Zeke snored softly.

"How many more duck hunts have you got?"

"Are you talking to yourself again?"

Burr knocked over his beer.

Damn it all.

"Do you want me to help you clean it up?"

"Zeke likes Labatt."

Zeke jumped down and started to lap up the beer.

"Should he be doing that?"

"It's his first one of the day."

"I've decided to give you another chance."

"I beg your pardon?"

"I've decided to give you another chance," she said again. Maggie Winston, Burr's vision of beauty, sat down on the dock and smiled at him. Late thirties, tall, willowy but not starved. Shoulder length black hair, like

Molly. Sky blue eyes like Burr, hiding behind glasses with big black frames, and her rose lipstick.

"How did you know I was here?"

"Eve told me."

Eve knows everything.

"Aren't you going to invite me aboard?"

Burr stood and offered her his hand. "Please come aboard."

"I'm not sure I want to."

Burr looked at his hand, then dropped his arm.

Maggie brushed her hair off her face. "I've really missed you, but now I'm not so sure this is a good idea."

I'm not so sure either.

"I do love you, or at least I think I do."

Burr sat.

Maggie took off her glasses.

Her glasses are a little thicker than I remember.

"I had this all worked out in my head. It's easy to get things worked out by yourself. With no one saying anything back. Now I'm not so sure."

"Would you like a beer?"

"No."

"Wine?"

"I'm telling you how I feel and you're offering me a glass of wine."

"I'm going to have another beer." Burr disappeared in the cabin.

"Do you still drink Kim Crawford?" Maggie said.

He looked up at her from the cabin. "From Memorial Day to Labor Day."

"You drink too much," she said.

Burr opened the ice box and fished around until he found the Kim Crawford, the Sauvignon Blanc in the black bottle that reminded him of Maggie. He filled one of his plastic wine glasses and climbed back to the cockpit. He handed her the Kim Crawford and sat down.

"Would you like to come aboard?"

She ignored him. "I've decided to give you another chance."

This is the third time.

Burr looked down at his feet and wiggled his toes in his Harken sailing shoes.

I've never had anything but a good time in these shoes, but my streak may be about to end.

"Did you hear me?"

Burr nodded.

"You were mostly a terrible boyfriend, but I think your long-term prospects are good."

I still don't want to get married.

"Aren't you going to say anything?"

"I'm not sure what to say."

She squeezed her knees together. "Are you trying to look up my skirt?"

* * *

"Where is Jacob?" Burr said.

"Where do you think?" Eve smiled at him.

"Clove cigarette in the alley."

"He doesn't smoke clove cigarettes. And you know it."

Burr held up his glass for another Dos Equis.

"Between your booze and his marijuana, it's a wonder either of you get anything done."

The waitress came by and took Burr's glass.

Jacob walked in and sat down next to Eve with a silly smile on his face.

They were sitting at a booth in El Azteco, East Lansing's finest and only Mexican restaurant. It smelled like garlic and refried beans. Burr had traded legal work with the owner, who had a nasty habit of serving underage college students and an even nastier habit of getting caught. Burr could never eat enough blue-corn enchiladas to work off the trade.

It's the same thing with Scooter and his clams with red sauce.

Eve glared at Jacob. "Don't smile like that."

He kept smiling.

"That is a silly smile."

The waitress brought Burr's beer. She raised her eyebrows at Eve, who returned the eyebrow salute.

"She'd like a Margarita," Burr said.

"No, I wouldn't."

The waitress left.

Burr took a swallow of his beer.

It's not Labatt, but it's as close as I'm going to get.

"Jacob, I need you to find Alexandra McCall."

"Who?"

"The new beneficiary on Nick's life insurance policy."

"I won't do it."

"Jacob," Burr said.

"I simply can't find the case we need for the Weisman appeal. That's what needs to be done."

"Is that why you're smoking dope?" Eve said.

"It relaxes me."

"While you're so relaxed, find Alexandra McCall," Burr said.

"I'm a writer of appellate briefs. And I can't find the case we need."

"Jacob, please."

"No."

The waitress showed up with the Margarita that Eve didn't order.

She licked the salt off the rim, then drank half of it.

"Feeling better?" Burr said.

"Not yet."

"If the change of beneficiary form isn't valid, what difference does it make?"

"Why isn't it valid?" Eve said.

"There's no witness," Jacob said.

"Why did Nick change it?" Eve said.

"No one seems to know who she is."

"They're all lying." Eve finished her drink and signaled the waitress with her eyebrows. She looked at Jacob. "If you're going to keep up with us, you need to excuse yourself to the alley."

"Keeping up with the two of you is a losing proposition," Jacob said.

"I need you to find Alexandra McCall," Burr said.

Eve licked the rest of the salt off her drink. "Why have you left the one you left me for?"

It's not Top 40, but it's a great song.

* * *

Burr had just finished lunch at the Boyne River Inn in downtown Boyne City. It wasn't the Arboretum, but he was a big fan of the pan-fried walleye with the tartar sauce that had chopped pickles in it.

He rubbed the chalk mark on the tire of his Jeep. Then he let Zeke out, who lifted his leg on the tire and finished the job. The two of them walked to a small white house two blocks from Lake Charlevoix. There was a light wind that smelled of freshly mowed grass.

I love that smell, as long as I'm not the one doing the mowing.

Burr knocked on the door. No answer. He knocked again. Still no answer.

"No one here, Zeke."

Burr knocked one more time.

"She ain't here."

Burr turned around. There stood a woman in a muumuu as big around as she was tall. She had short gray hair that went every which way. Her glasses had dented the bridge of her nose. Zeke barked at her.

"Hush up," she said. "You looking for Alex?"

"I am."

"She ain't here."

"You said that."

"I did."

"Do you know where she is?"

"Nope. Been gone about a month."

"A month?"

This is the address Jacob gave me.

"That's what I said."

"Do you know where she went?"

"Yep."

That's something.

"Where is she?"

She turned and started off. Her dress swung around after her.

"Excuse me," Burr said.

The big woman kept going, but not very fast.

"Excuse me," Burr said again.

She stopped and her dress swung the other way. "I'll tell you if you pay me for the last two month's cleaning.

Two hundred and fifty dollars later, Alexandra McCall's former cleaning lady told him where the disappearing beneficiary worked.

Burr, sans Zeke, walked up a flight of stairs and into the KHQ reception area. *Faith* played in the background.

A pert young woman greeted him.

"I'm looking for Alexandra McCall."

"She's not here."

"When will she be back?"

"She doesn't work here anymore."

A blond woman in her mid-thirties walked into the reception area.

"Can I help you?"

She was about five-five, with shoulder-length hair, parted nicely in the middle, framing a turned-up nose and bright red lipstick framing white teeth.

She was in the courtroom.

"Burr Lafayette." He offered his hand.

"Melissa Warren." She didn't offer hers.

She was here when Molly gave me the tour.

"I'm looking for Alexandra McCall."

Melissa nodded.

"Does she work here?"

"No." She chewed on her cheek. "Not anymore."

"Do you know where she is?"

She turned and started back where she'd come from, Burr on her heels. They walked past the studios Molly had showed him, past the sales bullpen, and into an office with glass walls. She shut the door behind them and sat at her desk. An ashtray full of cigarette butts to her right. A framed picture of Nick to her left.

Burr sat across from her. "What about Alexandra McCall?"

"Alex? She was in sales, but she left."

"When?"

"After Nicky died."

"Right after?"

"I don't pay too much attention to salespeople. Except when they need to collect from an advertiser." She lit a cigarette.

Burr looked at the picture of Nick.

"That was in the lobby, but it was too upsetting for some of the staff after he died."

"Do you think it was an accident?"

She tried to find a spot in the ashtray to knock the ashes off her cigarette.

"I'm just trying to find out what happened," Burr said.

"I thought you were looking for Alex."

"Do you think it was an accident?"

She looked at the end of her cigarette, then crushed it out. "Nicky never would pick bad mushrooms. He knew all there was to know about them."

"Where was Alex's desk?"

The business manager swiveled her chair around and pointed to an empty desk in front of Nick's office.

"Can I have a look?"

She turned back to Burr. "It's empty. She cleaned it out before she left."

"When was that?"

"About a week after Nick died. I came in one morning and her desk was cleaned out. We haven't seen her since."

"Isn't that suspicious? Or, at least odd?"

"Salespeople come and go. I can't keep track of them."

"Melissa, why do you think Alexandra McCall was on the new beneficiary form?"

She sat up straight. "What did you say?"

That got her attention.

"At the arraignment, the prosecutor introduced a change of beneficiary form with Alexandra McCall's name on it."

"I have no idea."

"Ms. Warren, why do you think Nick would put her on his life insurance?"

"Missy. And I have no idea."

I think I have a pretty good idea.

"Is she tall with long dark hair?"

"What difference does it make?"

Burr rolled his tongue around in his cheek. Missy looked away.

"Missy, are you at all interested in finding out what happened to Nick?"

She turned back to him and nodded.

"If it wasn't an accident, who do you think killed Nick?"

"Molly."

I'll make sure not to call her as a witness.

"Who does Alex look like?"

"Look like?"

"Yes, who does Alex look like?"

"Molly."

CHAPTER ELEVEN

"Burr, I told you I don't know who she is, and I have no idea where she is. And that's not why I asked you to come over."

Burr looked off into the woods, then back at Molly. She had on a royal blue sleeveless top, white shorts and rope sandals. Just a little lipstick. Her black hair fell on her shoulders.

"Don't you believe me?"

No, I don't.

"Of course I believe you."

Burr reached under the table and scratched Zeke's ear. He yelped.

"Sorry, Zeke."

Burr had called Eve after he'd left KHQ. Eve told him Molly needed to talk with him.

Which was fine with him. He had his own reasons for wanting to see Molly.

Burr had driven from KHQ down the east side of Lake Charlevoix to Molly's house. The trees broke up the afternoon sun, and the light puddled on the deck. She handed him a Perrier with lime.

At least she didn't give me an iced tea.

Burr scratched Zeke's ear again. Zeke pushed his head against Burr's fingers.

If he was a cat, he'd purr.

"It matters because Oswald may try to say you knew about Nick and Alexandra McCall. You were jealous and you killed Nick over it."

"There was nothing going on between them. I'd have known if there was."

"Why would Nick change his life insurance?"

"I have no idea."

"It looks bad," Burr said.

"I didn't murder Nicky."

I'm not so sure.

"I know you didn't, but it looks bad."

"I have no idea who she is."

Burr scratched Zeke's ear a little harder. He yelped again.

"Sorry, Zeke," he said again.

"Every time I answer, Zeke yelps."

That's because I don't believe you.

"Really?"

"This is all so horrible."

"I'm sorry, Molly, but I have to know."

"I don't know who she is." She went back into the house. She came out with an envelope and handed it to Burr. He took a piece of paper. It read "Notice of Foreclosure." Burr looked up at Molly.

I have personal experience with this.

"I don't have any money," Molly paced back and forth across the deck. "The station paid me Nicky's salary after he died, but they stopped." She paced back and forth across the deck.

"Why?"

"Davies said the station only had to pay me for two months after he died. It was in his contract."

"Davies told me you were a top salesperson in Detroit."

"I was great at it."

"Why didn't you work at KHQ?"

Molly stopped pacing. "Nick didn't think it would look good."

There was another reason Nick didn't want you working at KHQ.

"Look good?"

"He wanted my job to be his wife."

This guy had an ego that wouldn't quit.

"I was really good at my job, and now I'm broke. Nicky's dead, and I'm broke." She looked out the window. "And that part is his fault."

"How are you getting by?"

"I have credit at a few places." She started pacing again.

"Foreclosure takes a long time."

"What should I do?"

"Can you get a job?"

"While I'm on trial for murder?"

Burr reached in his wallet and took out his emergency Lafayette and Wertheim check. He wrote her a check for a thousand dollars.

"Just pay what you have to."

"Then what?"

"Would you please stop pacing?"

She looked at Burr, then sat down next to Zeke and scratched his ear. Burr studied his Perrier, then looked at Molly. "Tell me about Kelly."

"Kelly?"

"The prior Mrs. Fagan."

Zeke yelped.

* * *

Burr sat on the balcony of his apartment, nursing what was left of his martini. Zeke was curled up in the chair next to him. Burr had a grand view of downtown East Lansing, such as it was. It was hot and humid, but the breeze at six stories and the shade from his patio umbrella made it tolerable. That and the martini.

The door to the hallway that connected his apartment opened, then slammed shut. He counted to three, then it happened again.

The sliding glass door flew open. Eve stood there, hands on hips, Jacob behind her doing his best to look outraged.

Eve does outrage much better than Jacob.

"How could you?"

"I knew I should have locked the door."

"We don't have any money," Eve said.

"That isn't anything new."

"However much we don't have, we now have a thousand dollars less," she said.

"I beg your pardon," Burr said.

"Connie from the bank called. We're overdrawn but she went ahead and paid the check."

Good for her.

Burr had driven back the day before yesterday and worked on cases with clients who might actually pay. Labor Day weekend was coming up and he'd thought he could get out of town before the check cleared.

Wrong again.

Jacob squeezed around Eve. "How could you, Burr?"

"She doesn't have any money."

"We don't have any either," Jacob said.

Eve squeezed back in front of Jacob. "Molly Fagan is our client. She writes checks to *us*. We don't write checks to *her*."

"She doesn't have any money," Burr said again.

"Clients write checks to lawyers. Lawyers don't write checks to clients," Eve said again. She put her hands back on her hips.

Jacob inched his way forward.

Burr studied his drink. He thought the patio was getting too crowded with unhappy people.

"Jacob, we need to find Alexandra McCall."

"No," Jacob said.

"Eve, this is a list Molly gave me of their charge accounts. Can you find their addresses for me?"

"No," she said.

Burr finished his martini. He squeezed by the equally unhappy Eve and Jacob, then started for the galley kitchen, which reminded him of his boat, which was where he'd rather be.

"If we can't find Alexandra McCall and if we can't find out something about how the Fagans spent their money, we're never going to get paid."

"What do their charge accounts have to do with anything?" Eve said.

"There's more to this than poisonous mushrooms."

"If you're in there making yourself another martini, don't," Eve said.

Burr poured himself two generous shots. "Ice is overrated."

* * *

Burr had managed to sneak in while Eve was out. He looked out his window and made a point of doing nothing while Eve was gone. He had a little peace but not for long.

Eve and her coffee sat in the wing chair that may as well have had her name on it. She unfolded the Fagans' list of charges and dropped it on the desk.

"Burr," Eve said.

Burr turned around from doing nothing.

Eve smoothed out the list. "You and I go back a long way."

He nodded.

"I've done some things, many things, for you that I thought were stupid and silly. They almost always turned out to be the right thing to do." She smoothed out the list again. "But this ..."

"This?"

"Finding out about Nick and Molly's charge accounts is the silliest yet."

He didn't say anything.

"I'm not going to do it. And if you insist, I'm going to quit."

Burr started to say something.

"You and I go back a long way."

You just said that.

"You and I go back a long way," she said again. "But I've had it. I've had it with not getting paid on time. I've had it with your stupid criminal cases. I've had it with the stupid things you ask me to do." She paused. "And you drink too much."

"So far, I've managed to stay one step ahead of the posse."

"So far."

"Eve ..."

"Let me finish. It's not just that. Writing that check to Molly when you knew we don't have any money. That was it." Eve crumpled the list into a ball and threw it into the wastebasket.

Burr looked in the wastebasket, then reached into his pants pocket. He took out an envelope. He took out a piece of paper and set it in front of Eve.

"This is the notice of foreclosure the bank filed on Nick and Molly's house."

"Did you hear a word I said?" She made a point of not looking at the piece of paper.

"See the date?"

She didn't look.

"It's two weeks ago. Do you know what it means?"

"You're the expert on foreclosure."

I deserved that.

"My dear Eve, a mortgage doesn't just go into foreclosure. There are late notices. One after another. Then, finally, a notice of default. Finally, and I mean finally, this." Burr tapped the paper.

"You've never gotten that far with your silly building."

"Exactly."

"So?"

"So, Nick and Molly Fagan had some money problems that started before he died."

"Maybe it was just the house."

"Maybe."

"Do you think Molly knew?"

"Maybe."

"And that's why you want to know about the charges."

"Exactly."

Eve took the crumpled list from the wastebasket and smoothed it out. "You need to go see the bank about the foreclosure notice."

* * *

Spindrift drifted back in the current, her engine in neutral. When the bow started to swing broadside to the river, Burr slipped the engine back in gear and brought her nose back into the current. He gave the bridge tender another blast with his horn, but the tender waved him off.

He and Zeke had driven to Harbor Springs the night before. He'd provisioned this morning and singlehanded to Charlevoix. He'd hired someone to drop his Jeep off at the city docks. He was ready to tie up now, if the engine didn't stall and the damn bridge tender would open the bridge and let him through.

Twenty minutes later, the bells on the bridge rang. The crossbars went down, and the bridge opened, like the jaws of a dragon.

* * *

Burr followed the not-so-thin teller through the lobby and into the netherworld of the bank. Banks had always made Burr nervous, mostly because he was always late on something. Banks called it paying in arrears, which he thought was a polite way of saying *pay or die*. He didn't owe a nickel to the

Charlevoix State Bank. He hadn't tried to cash a check, which he thought showed uncommonly good judgment on his part. He hadn't even asked the bank to break a fifty, which he didn't have anyway. But he still had that 'I know I've done something wrong' feeling. He was fearless in court but a marshmallow in a bank.

The teller led him past three desks of worried-looking assistant vice-presidents to a corner office.

She knocked.

"Come on in."

The teller opened the door. "Mr. Lafayette to see you, sir."

He was lean and had brown hair with blond streaks and an end-of-summer tan. He had on a gray summer-weight suit, white shirt and club tie. The shirt showed off his tan.

He didn't get that tan sitting in here all day.

The banker came around the desk and shook Burr's hand. "Jack Flood." He pointed to one of the side chairs, then sat on the corner of his desk.

Burr looked around Flood's office. Not a bit spartan. Trophies with miniature golfers everywhere.

That's how he got his tan.

"It's nice to meet you."

"Mr. Flood, I'm here to see you about Nick Fagan's mortgage."

"Call me Jack."

"Jack, my client received a notice of foreclosure on their house on Lake Charlevoix."

"I signed it myself."

"That's why I'm here."

"Of course." Flood smiled back at Burr. "Do you have something for me?"

"For you?"

"The amount in arrears."

The first check Molly writes is going to me.

"I'm sorry we had to send the foreclosure notice, but we must stay current." The tan banker clapped his hands.

"Of course you do."

"If you give me the check, I'll get one of the girls to give you a receipt, and everything will be hunky-dory."

I may have heard someone say that when I was seven.

"I didn't bring a check."

"Cash? You brought cash? How wonderful." Flood clapped his hands again.

Burr shook his head.

"A wire?" A shadow came across the overdue banker's face.

"Jack, my client, Molly Fagan, just got the notice of foreclosure. This was the first she'd heard anything about it."

"Your client is Molly Fagan?"

Burr nodded. "How many months is the mortgage overdue?" Burr said.

Flood scowled. "Mr. Lafayette, the mortgage is in Nicholas Fagan's name. His name alone. If you don't represent him, or his estate, I can't discuss anything with you."

"How late is the loan?"

Flood walked around his desk and sat in his overstuffed chair. He folded his hands. "I can't say."

"Would you like to get paid?"

"Of course, but I can't talk to you about it if you don't represent Mr. Fagan's estate."

I bet he plays golf with Nickels.

"Molly Fagan is his sole heir."

"But she's not the executor."

"Who might that be?"

"Robert Davies."

Perfect.

"Mr. Flood, why didn't my client receive notice until now?"

"I really shouldn't be talking to you."

"Mr. Flood, if you have any hope of getting any money out of Molly Fagan, it would be better if you talked to me."

"The notices went to Mr. Fagan at the radio station. That's the address he gave us. The notice of foreclosure was also sent to the residence because that's the subject of the foreclosure."

"And when did the loan go into default?"

Flood straightened his tie. "I can't say."

"What if you could say?"

"I can't."

This guy would make a great witness.

"Mr. Flood, what is the policy of Charlevoix State Bank when it comes to foreclosures?"

"I beg your pardon."

"How many missed payments are there before you start foreclosure?"

"Six."

"Six months then."

"Yes."

The loan started to go bad at least three months before Nick died.

"Thank you." Burr started for the door.

"Mr. Lafayette."

Burr turned.

"Nick Fagan had another mortgage that's gone bad."

"Really."

"A house in Boyne City. He was the co-signer with Alexandra McCall. Do you know where we might find her?"

* * *

Burr slid closer to Maggie. His arm brushed against her breast, and he felt her nipple through her bathing suit.

Burr had rowed Maggie out to *Spindrift* around noon. He'd tied the dinghy to the mooring, started the engine and cast off. All by himself. He'd put her at the helm while he took off the sail covers and had her head up into the wind so he could hoist the sails.

"All you have to do is make sure the bow of the boat is on the same line as the wind vane on the top of the mast," he'd said.

That turned out to be more difficult than he thought it would be.

Maggie wanted Burr to teach her how to sail, but so far Burr was single-handing. They were just about to round Harbor Point and head up into the wind. She was back at the helm but having a hard time of it.

"This is a backwards steering wheel, and it looks like a long stick," she said.

She's the smartest person I know, but this isn't working out.

"It's a tiller, and it's attached to the rudder. When you move it to starboard, *Spindrift* turns to port." Burr pulled the tiller toward him. "Like this."

"Right and left?"

"Yes."

"Why don't you just say right and left?"

Burr was doing his best, but he was distracted by Maggie's orange one-piece bathing suit and cutoffs.

She pulled up one of the straps of her bathing suit. "I'm trying to learn how to sail, and all you're doing is ogling me."

"If *Spindrift* had a steering wheel, you'd steer her just like a car. It's different with a tiller."

"It's a dumb way to steer."

"All you have to do is remember that the boat is going to turn the opposite way you move the tiller."

"That flies in the face of everything I've ever learned about steering anything," Maggie said. She slid away from him.

"We're coming up to Harbor Point. When we get past it, harden up."

"I beg your pardon."

"We're going to sail closer to the wind. So, you push the tiller to port." Maggie glared at him.

"Push the tiller to the left. *Spindrift* will turn to the right."

The wind drifted in from the northwest under clear skies. Seventy-five degrees, crisp, and dry. A perfect northern Michigan Saturday afternoon in September. Burr hadn't made much progress with Molly's defense, but things were picking up with Maggie. This was the second time he'd seen her since the Fourth of July. Marriage hadn't come up, and Burr wasn't going to be the one to broach the subject.

They rounded Harbor Point.

"Push the tiller away from you a little. Like this." *Spindrift* edged up into the wind. "We need to watch out for the other boats."

"Just so you know, they're everywhere," Maggie said. "You do it." She stood and took two steps to the stern and looked back at Harbor Springs.

"It's beautiful. The water and the sky against the shore."

Burr nodded.

"I'm going to get this, but you need to slow down. The tiller thing is backwards, and I don't understand the jargon."

"It's not jargon."

"I'm a Ph.D. in ornithology. I know jargon when I hear it."

It's been this way for a thousand years.

She bent down and kissed him. "Let's try it this way." She took the tiller from him and put it between her legs. "I can steer with my thighs."

This was absolutely too much. Burr sat back against the gunwale and ran his hand along the varnished rail.

"I think I've got it." She pushed her thigh to the left and the boat went right. "I push the tiller to the left which is port, and the boat turns right. Which is starboard." She pushed the tiller the other way. "Now the other way. I've got it."

All Burr could think of was the six-foot tiller sticking out between Maggie's legs.

She took the tiller from between her legs and stood to the right of it. "Stand up behind me. Make sure I've got it right."

I don't think this is a good idea.

"Come on." She took Burr by the hand and pulled him to his feet. "Stand behind me and we'll steer together."

He stood behind her. She backed up against him. "Oh, someone's glad to see me."

"We need to watch where we're going."

"I am watching." She pushed back against him. "That feels nice. Now we'll just move our thighs a little. I've got this backwards steering figured out. Put your hands around my waist so we can steer together."

Burr could hardly contain himself.

"I've got it," she said. Maggie let go of the tiller. She undid her cutoffs and stepped out of them. She wiggled her bright orange bottom against him.

"Your turn."

"There's boats everywhere."

She turned and unzipped his shorts. She pulled at his boxers and freed him. "You're as stiff as the tiller."

"Maggie."

"No one can see a thing." She pulled the bottom of her bathing suit to one side and pushed herself on him. "That's very nice."

She put his hands on her breasts. She pushed herself all the way on him. "I'll steer the boat while you steer me."

CHAPTER TWELVE

Burr had just left Toski Sands, a small, pricey grocery store halfway between Petoskey and Harbor Springs. The manager had been delighted to see him about Nicky's bill until he found out that Burr wasn't there to pay off the five-thousand-dollar charge. According to the manager, a middle-aged man with the beginnings of a paunch, Nick bought steaks, chops, shrimp, cheese, and wine. Burr thought Nick could have paid half the price at Glen's Market, but he couldn't have charged it at Glen's. The manager said Nick had always been a slow pay, but the paying had stopped before he died. Or was murdered.

It was the same story at the Rexall Drug Store on Main Street in Charlevoix, the grocery store on the south end of town, and the cleaners. They were all mad, and the only one who had any chance of ever getting paid was the dry cleaner, who had two of Nick's suits, five sport coats, and a tuxedo, and he didn't have much of a chance.

Now they were on their way to Harbor Springs. Burr rolled down Zeke's window. The Lab stuck his head out and bit at the wind. He rolled down his own window and did the same thing.

A BMW honked its horn at them. Burr pulled his head back in. "Zeke, old friend, I'm glad you like it, but it's not for me."

Burr had had a fine, if unsettling, afternoon with Maggie. She'd gone back to her car to get Finn, her English setter, and they'd both come aboard the *Spindrift*. Maggie had sat across from Burr. Finn had sat next to Burr. Zeke, who still had a crush on Finn sat next to her.

"Zeke knows what he wants, even if you don't," Maggie had said.

Burr had reached across the cockpit and held her hand. He knew it was sophomoric, but it was the best he could do.

I did miss you.

Burr asked her to spend the night. She shook her head no.

"We have to get a few things straight first."

Burr didn't ask what. She didn't say, but he had a pretty good idea what they were. He'd ruined everything when he asked if they could date with a view toward marriage. She left in a huff, Finn at her heels. Zeke would have gone with them if Burr had let him.

He looked over at Zeke, who'd stopped chewing the wind. His ears flapped.

"I'm pretty sure I'm not marriage material."

They drove into downtown Harbor Springs, not a single parking place on Main Street, but it was Labor Day weekend. Burr turned onto Third Street and took a spot reserved for mail trucks at the Post Office.

He cracked the windows for Zeke and walked the two blocks to Gurney's Bottle Shop, where Nick had charged booze. Gurney's made the best sand-wiches in northern Michigan, and there was a line out the door. Burr always had the Train Wreck — roast beef, ham, turkey and salami.

He found Bill Gurney next to the cash register, putting the pickle that came with the sandwich into a plastic bag.

"This isn't a good time."

"Five minutes?"

Gurney was a short, slight man who needed a tan. He looked up at Burr. "Not right now."

"Two minutes?"

"The line's out the door, and we're almost out of bread."

Gurney's baked their own bread every day, and they made sandwiches until they ran out of bread which, in the summer, was nearly every day.

"It's about Nick Fagan."

"I'm never going to get paid, am I?" Gurney said, not asking.

"No, you're not."

"Then there's nothing to talk about."

"I represent Molly."

"In the murder trial?"

Burr nodded.

"I don't know anything about it."

"You might be surprised."

Gurney put another pickle in a bag, tied it shut and brought a sandwich maker over. "I'll be right back."

Gurney led Burr to the walk-in cooler at the back of the store. "Two minutes."

I won't last more than two minutes in here.

Burr had known Bill Gurney for as long as he'd owned the store. He bought all his booze here.

"It's about Nick Fagan's charge."

Gurney bit his lip. "At the beginning, he paid it off every month. Like clockwork. Then it slipped. Thirty days. Sixty days. Ninety days." Gurney put his hands in his pockets. "Then never."

"When did that happen?"

"I'm not sure. I got the last check five, maybe six, months ago."

Just like everyone else.

"What happened?"

"What do you mean what happened? He quit paying. He said he could pay with advertising. I traded with him. For a while. Then I cut him off."

"Did he say why he couldn't pay?"

"He entertained clients, I think. I know he had station parties. To promote the station. I never saw him have a drink."

"Was the charge in the station's name?"

Gurney shook his head. "I probably should have done that, but radio stations are always slow pay. I thought it would be better if it was in his name. It worked. For a while."

Burr shivered.

"The thing about Nick was that he was short."

What does that have to do with anything?

"Short. Like me. Except he didn't like it. Me, I don't care. But he didn't like it. He had lifts in his shoes. Did you know that?"

Burr nodded, shivering.

Bill isn't a bit cold.

"Like Napoleon. Most driven guy I've ever seen. He was going to make KHQ the biggest, best, most successful station up here, and he did." Gurney looked at Burr. "Are you cold?"

"Cold? No."

"Your teeth are chattering. He was also the best salesman I ever met. I wanted to believe him. He was just so sure of himself." Gurney pushed a six-pack of Corona toward the glass doors on the self-serve side of the cooler. "That stuff really sells. Or maybe he was so sure of himself because he wasn't so sure of himself."

I've got to get out of here before I freeze to death.

"Maybe down deep he had something to prove. To himself maybe. Maybe he wasn't so sure of himself."

I don't care about anything except getting out of here.

Burr started for the door.

"He seemed so sure of himself. Hard guy to like, but easy guy to admire." Gurney filled the display with more Corona, then Heineken. "You sure look cold."

Burr walked out of the cooler, out the back door and into the rain. By the time he got back to the Jeep, he was soaked. He hadn't seen rain coming, and his seat was wet because he'd left his window cracked for Zeke.

"I don't know any more than when I started except now, I'm cold and wet."

He drove toward Harbor Point in the rain. The defroster never worked right and didn't now. The windows fogged up and he had to wipe off the windshield with his hand. The back window was hopelessly fogged.

He and Zeke parked in the garage in one of his aunt's stalls and had to ride a bike to Cottage 59 — no cars allowed on Harbor Point. By the time he got there, he was wetter than he ever remembered being when he was fully dressed, except for the time he fell off the Irish gas dock. Zeke, who'd trotted alongside the bike, was soaked, but he looked like he was quite enjoying himself.

Burr parked the bike, climbed the porch and knocked.

Kathryn Lafayette, his father's sister and his only living relative save Zeke-the-Boy, answered on the third knock.

"Did you fall off the gas dock again?"

Burr stepped inside. Zeke followed him and shook off.

"Let me get you a towel." His aunt disappeared and came back. She dried Zeke off. "I don't want you to catch a cold. Not at your age."

Aunt Kitty was eighty, never married, but always in demand. She'd graduated from the University of Michigan Law School when women lawyers were few, if any. She'd fought the developers in northern Michigan long before it was fashionable and mostly on her own nickel.

His grandfather, the original Aaron Burr Lafayette, had built Cottage

59. It was the last cottage at the end of Harbor Point, if you could call a seven-bedroom, five-bath house a cottage. It was one of the few that faced both the bay and the big lake. All the views were spectacular, but none were as good as the view from the turret.

She lived here year-round. Cottage 59 was all that was left of the family fortune, and it was drafty in the winter.

* * *

Burr had grown up with more than enough, but it didn't last.

His grandfather, the first Aaron Burr Lafayette, had moved to Detroit after the family bank had failed for the fifth time. Planter's Bank of Baton Rouge had made a fortune lending to sugar planters, but it was a boom-and-bust business, and the planters had a cavalier attitude about paying back the money they'd borrowed.

Aaron had moved to Detroit when he was twenty-five. He'd hired at Fords. It turned out he had a gift for metalworking. He started his own shop, milling the heads for Henry Ford's Model T. He came up with the jigs to machine crankshafts, and he ended up with a piece of Ford's crankshaft business.

But what put him over the top was the broach. Aaron figured out how to cut a square hole in metal. He did it by piercing the metal with a hardened steel point with a square shape that got ever so slightly bigger as it pierced the metal. He got a patent on his tool and founded Colonial Broach in the '30s on the east side of Detroit, near the site of the old Chrysler plant.

Five years later, he invented the tap, the tool that puts threads in metal. Detroit Tap and Tool was born.

Aaron and his wife, Amelia, built a grand brick home on Lake St. Clair in Grosse Pointe Park. They had two children, George and Kathryn. Amelia died of tuberculosis. Aaron did his best to raise his two children. They were chauffeured to school during the Great Depression.

Aaron had a stroke a week after he was robbed at gunpoint. It was a Friday afternoon. Everyone was paid in cash then, and he'd just gotten back from the bank with the payroll. He was held up in the parking lot of Colonial Broach. He died two weeks later. George took over, but he didn't have the ability or the interest in metal that his father had.

It didn't really surprise anyone when the companies Aaron had founded went under. It was less surprising when George ran his Coupe de Ville head on into a bridge abutment on the Chrysler Freeway. The police were kind enough to call it an accident. Burr's mother, Miriam, died of a broken heart.

George and Miriam left their only child, Aaron Burr Lafayette, with enough money for a good education and precious little else.

* * *

"Follow me up to the turret. I have a space heater up there."

Burr followed his aunt's white ponytail. She was tall, thin and tan. She had Burr's pointed nose, or rather, he had hers. They had the same eyes. She called them cerulean.

She stopped at the foot of the stairs and turned to him. "Make me a martini, would you, please." She started up the stairs, Zeke at her heels.

Traitor.

The old refrigerator ground away in the kitchen, the compressor on top, four spindly legs holding it up.

"This thing is as old as you are."

"I heard that."

Burr filled two rocks glasses with ice, then poured two shots of Bombay into each glass. He poured a capful of dry vermouth, threw it down the sink, and dripped what was left into his aunt's glass. He dropped an olive in her glass and finished making his drink.

Burr climbed two flights of stairs to the third floor, then through the bedroom to the turret. Aunt Kitty had the space heater on, Zeke lay in front of it, far enough away so his fur wouldn't catch fire but just barely.

It smells like a wet dog in here.

Burr handed his aunt her martini and sat across from her. The turret looked out over the harbor, Little Traverse Bay and Lake Michigan. Burr thought it had the most spectacular view in Harbor Springs. He loved the turret, but it haunted him.

This had been Burr's father's room, and Burr had never made peace with what had happened.

Aunt Kitty sipped her drink. "Still too much vermouth but you're learning."

If there was any less vermouth in that drink, it would be straight gin.

Burr slid his chair closer to the heater.

"It's wonderful to see you, but I suspect there's a reason you're here. Especially in the rain."

"What do you know about Nick Fagan?"

"That awful short man?"

"He's dead."

"I know. You're defending his wife. And you're not a criminal lawyer."

"I wasn't the last time either."

"Don't be smart with me."

"What about Nick Fagan?"

"He had an ego as big as a barn."

"That's what I hear."

"And that partner of his. Davies. What a stuffed shirt."

"And?"

"And? He was born on third base and thinks he hit a triple."

I haven't heard that one in a while.

"Davies' father got an FM license in Detroit when the FCC was literally giving them away. He put it on the air on a lark, and Robert, don't-call-me-Bob, fell into it." She sipped her martini, then took a big swallow.

"Do you know if KHQ had money problems?"

"If they did, Davies would be the last to know. He thinks money comes in like a God-given right. I knew his father. Smart man. Knew all about money."

Aunt Kitty swirled the ice in her glass. "His partner, what's his name, Harvey. That's it, Harvey. Nothing gets by him."

"The Porn King of northern Michigan?"

Aunt Kitty scowled at him. "He's a fine man, started from nothing. If there's anything going on at that radio station, he'll know. Go see him."

"I did."

"See him again."

Aunt Kitty looked out the window. "It's really coming down now. That's what happens when the wind goes to the southeast."

"Did Nick have any friends?" Burr said.

"I don't know. A man like that doesn't have friends. Admirers, sycophants and hangers-on. Probably not too many friends."

"Who do you think might have killed him?"

"It seems like Molly had a pretty good reason."

"Other than her."

"This is exactly why you shouldn't be doing this. One of these days you're going to lose." She put her hands in her lap. "If you're looking for suspects, I'd take a look at Nick's competitors."

Burr arched his eyebrows.

"Every radio station owner up here despised him. He took their customers." She handed Burr her glass. "A dividend, please." Aunt Kitty looked out the window again. "There's dry clothes in there." She pointed at his father's bedroom. "You're about the same size."

* * *

Burr spent a fitful night in his father's old room and drove back to East Lansing the next morning. He and Zeke snuck into his apartment, and he put himself to bed. He worked on his paying cases, not that there were very many, for the next three days.

Then he drove back to Molly's. At Alma, the median on 127 had been full of New England asters, big showy wildflowers with purple petals with a yellow center, the last wildflower of the season. By the time he reached Grayling, some of the aspen had a few yellow leaves, and the odd maple had a red leaf or two. The clouds broke up at Gaylord, and by the time he parked the Jeep, they were gone, a crisp, early fall day. It wasn't cold enough for his Barbour jacket, but Burr thought he could probably use a sweater.

Burr sat across the kitchen table from Molly. "This is a nightmare," she said, somewhere between angry and crying. "I didn't kill Nicky."

I'm not so sure.

Burr looked out at Lake Charlevoix, the waves washing in, not a care in the world.

"Don't you believe me?"

You may not have killed him, but there's something you're not telling me. Or something you're lying about.

"I believe you, but you were seen putting something in the veal morel. You didn't eat any of it, and it looks like Nick tried to change the beneficiary on his life insurance policy. We can't find Alexandra McCall, and he may have been having an affair with her."

"I looked through his desk after he died, and I didn't find the form."

"But Davies found it."

"Don't you believe me?" Molly said again. She put her hands on Burr's hands.

That's melodramatic.

"Of course I do, but I need a little help."

"I didn't put anything in those awful mushrooms, and Nicky would never cheat on me."

"He cheated on his first wife."

Molly pulled her hands back. "That was different. They weren't happy."

"And you were? You and Nick?"

"Yes. And that's why I don't know who what's-her-name is."

"But she worked at the station."

"So did twenty other people."

"Did you go with Nick that day? To look for morels?"

She shook her head.

"Do you know where he went?"

"What difference does it make where he went?"

"Molly, I'm trying to help. It probably doesn't matter, but it might." Burr looked back out at the lake then back at Molly. "Did he go with anyone?"

"No."

"How do you know?"

"He'd have told me."

Right.

"Did he go anywhere between the time he finished looking for morels and the time he came home?"

"I don't know."

"Where might he have gone?"

"He might have gone to Car Wars."

"Car Wars?"

"All the car dealers set up at the Petoskey fairgrounds and have a big sale. KHQ did a remote."

"Car wars?" Burr said again.

"It's a play on *Star Wars*. It's just a big car sale. Most of the radio stations were there."

"Where else might he have gone?"

It was Molly's turn to look out the window. "He might have gone to the station. He was always going there."

"What happened to the mushrooms when he got home?"

"I washed them. Then I put them in a Ziploc bag and put them in the refrigerator."

"Then what?"

Molly turned toward Burr. "What difference does it make?"

"I'm trying to establish the chain of evidence."

She leaned toward him. "What?"

"Is it possible someone could have tampered with the mushrooms between the time Nick picked them and the time you took them into the kitchen at the Arboretum?"

"I put them in my purse when we left for the restaurant. I took them into the kitchen and gave them to Cat."

"The cook?"

Molly nodded.

"And that's the last time you saw them?"

She nodded again.

That's not what Cindy Showalter said.

Burr walked to the deck and looked out at Lake Charlevoix. "Cindy Showalter said she saw you put something in the veal morel."

"I didn't. I swear." She cracked her knuckles.

That is annoying.

"Why would she say you did?"

"I don't know."

"But you did go back into the kitchen."

"Just to check on things. Nick was so fussy."

That, I believe.

"So, someone in the kitchen put something in with the morels, or ..." Burr looked back out at the lake, "... he picked some poisonous mushrooms."

* * *

The next afternoon, Burr took Boyne City Road south, winding in and out of the woods, a cornfield every now and then, the blue of Lake Charlevoix sometimes in sight and always on his right. They passed the Horton Bay General Store and Hemingway's haunts. Two miles further down the road he turned in at a sign marked "Revels" and drove through oaks, ashes, maples and hemlocks.

"Zeke, this driveway is in better shape than just about any road I've ever been on."

The driveway ended in a circle drive, the center overflowing with perennials in red, purple, orange, and yellow. Burr parked behind a late model Benz.

"This place is a castle."

Burr knocked on a Volkswagen-size front door. The cottage, not a cottage by any stretch of the imagination, was all fieldstone on the first floor, full logs on the second. Two dormers peeked out of the shake roof.

They look like eyes.

Harvey Wall answered the door. Burr walked back to the Volkswagen front door. Harvey looked over Burr's shoulder at the Jeep. "They still make those things?"

Burr nodded.

"I had one for a while. Back window never worked right."

Burr followed the porn king of northern Michigan down a hall with bright hardwood and an oriental runner to the great room with a floor-to-ceiling stone fireplace on one side, Lake Charlevoix on the other. Dining room and commercial size kitchen on the right. A breakfast room on the lake side with a table and chairs in a bay window.

There's money in porn.

Wall took Burr out to the deck. They sat in wicker chairs underneath a pergola. A wood-chip path ran down to the water. There were myrtle and ivy where the lawn might have been. The wind had died, and it was dead calm. Lake Charlevoix looked like a blue sheet of glass.

"Something to drink?"

If I have anything like what I had last time, Zeke will have to drive.

"Water."

"Water? There's a lake full of water."

Harvey walked over to the bar at the edge of the pergola, his back to

Burr. Burr heard ice, bottle and glass noises. Harvey came back and handed Burr a tall glass with ice, full of something clear with a lime squeeze.

I don't think this is ice water.

"Here's to finding Nicky's murderer. Let's hope it's not Molly. Cheers." Harvey clanked Burr's glass. "Nothing like a gin and tonic with what's left of summer."

Burr took a drink.

This is all gin.

"There's no reason to ruin perfectly good gin with tonic."

Burr nodded. "Can you tell me anything about the competition?"

"The competition?"

"I hear Nick wasn't well loved by the other stations."

"That's the understatement of the year."

Burr nodded again.

"Me, I don't have much competition. I took care of the ones I had. The other stations had the pie all cut up the way they wanted until Nicky came along. He turned everything upside down."

"What did they think about it?"

"They hated him. Couldn't believe one station could take all their business away. Which is what he did. Collecting, though, that's something different. We talked about that last time." Harvey finished his drink and stood. "How about a refill?"

That'll be the end of me.

Burr shook his head. Harvey took Burr's glass to the bar. "They all hated him. Every single one," he said, his back to Burr.

"Did anyone hate him enough to kill him?"

"Melissa is the one you should ask. She knows all of 'em. Worked for a few before Nicky hired her away."

Harvey handed Burr a brand-new gin and tonic with a grapefruit-size wedge of lime. Burr picked out his lime and squeezed it into the drink. "I like mine with lots of lime. You should ask Melissa," he said again.

Burr squeezed his lime.

"I think she had a crush on him. They all did."

Harvey banged on the pergola again.

"Did anyone hate him enough to kill him?"

Harvey looked down the path. "I never liked grass," Harvey said. "If you want grass, buy a place at Belvedere or the Chicago Club. That's where my stuffed shirt of a partner is. You have to have grass. Lots of rules there. They didn't want me there." Harvey smiled at Burr. "Because I'm in adult entertainment. Plenty of 'em come to my places." Harvey drank half his drink. "A couple guys really hated him. Guy who owns the country station. Fought us from the get-go. Way back to when we applied. Same thing with the AC. You know what that is."

Burr shook his head.

"Adult Contemporary. Pop music. Not too hard, not too soft."

Burr nodded.

"Nick pretty much put the other Top 40 out of business. Just a Class A FM. Only 3,000 watts. KHQ is a Class C, a hundred-thousand-watt flame-thrower. You can hear it all the way to the North Pole. Big signal. That had something to do with it."

"Anyone else?"

"TV stations weren't too happy either. We're losing now, though. We just don't have the juice without Nick. Damn thing might be good for a write-off now." Harvey finished his drink, then reached for Burr's glass. Burr hung onto it for dear life.

"I'd rather have the money, but I can use the write-offs. The IRS is always after me. I got a cash business, and they know it."

Harvey Wallbanger banged on the pergola.

* * *

Burr sat across from Maggie at the Gandy Dancer. She had on a black, above-the-knee dress with a V-neck, a forest green jacket, dangly gold earrings, a gold chain necklace, and black heels high enough to get Burr's attention. A little lipstick and a little eye makeup, but that was all she needed.

She'd invited Burr to dinner at the Gandy Dancer, the old train station in Ann Arbor, just about the best restaurant in town, and the reincarnation of the Michigan Central Railroad Station, circa 1876. Fieldstone walls, high ceilings, slate roof, and floor to ceiling windows overlooking the railroad tracks. The Gandy Dancer was famous for its seafood and infamous for its prices.

I can buy a glass of wine for the price of a train ticket to New York.

Burr was doing his best to nurse his first martini. He desperately wanted another, but he thought it was too soon, even for him.

"Go ahead. Order another one," Maggie said.

"You said I drink too much."

"It's just ice." She waved the waitress over. "Could he have another, just like this one?"

"This one is fine."

"I'll drive." Maggie swirled her vodka on the rocks but didn't drink any. "This is how you nurse a drink."

What's going on?

Burr's martini came along with the calamari he'd ordered. He wasn't a big fan, but it was Maggie's favorite.

How can anyone say I'm self-absorbed?

She squeezed lemon on the calamari, picked a piece up with her fingers and dipped it in the red pepper sauce. She bit half of it and chewed it slowly. "I couldn't wait to put it on my plate. Have some."

"I think I'll have an olive first."

Burr ate one of his olives. Maggie kept after the calamari. Somehow, she'd gotten a dab on her nose.

"Is there something wrong?" Maggie said.

"No. No. Everything's fine."

"Why are you looking at me like that?"

"You're so pretty."

"Why, thank you." She put her hand on top of his. The waitress came back. She couldn't help but stare at Maggie's nose.

"Is there something wrong?" Maggie said.

The waitress touched the end of her nose. Maggie touched her own nose, then wiped it off with her napkin.

"Burr Lafayette," she said, "how could you?"

"It looked good on you."

"Are you ready to order?" the waitress said.

"I'd like another Stoli on the rocks. Then we'll be ready."

"Nothing for me," Burr said.

"Please bring him another one of those." Molly pointed at Burr's glass. The waitress left.

"I don't blame Molly for murdering her husband."

Where did that come from?

"If he was running around on her, he deserved it."

"I beg your pardon."

"There's no excuse for that type of behavior."

Burr fished out an olive.

If I run out of olives, I'm going to have to eat some of that calamari.

"Maybe his needs weren't being met," Burr said.

"What therapist told you that?"

Maggie dipped another piece of calamari in the sauce, careful about her nose. "Try some." She pushed the plate toward Burr.

Burr reached for the calamari but was saved by the waitress and their drinks.

What luck.

"I think we're ready to order," he said.

"I'd like the scallops with a Caesar salad," Maggie said.

Burr ordered the salmon and a bottle of Pouilly-Fuisse. The waitress nodded and left.

"My ex cheated on me. I'd have killed him if I could have gotten away with it."

"I think divorce is probably a better way to handle it." He pulled out another olive.

"Divorce was too good for my ex. Maybe for you, too." She patted his hand. "I'm kidding. About you. Not my ex."

Hell hath no fury like a woman scorned.

"I hope the jury isn't full of people like you."

Half a bottle of Pouilly-Fuisse later, the entrées arrived. A bottle and a half and an hour and a half later, Burr sat on the couch next to Maggie.

Between the two of them and Zeke, they'd somehow managed to make it to Maggie's house, a red brick colonial just off Washtenaw near Hill Street.

Zeke still had a crush on Finn, largely unrequited.

Maggie snuggled up next to him. Her earring brushed against his cheek. She kissed him on the mouth, and he tasted her lipstick. Her tongue darted in and out of his mouth. Then she put her hand on him.

Burr ran his hand up her bare leg, tracing circles on the inside of her thigh with his finger. Then he ran his fingers along the edge of her panties, smooth and silky with lace at the edges. He took his other hand and found the zipper on the back of her dress.

Maggie brushed his hand away. Burr didn't take the hint and reached for her zipper again. She turned her shoulders so he couldn't reach it. She kissed him, then wiggled away. "I want to make love with my dress on." She pulled up her dress and Burr saw her white satin panties with pink lace. She unbuckled his belt.

"It's all right if you don't want to marry me."

Where did that come from?

"But I think you'd make a much better husband than boyfriend." She laid back on the couch and pulled him toward her. "You have good genes and I want a baby."

That's why she ordered me another martini and a bottle of wine.

Maggie unzipped his pants.

Burr lost all his desire.

CHAPTER THIRTEEN

Burr sat at his desk and drummed his fingers. "Zeke, old friend, every time I take a step forward with Maggie, the next thing I do is take two steps back."

Zeke looked at Burr from the blue leather couch.

"She shocked me. That's what she did. It's all well and good to want to get married. I get that. If that's what she wants, that's fine. I'm just not ready. Not now." Burr took a deep breath. "Probably not ever. But that's not the point. I was clear about that. Mostly. And it's fine to want to have a kid. I get that. And I get ticking clocks. Are you listening?"

The dog lifted his head and cocked his ears.

"Of course you are." Burr shook his head. "I'm not saying I wouldn't do it, but the timing is terrible. How am I supposed to do it, then and there, when we're all ready, and then I'm going to be the father of her child. That's not how it works. And Zeke, old friend, that's why it didn't work. I can't think about making a baby when I'm about to make love. That's not how it works."

He turned around and watched the raindrops run down his office window, a soft, end of summer, beginning of fall rain. They splashed on the window, then ran down the pane in squiggly lines, nowhere to go, until they puddled on the windowsill. He looked up at the ceiling.

"Damn it all."

Zeke snored softly on the couch.

"I'm glad it's not raining on you."

The ceiling corner on the southwest corner, where the water came from, was dark, almost black. A drop grew out of the ceiling, then dripped into the martini glass on the floor.

"That's a poor use of a good glass," Burr said.

"Roof leaking again?" Eve said, from the doorway.

"No."

"I put it there to catch the drips from the roof that doesn't leak," Eve said.

Very funny.

"If it did leak, at least the floor won't get ruined."

"Thank you," Burr said, his back still to Eve.

"This building is going to be the end of you."

Burr turned around. "I thought we were in this together."

"You should never have bought this silly building. I told you not to buy it."

Sometimes I'm not a good listener.

"Sometimes you're not a good listener," Eve said. She had on a black sleeveless top, jeans, tennis shoes, and a smudge on her nose.

This must be a gardening day.

Burr touched the tip of her nose.

She blushed under her tan, rubbed her nose and sat in the blue leather wing chair she always sat in. "You have to get the roof fixed."

Burr looked out at the rain.

I never should have bought this building.

He turned back to Eve. "I was thinking …" he said.

"You need to call the roofer."

I haven't paid him for the last time he was here.

"I was thinking," Burr said again, "that radio stations aren't really real. They're …"

Jacob burst in and collapsed into his wing chair.

There was a boom outside. Burr turned back to the window. Lightning flashed to the west and there was another boom.

Jacob threw a fistful of papers in front of Burr.

Burr ignored them. "Radio stations aren't really …" he said again, "they're …"

"Stop it, Burr," Jacob said. "What's real is the leak over my desk. You've spoiled my brief."

"I didn't spoil anything."

"How can I possibly do my job and get us paid when your miserable building has ruined my brief."

"If you're not going to call the roofer, I am," Eve said.

Maybe I can find a roofer that I don't have to pay right away.

"I'll take care of the roof," Burr said. He picked up his pencil, but Jacob grabbed it before Burr could tap it.

"We have great views here on the top floor," Burr said.

"That's where the roof leaks," Eve said.

Burr looked up at the leak.

That glass is going to overflow.

"I'll take care of it," Burr said.

"As soon as Burr doesn't get it fixed, I will," Eve said.

"I'll take care of it," Burr said. He reached for his pencil which wasn't there.

Jacob tapped Burr's pencil on the desk.

"Would you please stop that," Burr said.

"Now you know what it's like," Eve said.

Burr reached into his pocket and took out a piece of paper. He unfolded it and put it next to Jacob's soggy brief.

"This is a list of KHQ's competitors. All of the masters of illusions. Someone on this list knows something. Jacob, I need you to sort out the reality from the illusion."

"I won't do it." He started tapping again.

Burr snatched the pencil from him.

* * *

Burr sat in the reception area and waited. And waited. The station played *Mamas Don't Let Your Babies Grow Up to Be Cowboys, Love's Been a Little Bit Hard On Me,* and *A Country Boy Can Survive.* Three in a row. Then commercials.

I never thought I'd rather hear ads.

Buck Houston and his rich, clear baritone with just a touch of a drawl came back on. "Seventy-five and partly cloudy in Traverse City, seventy and sunny in Petoskey. Sixty-eight and partly cloudy in Mackinaw City. It's sunny and seventy-five here in Gaylord's Alpine Village. I'm Buck Houston and here's another three in a row from K-92 Continuous Country."

He's got some voice.

Jacob, after more grumbling, had gotten Burr a list of KHQ's competition and the stations that had been at Car Wars. Burr had driven to Gaylord that morning. He'd parked downtown in front of a brown A-frame with red and yellow gingerbread trim, the home of WKLH-FM. He'd been waiting to see Buck Houston for the better part of an hour. He thought he'd rather lose his hearing than listen to another country song.

A small, thin man in a white shirt and a thinner black tie came out of the studio.

Burr stood. "I'm here to see Buck Houston."

"That's me." The small, thin man's voice boomed. Burr shook a limp hand.

"This is all an illusion," Burr said, mostly to himself.

"What?"

"Nothing. Just that radio stations are illusions. Theatre of the …"

Buck cut him off. "Come on into my office." He led Burr down a narrow hall past the studio, then opened a door to another studio. "Jack, spell me for a minute." Buck walked past two more studios then an open area with desks but no people.

"Salespeople can't make any money in the office. I throw 'em all out at nine. They probably go to the movies, but at least I don't have to look at 'em wasting time. No illusion there." Buck opened a door at the end of the hall and sat behind a desk he could barely see over and an ashtray full of cigarette butts that he couldn't see over. He lit a cigarette.

Burr sat across from him.

"You're here about Fagan, right?"

Burr nodded.

"Miserable son-of-a-bitch. Little guy with a big ego. Waltzed in here like he owned the place." Houston tapped the ash of his cigarette in the ashtray, but it spilled on his desk. He ignored it. "Not in my office but around here. Up north."

"I beg your pardon."

"Moved up here from Detroit. Acted like he owned the place. Cocky little bastard."

"Did KHQ hurt your business?"

The little man looked at his cigarette, stubbed it out, lit another. "My business? No. Not a bit. Country and pop don't mix, audience wise. My signal is as good as his." He looked at his burning cigarette. "Was. I guess it was. Since he's dead. His signal still is though. I guess."

"KHQ didn't hurt you at all?"

"I go from the straits to Cheboygan to Petoskey to Traverse City. Hard to get hurt when you got physics like that."

Burr watched the ash burn down on Houston's cigarette. "I heard he turned everything upside down."

"He may have taken a little off the bottom of my audience. The kids. But they don't buy anything. A country audience is the best there is. Thirty-five plus. They all got jobs. Mostly. And you know what?"

Burr didn't.

"They do what you tell 'em to do. You tell 'em to go somewhere. Like a car dealer. They go. Grocery store. Same thing. Best audience there is. They do what Buck says. Good thing they don't know who Earl Hickey is. That's me. I own this place, but the world thinks I'm Buck Houston."

"Did they do what you said at Car Wars?"

Houston dropped his cigarette. "What's that?"

Burr watched the cigarette burn scorch Houston's desk, but it wasn't the first one. "Car Wars," Burr said again.

"How do you know about Car Wars?" Houston picked up the cigarette and stubbed it out in the ashtray. "My secretary says I'm going to burn the place down."

"Was your station there?"

"Of course we were."

"Were you there?"

"I did the broadcast. Star of the show."

"Was Nick at Car Wars?"

"He was always at the big ones."

"Did you see him?"

"Not hardly."

"What stations did Nick hurt?"

The small man with the big voice shook another cigarette out of the pack. He looked at it, then put it back in. "Doctor says I got to cut down." He shook the cigarette back out and lit it. "Hurt. Probably everybody. Everybody but me. Especially WBAY in Petoskey. Little corn popper class A Top 40. Killed old Julie. I have a hundred thousand watts, just like Nicky had. Couldn't touch me." Houston looked out the window then back at Burr. "My biggest problem is this stupid Alpine Village building thing in Gaylord.

City's been good to me but how do you make an Alpine Village go with country?"

* * *

WBAY was sandwiched between a nail salon and a therapist's office, on Howard Street, at the edge of downtown Petoskey. The receptionist took Burr back to the general manager's office.

A freckled redhead in her forties was looking out her window. She flicked her cigarette out the window then met him at the door. "Julie French." She shook his hand.

That's a handshake.

Burr introduced himself and told her why he had come, everything except the *did you kill Nick Fagan* part, but Julie French was no fool.

"If I stand here on my tiptoes and look this way, I can just about see the bay," she said.

Her hair fell on the shoulders of her emerald shirtdress. Her cream pumps, even with a sensible heel, didn't hurt anything.

"We call the station the Bay, but you probably know that."

"I like the music."

She turned toward him. "Aren't you a little old for Top 40? I shouldn't have said that." Her cheeks turned red.

That covered up her freckles.

She sat at her desk, a table really, blond with shallow drawers. "How about if I just keep making things worse." She crossed her legs and looked right at him. "You're really not here about the music."

Burr sat a little straighter in his chair. "Not really."

"Nick Fagan," she said, not asking.

"I represent Molly Fagan."

"Lovely woman. Why she married him, I'll never know."

Nick was a popular fellow.

"How can I help?"

Burr leaned forward. "I'm trying to find out about Nick's enemies. Who might have hated him enough to kill him?"

"Other than Molly?"

Burr leaned a little further forward. "Molly didn't kill Nick."

"She had every reason to." She walked behind him and straightened a painting on the wall.

"Degas?" Burr said.

"The ballerina. I love it. And the Monet." She touched the frame of another print. "The girl in the summer dress."

This isn't like any office I've ever been in.

She turned back to Burr. "I have a closetful. More paintings than walls. I put them up, take them down, move them around."

"I've always liked Monet," Burr said.

"This is just a radio station," she said. "A little one. We only cover Petoskey and Harbor Springs, and part of Charlevoix. It's not art, it's pop culture. I try to make it like pop art."

"I never thought about it like that."

"There are bills to pay."

"Did KHQ hurt that?"

She looked back at Burr. "At first. But we got over it. Nick made us better. We had to get better to stay in business. We have loyal advertisers who stick with us."

That's not what Buck Houston said.

"So, you didn't get hurt?"

She straightened the Monet, which didn't need straightening, then sat back down behind her desk.

"I didn't get hurt. The station got hurt a little. I'm not the station. Nick was KHQ." She looked down her nose at him.

I don't think I'd like to be on her bad side.

"I didn't like Nick Fagan, but I didn't kill him."

"Do you have any ideas?"

She started to say something, but Burr cut her off. "Other than Molly," he said.

"Other than Molly," she said. "The only one who really got hurt was Earl at K-92. Nick went right after him, and he's never recovered."

"That's a country station."

"I know, but the coverage areas are about the same. Nick went after him and all his big advertisers."

"You think Buck might have killed Nick?"

"Buck Houston. What a cornball name. He hated Nick. I'm surprised cigarettes haven't killed him. He's a little jerk with a big ego, and he's just mean enough to do it."

"Were you at Car Wars this year?"

"We're there every year. It's in our backyard."

"Were you there?"

"I'm there every year. All our big car dealers are there."

"Did you see Nick?"

"I went out of my way not to see him." She walked to a Cezanne, the one with the old man smoking a pipe and playing cards. She cocked her head then straightened it.

* * *

Burr took US-131 south, past Boyne Falls. At Kalkaska, he turned east on M-72. A mile later he turned right and ended at what looked like the smallest radio station and the tallest tower he'd ever seen.

"Zeke, if there was a tower of Babel, this is it." Burr cracked the windows and got out.

He parked in the shade on the side of a white cinder block building about the size of a shoebox. It had a flat roof, a fuel tank on stilts, and was desperate for a fresh coat of paint.

Burr walked up the crumbling sidewalk, opened the peeling screen door and walked into a reception area the size of a closet with no chairs and no one in sight. He turned the knob on the only other door in the room. It had a peephole, and it was locked. He knocked. No answer. He waited, knocked again, and waited.

A shoebox-sized speaker mounted on each side of the door played *She Loves You.* It was an instrumental arrangement by a full orchestra, but the speakers made it sound tinny. Then a downtempo version of *Summer Wind* by a big band, followed by *Swinging on a Star,* also a full orchestra.

I didn't think it was possible to ruin those songs.

Burr peeped through the peephole. An eye peeped back. Burr jumped. The door opened.

A big man, big in every way, came out. There wasn't room for both of them in the reception area. The big man stood in the doorway, squashed in the door frame. He was chewing on a pipe, surrounded by a cloud of smoke.

"And you are?" he said.

"Burr. Burr Lafayette."

"Do I know you?"

Thank heavens, no.

The music stopped and a mellifluous voice came on. "This is Don James. More beautiful music on WMBN after the news." Then. "It's seventy-two and sunny in Traverse City. Now the news."

"Do I know you?" the big-in-every-way-man said.

"I represent Molly Fagan."

"Oh." He backed out of the doorway and let Burr squeeze into a reception area not much bigger than a coffee cup.

Burr followed the big man and the smoke down a hall and into a room only slightly bigger than the reception area. Reel-to-reel tape machines hung on two of the walls. The third wall had a blue cabinet that covered the wall. It was stacked with long, flat machines with blinking lights.

The man squeezed behind the machines, sandwiching himself between the desk and a window behind him. He opened a desk drawer, took out a clipboard and crossed something off. One of the machines spun around slowly, not in any hurry.

Burr listened to the Tigers' score. They'd lost to the Yankees again. The machine stopped. Another started. Burr listened to the weather. Another machine started. An instrumental version of *Standing on the Corner*.

The man looked up at Burr. "I don't remember inviting you in here, and I don't like strangers."

"Mr. ..." Burr said.

"Mason," he said. "Sterling."

Which one is his first name?

Another machine started. This time it was *The Lonely Bull*.

At least it's Herb Alpert.

"Where is everyone?" Burr said.

"Who?"

"All the people. The ones who work here."

"I work here."

"What about the disc jockeys, the news guy, the weather girl."

Mason Sterling or Sterling Mason smiled. He swept a big hand around the room. "They're all here. All captured on tape."

"This is all there is?"

"All?" The big man slammed the clipboard on his desk. He pointed at the blinking lights. "That's the brains of WMBN." He stood, slid over to it and stroked it lovingly. "This is the automation system. It runs everything. All those tape machines." He pointed to the spinning machine. "I tell it what to do and it does it. *'Michigan's Beautiful North.'* Relaxing music and everything you need to know."

"WMBN," Burr said.

"Exactly."

"Mr. Mason," Burr said.

"Sterling."

How do I find these guys?

"Mr. Sterling ..."

"Sterling is my first name."

I finally learned something.

"Sterling, I'm told that Nick Fagan wasn't exactly loved by the competition, and I'm trying to find out if any of them might have been mad enough to murder him."

Sterling walked to Burr and looked down at him. "And you think I might have done it?"

This guy seems just about crazy enough to do just about anything.

"Of course not. I mean the competition."

"Of course." The big man smiled and wedged himself back in his chair. "We don't compete with KHQ. They have the teenybopper audience. WBMN has the mature audience, the ones with the money."

"Don't all radio stations compete with one another?"

Sterling folded his hands on top of the clipboard. They covered it completely. "My audience is affluent and age thirty-five-plus." He cleared his throat. "Although the salespeople at the other stations call it fifty-five-to-dead."

I'd say they have it about right.

"I certainly don't think you had anything to do with it. But I thought you might have an idea who might have."

Sterling nodded knowingly. Then he rattled off all the stations north of Clare and west of I-75.

That's a big help.

"Sterling, is there anyone who stands out on the list?"

"Stands out?"

"Someone who was really hurt by KHQ. Someone who might have wanted Nick dead."

Sterling nodded. "Julie. Julie in Petoskey. She hated Fagan."

Julie and the Impressionists.

"Her station is Top 40. Just like Nick's was. Still is, I guess. Just like Nick's but without the signal. He destroyed her."

"Really?"

"Really. She doesn't own the station. She has a little piece. Ten percent. And now it's worthless. She's a redhead. Bad temper."

"Really?"

"Really. And then there's that idiot at K-92. Calls himself Buck Houston." He shook his head. "Nick killed him. I'm surprised the cigarettes haven't killed him first."

"Even though it's country."

"Same coverage area. He'd get the big coverage buys. Not anymore. Me? Not that you asked." Sterling looked out the window. "Did you see that tower out there? I still get the big coverage buys." Sterling looked at his clipboard then cleared his throat. "And I have almost the perfect business. Not that you asked." The big man smiled at Burr. "You know what the perfect business is?"

Burr shook his head.

"The perfect business is no customers. And no employees." He smiled. "I've got the no employees part of it with Otto here." He stood and patted the cabinet with the blinking lights.

Another illusion.

Sterling waved his pipe. "I don't quite have the no-customers part of it yet. I'm down to one salesman. He's obnoxious but he's good. I only let him in the station when he brings in a contract."

"That sounds like a great business model," Burr said.

"It truly is."

"What about Car Wars?"

"That miserable thing. I had to go. My salesman couldn't cover it by himself."

"What's miserable about it?"

"There's people there. People everywhere. But I had to go."

"Is there anyone else who might have killed Nick?"

Sterling rubbed his chin. "How about Molly?"

* * *

When Burr opened the door to KHQ, he saw Melissa Warren blowing smoke rings, white halos drifting across the room. She saw him and pretended to shoo away a fly. The halos melted away.

Burr sat down in front of her, another overflowing ashtray between them. The business manager made room for her cigarette in the ashtray and stubbed it out.

Why do they all smoke?

She looked at Burr but didn't say anything.

"Were you here at the station on the Saturday of Car Wars?"

She nodded again.

"Did Nick come in while you were here?"

She shook her head. She picked up her cigarettes, but put them back down.

Thank heaven for small favors.

"How long were you here?"

She scrunched her nose. "I don't really remember. In the afternoon. Probably from about noon to five."

"And you didn't see Nick come in?"

She shook her head again. She picked up her cigarettes and lit one.

* * *

The next day, Burr asked Sammy Fairley for a table for one.

"Burr, old friend, good to see you. Of course, I have a table for you. As long as you're not here about that awful Nick Fagan business."

"I'm here for your signature martini. But I do have a few questions." He put his arm on Sammy's shoulder, which took some doing, Sammy being at least a foot shorter than Burr. He looked down at Sammy's black comb-over.

I hope I don't end up like that.

"I can't help you," Sammy said, still smiling.

"I'm sorry to drag you into this, but a few questions now are going to help keep the Arboretum out of things later."

Sammy led Burr to a window table. It was early and the restaurant was mostly empty.

"Maybe the bar would be better," Burr said.

Burr followed Sammy across the dining room, past the baby grand to the long, almost black, mahogany bar. Rudy smiled his yellow-toothed smile and mixed Burr a martini.

"I'll have the usual," Sammy said.

The bartender set an overfull rocks glass in front of Burr and a yellow drink with a red straw in a highball glass full of ice in front of Sammy.

"To the Arboretum," Burr said.

"To no bad press," Sammy said.

They clinked their glasses.

"I didn't know you like screwdrivers," Burr said.

"I don't."

"What's that?"

"A tennis ball."

"That's what Zeke-the-Boy drinks."

"It's refreshing."

"So is a cold shower."

"Orange juice and 7-Up keep me on my toes."

I don't want to be on my toes.

"I know you don't want to be involved, but Nick Fagan was poisoned here."

"We didn't poison him. His wife did."

So far, it's unanimous. Except for Molly.

Burr ate an olive. It was too soon to eat an olive, but these were desperate times. "I need to talk to the people who saw what happened with the morels."

Sammy stirred his tennis ball with the straw.

Burr stirred his drink with his finger. "If no one is sure what really happened that night or isn't really sure what they saw, that helps Molly."

"Helping Molly may not help me."

"It's part of the chain of evidence. If someone spiked the mushrooms, or even if I can show that someone could have when they were out of Molly's control, that really helps."

"It doesn't help me," Sammy said again.

Burr ate another olive.

The short restaurateur sipped his tennis ball through his straw. "So far, the Arboretum has stayed pretty much out of it, and I want to keep it that way."

"I just want to talk to the people who were here that night. The waitress, the kitchen staff, Cat. Maybe the piano player — Hoagy."

"None of them are here right now."

"How about Cat?"

"She'll cut your throat."

Burr studied his last two olives then took a drink. "Look Sammy, the prosecutor has a witness, someone from the kitchen, who said she saw Molly put something in the mushrooms. I need to talk to her."

"If that gets out, it will ruin my business."

"How long have you owned the Arboretum?"

"Seventeen years."

"Help me, and I'll do my best to keep the Arboretum out of it."

Sammy pushed his glass to the bartender. "Top this off with Grey Goose."

A preppy couple, he in a blue blazer and she in late season Lilly Pulitzer, came in.

They go nicely with the wallpaper.

Sammy drank the rest of his adulterated tennis ball. He had the bartender freshen Burr's martini, then made his way to the couple.

Burr and his drink walked through the double doors to the kitchen. It was at least twenty degrees warmer than the restaurant. It smelled like fish.

The kitchen had a wall of refrigerators and freezers, stainless-steel counters and tables, and floor to ceiling cupboards. There was a gas stove the size of a double bed. There was no one in the kitchen except Cat Garrity. She stood on her tiptoes in front of the stove, stirring a pot the size of a wading pool. She dipped a ladle, took the cigarette out of her mouth and tasted tomato something or other. She made a face, tapped the ash of her cigarette into the pot and stirred again. She turned and looked at Burr.

"You weren't supposed to see that."

"I've always thought ashes gave tomato soup a little bite. Brings out the basil."

"It's tomato bisque."

Better yet.

Cat sucked on her cigarette and stirred again. She was barely five feet tall, maybe five-five with her hair piled on top of her head. She moved in quick strokes, and her eyes darted when she spoke.

"If you're here about the whitefish or the bisque, we can talk, otherwise get out."

"I need a little help."

"Not from me you don't." She looked at the ash on her cigarette. She tapped the cigarette on the rim of the pot so that the ash fell on the floor. "The soup only needs a smidge of ash."

"I'm here about the Baked Alaska."

"No, you're not."

Cat's Baked Alaska was almost as legendary as her planked whitefish and her veal morel. Burr liked it because of the fire.

Fire makes everything taste better.

"Those mushrooms just about ruined us."

"I'm sorry."

"They weren't morels. Couldn't have been. Morels aren't poisonous."

Burr drank some of his refreshed martini.

"Thank God he didn't die here."

Burr nodded.

"Did you see anyone put anything in the bag Molly brought in?"

She shook her head. "I can't talk to you right now. The crew is due any minute."

"Cindy Showalter testified that she saw Molly put something in the mushrooms."

Cat's eyes darted around the kitchen. "Who knows what she saw." Cat crushed her cigarette in yet another overflowing ashtray. "Burr, you and I go way back. You should have been thrown out of the bar more than once, and you're the only reason Baked Alaska is still on the menu. The official position is nothing happened here. Nick Fagan may have been poisoned, but it didn't happen here."

"That's not what Oswald thinks."

"Who?"

"The prosecutor."

"Nothing happened here."

"What if you're called as a witness?"

"That's what I'll say."

Burr fished an olive out of his drink. "Even if it's not true?"

"Doesn't this help you?" Cat said.

"Probably."

"Then you should stop right there." She lit another cigarette.

"Molly came in here. With the mushrooms."

"I never liked Nick Fagan. He'd come in here, spend a fortune, and charge it. We'd go to get paid and he'd make us take it out in advertising. Cocky little son-of-a-bitch."

"Why did you let him do it?"

"Sammy did. He's a sucker for that."

"It's his place."

"Not really." She stirred the soup with her other hand. "He owns most of it, but I'm the one who lent him the money to keep it going."

Can't something be simple? Just once.

"Who do you think murdered Nick?"

"I didn't like him, but I didn't wish him dead."

That's what they all say.

"Who do you think murdered him?"

"I suppose it coulda been an accident. But if you ask me, it was probably Molly." Her eyes darted around the kitchen. "The staff will be here any minute. Shoulda been here by now." She tapped her ash in the bisque again.

CHAPTER FOURTEEN

Burr sat in his favorite booth in Beggar's Banquet, the one closest to the door. He could see the door and out the plate glass window, a perfect spot for someone who would rather be outside than inside and who was nervous when he sat with his back to the door.

He'd had quite enough of the cast of characters at the Arboretum, not to mention Nick's competition. After his less than helpful meetings with Sammy and Cat, he'd sat at the bar hoping against hope that Cindy Showalter, the witness who'd testified that she'd seen Molly put something in the mushrooms, would show up. She didn't. But Hoagy did, who said he hadn't seen Molly do anything suspicious.

Piano players know everything, but they never say anything.

He'd had two more martinis and a very fine Baked Alaska with extra fire.

He and Zeke had spent the night on *Spindrift*, Burr in a down sleeping bag, Zeke sprawled on the bunk across from Burr.

The next morning, he and Zeke drove back in the September fog, which lifted by Gaylord. The fog from Burr's martinis had lifted by Clare. By the time he'd gotten to Mount Pleasant, it had clouded over. By East Lansing, it was raining.

He'd just ordered his third Labatt when Eve came in. She sat across from him and bumped into Zeke. "It's Five Alarm Chili Day," Burr said.

The waitress came over. Burr ordered Eve a Bloody Mary with a pickle.

"I don't drink while I'm working."

"Neither do I."

"I beg your pardon."

"I'm not working. I'm at lunch."

"You drink too much, and it's going to be the end of you," Eve said.

Jacob stumbled in with his parachute-size umbrella, black with a mahogany handle. He took off his Burberry raincoat, his fedora, circa 1960, and sat down next to Eve. He put his umbrella, still open, in the next booth.

"It's bad luck to bring an open umbrella inside," Eve said.

"Nonsense," Jacob said. He wiped the rain off his forehead with his handkerchief.

"So far, that's the only luck we've had," Burr said.

"Is that why you're drinking your lunch?" Jacob said.

"It's Five Alarm Chili Day," Burr said.

"That will burn your insides up," Jacob said.

Beggar's wasn't Burr's favorite restaurant. It was dark — very dark. Dark walls, a dark ceiling, dark floor and dark booths. The only light was right next to the windows. There was so much seating that Beggar's always looked empty even when it wasn't.

But Beggar's did have Labatt on draft, and every now and then, they had five-alarm chili, the hottest chili Burr had ever had. Chili and a beer for a buck, Beggar's world-famous Sympathy for the Devil special. Bob, the owner, always called him when it was on the menu.

Jacob sneezed. He looked under the table. Zeke wagged his tail.

"I knew it."

The waitress brought Burr's chili, a bowl of oyster crackers and a glass of ice water. He ate a spoonful. "Perfect."

"The roof is leaking again," Eve said.

"On my desk," Jacob said.

"That's because it's raining." Burr took another spoonful of the chili. He looked at the ice water but drank his beer. "We're nowhere with this case. Nowhere. We can't find Alexandra McCall, and we have no suspects." Burr crumbled some oyster crackers into his chili.

"Probably because she did it," Jacob said.

Jacob is always so positive.

"I met with Nick's competition, at least the ones that Nick probably hurt the most. Molly told me that she thought Nick went to a big car sale after he went looking for morels. They were all there so it's possible that one of them could have spiked the mushrooms in Nick's car. Possible but not likely. Then I went to the station and met with the business manager. She said she'd been at the station that morning, but Nick didn't come in." Burr took a bite of his five-alarm chili and washed it down with his beer. "So there is a possible break in the chain of evidence, but it's not likely. Especially if Nick locked his car."

"It could have been an accident," Eve said.

"According to both experts, there's no way it could have been an accident," Burr said.

"I can't work at a wet desk."

"You came over here in the rain to tell me that?" Burr said.

"Yes," Jacob said. He wiped his forehead again and folded up his handkerchief.

"No," Eve said.

Burr cocked his head.

Eve reached in her purse and handed Burr an envelope, already opened.

"Oswald's witness list," Burr said.

Eve nodded.

"The trial starts in thirty days," Jacob said.

Burr read through the list. "Damn it all."

"Now what?" Eve said.

"Now I'm going to take a nap."

* * *

The snoring woke Burr up. He didn't know if it was Zeke snoring at the end of the couch or his own snoring. His mouth tasted like the chili he shouldn't have eaten and the fourth beer he shouldn't have drunk. The rain had stopped. There was still daylight but not much. He reached over and scratched Zeke's ear. Then he took the witness list out of his pocket and looked at it again.

"Damn it all."

He scratched Zeke's ear again. Zeke yelped.

"Sorry, Zeke." Burr looked at the witness list for a third time. "It's all here. Oswald's grand plan." Burr laid back down and tried to go back to sleep.

Ten minutes later, he got up and sat at his desk and picked up the witness list again. They were listed in alphabetical order, but Burr put a number in front of each one. "That's the order he'll call them."

Zeke looked up from the couch but didn't say anything.

"They're all here, the whole sorry lot, including Cindy Showalter and

Alexandra McCall. Oswald knows where they are, but I don't." He turned around and looked out his window. It had started raining again

"At least my desk isn't getting wet." He crumpled up the witness list and threw it in the wastebasket.

* * *

Burr spotted Maggie sitting by herself at a corner table at the Cottage Inn, a ten-minute walk from the diag. The Cottage Inn was Ann Arbor's most famous pizzeria.

She'd never order pizza for lunch. Has to be a salad.

He sat down beside her.

"What are you doing here?"

"I'll buy your lunch."

She pushed her chair back. "How could you possibly know I was here?"

"I saw you come out of your office."

"You followed me?"

Burr looked out the window then back at Maggie.

"You don't want to get married. You don't want to have a baby, but now you're stalking me."

If she were a teakettle, steam would be coming out of her ears.

"I was hoping we could talk a little."

Maggie took her glasses off and glared at Burr.

Not a good sign.

"We have nothing to talk about."

Burr hadn't seen or talked to Maggie since the disaster at her house. She's refused to talk to him, much less see him. The truth of the matter was that Burr had missed Maggie. He didn't think he would, but he did, and even if he still didn't want to get married or be a father again, he did want to see her. Desperately.

He was about to run his hands through his hair but thought better of it.

I'm going to stop these silly tics.

"I've been thinking about what you said. And that night."

Maggie looked at her menu.

"I'm sorry," Burr said.

She put her menu down and looked at him. "Unless you have a ring in your pocket, we have nothing to talk about."

Burr winced.

Maggie looked over Burr's shoulder and smiled.

Burr turned around. A thirty-five-ish man walked up to Maggie and kissed her on the cheek.

She looked at Burr. "This is Dr. McMasters." Then at McMasters. "My friend was just leaving."

* * *

Burr looked over at Zeke, napping on the couch again. "He's younger than me, but he's not as good looking." He swiveled in his chair and looked out his window at another September rain. More a drizzle than a rain. "It's almost duck season."

Zeke sat up when he heard "duck."

"I've got a client who may well have murdered her husband, and a girlfriend who isn't, but we do have duck season. That's something."

At the second "duck," Zeke jumped off the couch and limped over to Burr.

Burr scratched the aging Lab's ear.

"What kind of world would it be if I couldn't talk out loud to a dog. Who pretends to listen."

Zeke crawled in the knee hole of Burr's desk and laid at, mostly on, Burr's feet. Burr leaned under the desk and looked at Zeke. "She didn't have to get a boyfriend so soon."

"What did you expect her to do?"

Burr cracked his head against the desk. "Damn it all." He banged his head one last time, then sat up, Eve and Jacob sat across from him.

How much of that did they hear?

"What were you prattling on about underneath there?" Jacob said.

"Ducks," Burr said. "And duck season."

Eve smiled and looked at Burr but didn't say anything.

Burr smiled back at her.

There's probably nothing I've ever said that she hasn't heard, or anything I've ever thought that she doesn't know about.

"I like a perennial garden with full sun. And all that goes with it," Eve said.

"I beg your pardon," Jacob said.

"Burr knows what I mean."

"I assume there's a reason you asked us in here," Jacob said.

"I didn't," Burr said.

Jacob twisted one of his steel-wool curls. "It's raining, you know."

"It's drizzling."

"A drizzle is a rain."

Burr turned back to the window. "It's not raining hard enough to leak."

"I'm sure it's raining in my office," Jacob said. "I put the patio umbrella from my deck in your office. You can work under that if the roof is leaking."

Burr turned to Jacob. "Which it isn't. Because it's not raining."

Eve clapped her hands. "Stop it. Both of you." Burr and Jacob jumped. "We don't need to talk about the drizzle or the rain or the leaky roof." She looked at Burr. "Or performance issues." Burr looked at his feet.

"Molly's trial is going to start in less than a month, and for the life of me, I don't know what you've got in mind for her defense," Eve said.

Burr took Oswald's balled up list out of his desk. He set it down in front of him and did his best to flatten it out. "Unless I'm missing something, Oswald has a straightforward case. Means, motive, and opportunity."

"Oswald will try to prove that Molly killed Nick for the life insurance. Or, more likely, because she was jealous of Alexandra McCall." Burr looked at Jacob. "Oswald knows where she is. And we don't. And now we have to wait until the trial to question her."

"Molly killed him with poisoned mushrooms, which she put in the veal morel. Right when Cindy Showalter was looking," Eve said.

Burr picked up the witness list. "It's all very tidy for Oswald. For us, it has to be one of two things. Either it was an accident or someone other than Molly did it."

"Unless Molly did do it," Eve said. She reached for her earring. Burr shook his head. She put her hand back down. "What do we do?"

"We wait." Burr crumpled up the witness list again.

* * *

The mallard glided around the pond in lazy circles. Burr looked at Zeke and watched the duck in the reflection in Zeke's blue eyes. The mallard beat his wings once, twice, then he was gone.

Victor Haymarsh leaned his shotgun, a beat-up 870 almost as beat up as Burr's, against the side of the stake blind. He was fifty-five and looked it. Short and stocky with leathery skin and a graying ponytail that ran halfway down his back.

Victor lit a cigarette, then offered one to Burr, who took it. It was from the pack that Burr had just given Victor, the ceremonial offering of tobacco to a chief. Neither of them smoked except during duck season.

"You could have killed that one," Victor said.

Burr blew the smoke out of his lungs and nodded.

"When I hunt, I shoot."

Burr nodded again.

"That's the difference between you and me."

Victor Haymarsh, half Ojibwe, half Potawatomi, was Burr's oldest friend. Their grandfathers had taken them hunting at the Holiday Pond in Walpole Marsh, which was where they were now. Walpole Island was just across from Algonac on the Canadian side of the St. Clair River, an hour north of Detroit but a world away, the unceded land of the First Nation.

Burr had met Victor at his house on the Johnson River at five this morning. They'd taken his sixteen-foot camo'd boat with the twenty-five-horse Evinrude down the river. They pulled it over the dike into Walpole Marsh, the largest freshwater marsh east of the Mississippi. Victor had poled the boat up the channel into the Holiday Pond. It had been in Victor's family for seventy-five years.

They'd set seventeen decoys. Victor always used an odd number. He said it brought in the singles better because they wanted to pair up.

Burr thought it was nonsense, but he went along with it.

Burr and Victor hid in the blind, sitting on rusty folding chairs, Zeke at Burr's side. Victor had brushed the blind with this year's cattails, still green in late September.

It was fifty-two and clear, not a breath of wind. They sat and smoked.

The wind came up from the southwest at about 8:30, and that's when the ducks started to move.

A pair of wood ducks swung over the pond. They circled once, then started to fly off. Burr stood and shot the drake. It fell into the cattails on the other side of the pond. Burr opened the gate to the blind. Zeke ran out on the two-by-six dock. Burr gave the dog a line, then "Fetch." Zeke looked at him, then jumped into the pond. He swam on the line Burr had given him, steering with his tail.

"His last year?" Victor said.

"No."

"He's getting old, like the rest of us." Victor stood and turned at the waist. He couldn't bend his right leg.

Zeke made it across the pond and disappeared into the cattails. They quivered and shook where Zeke searched for the duck.

"That's hard on a dog, slopping through the muck."

"He'll be all right." Burr lit a cigarette.

The cattails stopped moving.

They watched and waited.

Ten minutes later, Zeke swam out of the cattails with the dead wood duck in his mouth. He swam back to the blind, walked up the dog ramp and presented the duck to Burr.

"Good dog, Zeke."

Zeke walked over to Victor and shook himself off.

"Just like I taught him," Burr said.

Victor looked at Burr. "Work and love."

Burr looked at him.

"Work and love," Victor said again.

"I beg your pardon."

"Freud," Victor said.

"Freud said that?"

Victor lit another cigarette. "Freud said we all need two things to have a meaningful life. Work and love."

"I see," Burr said, who didn't.

A dozen mallards circled the pond.

There's ducks everywhere, and he's talking about Sigmund Freud.

"We all need those two things," Victor said.

"Of course," Burr said.

"You do, too," Victor said.

The mallards swung in a tighter circle. Burr crouched and hid his face. He blew softly on his call.

"The way I see it, you've got some work to do," Victor said.

I thought we were duck hunting.

"You've got an old dog, a Jeep and not much of a law practice."

The ducks dropped down a little. Burr called a little and turned to Victor.

"I have a son."

"Who you see part time."

One of the hens cupped her wings. "They're coming in," Burr said, whispering.

"I think you need to straighten yourself out," Victor said.

"Be quiet," Burr said.

"You need to get your work right and find someone."

"My practice is fine. I have my own office building."

"It leaks."

The ducks dropped their feet, bright orange in the sunlight.

"And I have a girlfriend."

"Who you won't marry."

I had a girlfriend.

The ducks hovered above the decoys.

"Now," Burr said.

He and Victor stood and shot.

"Zeke, fetch."

* * *

Burr and Zeke waited in Nick's office. Zeke napped on the couch.

"Zeke, old friend, my guess is Nick didn't use that couch for napping."

They had driven up from East Lansing the night before and stayed at the Charleboyne Motel just outside Charlevoix. It was nice enough, too nice to allow dogs. There was a back entrance, so Burr thought they couldn't be serious about their silly rule.

Burr wanted to talk to Melissa one more time. She seemed to know more about Nick, KHQ, and the money than anyone else.

The receptionist had told him Melissa should be back any minute and let him wait in Nick's office.

Burr knocked on the one-way window to the studio. The disc jockey turned around. Burr waved at him, but he didn't wave back. Then he waved at the disc jockey through the one-way window. He still didn't wave back. Burr looked through the one-way window to Melissa's office. The receptionist was putting the mail on Melissa's desk. She turned. Burr waved, but she didn't wave back either.

I guess that's how one-way windows work.

Burr sat down at Nick's desk and opened the top drawer. Pens, pencils, paperclips. Then the other drawers. Nothing interesting until he got to the lower double drawer on the left. It was locked, which was enough to make it interesting. He straightened out a paperclip and had just started on the lock when Melissa came in.

"I have the key."

If she's got the key, it can't be too interesting.

"Is there something you want? Other than what isn't in that drawer?"

Burr pulled on the knob again.

"Here, let me show you." Melissa stood.

"No, that's all right."

She started around the desk.

"No. No. I don't need to see it."

The business manager stood next to Burr and opened the top drawer. She took out a key, unlocked the drawer and opened it. Burr peered in. There were about a dozen manila folders.

"Go ahead," Melissa said.

"It's all right."

"I insist."

There can't be anything here if she's showing me.

Burr took out the files and flipped through them. Employee files, expense reports, client proposals. He put the files back in the drawer. Melissa shut the drawer, locked it and kept the key.

"What was it that you wanted?"

"I'm trying to find out all I can about Nick and the station for the trial."

She nodded.

"One thing keeps coming up. Over and over."

"Yes?" She pulled her hair back, but it fell back to her chin.

"Money."

"Money?"

"More like no money. It seems that Nick had charges, personal charges, everywhere."

"That's not unusual."

"Of course not. But he didn't pay them, and when he did, he was late."

"I wouldn't know about his personal life."

"It's just that for someone who was so successful and who wanted everyone to know how successful he was, I'd have thought he'd pay his bills on time."

"Nick was busy. I don't think he paid much attention to it."

Burr nodded. "KHQ's vendors got paid late. That's your department, isn't it?"

Melissa fussed with her hair again. "That is my department. I did what Nick told me to do."

"Which was to pay late?"

"Nick was running a business. Managing cash flow was part of it. Our vendors were, are, happy to have our business."

"Did his partners know? Davies and Wall?"

"I'm sure they did."

Burr looked through the one-way window of the studio, the jock's back to him.

"It just seems odd that the biggest station up here would pay its bills late."

"We do it because we can," Melissa said.

She hasn't said anything about the receivables.

The disc jockey turned around and looked at Burr. Burr waved at him. The disc jockey didn't wave back.

"He can't see you," Melissa said.

Burr looked at Melissa. "I really need to talk to Alexandra McCall before the trial starts. Any idea where she might be?"

The business manager shook her head.

"Any forwarding address?"

She shook her head again.

"Did you ever see them together? Nick and Alexandra."

"I'd rather not say."

"Why?"

"Nick's gone. What good can come of it?"

Burr put his hands on Nick's desk, face down. "The good that can come out of it is that you can help Molly Fagan."

"What if she did it?"

"Is that what you think?"

Melissa didn't say anything.

"Did you see Nick and Alexandra together?"

She still didn't say anything.

"Melissa."

She looked away.

"Melissa," Burr said again.

She looked back at him.

"What did you see?"

"What I saw won't help Molly."

"What was it?"

"I saw them together. Nick and Alexandra. That's why she left. Nick sent her away. Molly made him do it. That's why there's no forwarding address. There was one, but Nick tore it up."

"Where did you see them?"

"Do we have to talk about this, Mr. Lafayette?"

"We do."

Melissa put her hands back in her lap. "I don't want to."

"You can talk to me now or on the witness stand."

"My testimony won't help you."

Burr drummed his fingers on Nick's desk. "Did Nick and Alexandra come in here to his office? By themselves?"

She nodded.

"Do you know what they did in here?"

Melissa shook her head.

"They could have been meeting about business. Sales and clients. She was a salesperson," Burr said.

She shook her head.

"How do you know? You couldn't see in here, could you?"

"She came out, rumpled. And Nick. He was flushed."

Oswald will have a field day with this.

"That doesn't prove anything," Burr said.

"Maybe not."

"Did you ever see them after hours?"

She nodded.

* * *

Burr drove over the drawbridge and down the east side of Lake Charlevoix. The wind blew hard down the lake. The waves had kicked up, whitecaps everywhere. The aspen and birches had all turned yellow, and the wind was blowing the leaves off.

Burr cracked the window for Zeke, and the cold air rushed in. It smelled like the lake and falling leaves. Burr turned the heater on for the first time since spring. It smelled like burning rubber and barely worked.

"Now it's really fall, Zeke."

He parked in front of Molly's house. She let him in and they sat in the living room across from the fireplace. Burr watched the waves roll onto the beach.

She had on a burnt orange crewneck sweater over jeans, orange socks, and floppy house slippers. A little mascara and a touch of lipstick.

Burr looked over at the fireplace. It wasn't quite time to light a fire, but it would be soon.

I'm ready for cold weather and duck season.

He told her what Melissa had seen at the office.

She doesn't look surprised.

"Oswald is going to try to prove that you poisoned Nick because he was having an affair with Alexandra McCall."

"I didn't poison Nick."

Here goes.

"It just looks that way."

Molly leaned toward him. Her hair fell over her breasts. "Whose side are you on?"

"The life insurance was one thing. Juries aren't interested in life insurance. I could argue my way around that, but an affair and a jealous wife is altogether something different."

Molly pushed her hair back over her shoulders. "Nicky wasn't having an affair."

"Do you really believe that?"

"Yes."

Burr stood. "Maybe not, but Oswald has witnesses who are going to testify that he was."

"Well, he wasn't."

Burr walked over to the windows. The waves bunched up when they reached the shore and broke on the beach. Burr could hear the surf pounding.

It must really be roaring on the big lake.

"Then there's the kitchen help who said she saw you pour something into Nick's veal morel."

"It was the spices he liked."

Burr turned back to Molly. "You told me you didn't put anything in it."

"I didn't think anyone saw me."

"For God's sake, Molly, I can't defend you if you're going to lie to me."

"It was just spices."

"If it was just spices, why didn't you tell me."

She looked at her feet. "I thought it might make things look worse."

"Bingo."

"They were the ones he liked. I made them up for him."

"You made his own special poison."

"You're supposed to be on my side."

"For God's sake, Molly, I can't defend you if you're going to lie to me."

"I'm not lying."

"What would you call it?"

"Stop it, Burr. Stop it."

"Why did you have a separate bag? Why didn't you put the spices in with the morels?"

"There wasn't time. Nick came home with the morels, and we had to leave right away."

Burr put his hands in his pockets. "I'm trying to get you acquitted, and I can't do it if I can't trust you."

She looked back at him but didn't say anything.

"Your whole life has been turned upside down, but your sweater and socks match perfectly."

Molly stood. "Are you kidding me?"

"And you're wearing fluffy slippers."

"My sweater and socks make you think I killed my husband?"

"How could you not know about Nick and Alexandra."

"Nicky could be very secretive."

"I thought you said he wasn't having an affair."

"He wasn't."

"That's how you started with him."

"That was different." She cracked her knuckles.

"How?"

"Nicky and I loved each other."

"Did you love him so much that you couldn't stand to see him with anyone else?"

"Why are you doing this?"

"I'm not doing anything. This is what's going to happen at the trial."

"I'll make the jury believe me."

"The last person who is going to testify at your trial is you." Burr turned back to the window.

If I had a lawn, I'd have to rake it.

"Are you going to help me?" Molly said.

Burr ran his hands through his hair, front to back.

"Are you?"

He nodded, still facing the window.

"How could the station and Nick be so successful, but neither paid their bills?" He turned to Molly. "Did you have any money?"

"Some. Never enough."

"Some?"

"Nick said it was growing pains."

"Growing pains?"

"The station was growing so fast, it needed money to keep growing."

"For what?"

"Advertising. And promotion."

Burr shook his head. "You were growing so fast you were broke."

"I don't think Nick liked paying anyone. He lorded it over them."

He was a little Napoleon.

"I know this sounds like a cliché, but he didn't grow up with much so it all meant a lot to him."

That I believe.

"He said radio stations are illusions and the best illusion wins."
It sounded better when I said it to Jacob and Eve.

"How can this be happening? How can Nick be dead and I'm the one accused of murdering him?" Molly walked up and stood next to him. She pressed her palms on the window and looked out. "I like it when the lake is rough."

* * *

Burr stopped at the Villager in Charlevoix after leaving Molly's. The restaurant was on Bridge Street, two blocks from the courthouse and another two blocks from KHQ.

The Villager wasn't fancy, but it was far from a dive, and it had Labatt on tap, which, at the moment, was all Burr cared about. He had no idea what his defense was going to be, but he knew "accident" wasn't going to take him very far.

He sat at a window booth and looked across to Round Lake. There was a light chop; the lake was gray under a gray sky.

Five or was it six beers later, he climbed into his Jeep. He'd just crossed the drawbridge when the flashers came on.

"Now what?"

A sheriff's deputy knocked on his window. He was in his early forties, lean, and looked like he didn't know how to smile. Burr rolled his window down. "Driver's license," the deputy said.

"Is there a problem, officer?"

"I don't know. Is there? Where have you been?"

"I've been meeting with a client," Burr said, as sincerely as he could.
I don't like cops.

"At the Villager?"
I left that part out.

"Step out of the car, sir."

"Is there a problem?" Burr said again.

"Only if you blow more than a point 08."
This is the last thing I need.

Burr didn't move.

The deputy put his hands on his equipment belt, all thirty pounds of it. "Step out of the car, sir,"

"I'm sure we can work this out."

"I saw you come out of the Villager. You just about backed into the car parked behind you, and then you pulled out in front of another one." The deputy leaned in the Jeep. "And you smell like a brewery."

"I am not drunk," Burr said, who might have been.

The deputy studied Burr's driver license. "Look, Mr. Lafayette, I have a feeling you're going to blow at least a point 08 in which case, I'm going to have to arrest you and then figure out what to do with your dog." He looked at Burr's license again and then back at Burr. "Where are you going?"

"Just around the corner."

"That's what they all say." He straightened his hat. "Look, you go straight home. In fact, I'll follow you. The next time this happens, you're going to straight to jail." He handed Burr his driver's license.

CHAPTER FIFTEEN

"Your Honor, I ask that Mr. Hagerty be excused," Burr said.

"On what grounds?"

"Your Honor, I believe Mr. Hagerty likes WKHQ."

Judge Nickels rolled his eyes. "What can that possibly have to do with anything?"

Burr looked at Sean Hagerty, a gangly young man with crooked teeth. Then he looked back at Nickels. "Your Honor, Mr. Hagerty has testified that he is a big fan of KHQ, Mr. Fagan's radio station, and particularly KHQ's morning show, which Mr. Fagan hosted."

"What does that have to do with anything?"

"Your Honor, I believe Mr. Hagerty likes WKHQ so much and had such admiration for Mr. Fagan that he will be prejudiced against my client."

"I hardly think so."

Burr took two steps and stood in front of the judge. "It's called a halo effect. It makes it impossible for …"

"I know what a halo effect is." The judge peered at Burr over his glasses. "I am inclined to grant your request."

Oswald stood. "Your Honor, as I'm sure you know, WKHQ is the most popular radio station in northern Michigan, especially in Charlevoix County."

"So, I'm told."

"If you excuse every juror who likes WKHQ, there won't be anyone left in the jury pool," Oswald said.

Nickels took off his glasses. "Mr. Lafayette?"

Burr rocked back and forth, heel to toe. This was the first day of Molly's trial, and all was well. At least it was as well as it could be, given that his client was on trial for murder, he had no suspects, Jacob couldn't find Alexandra McCall, he was fairly certain Molly knew more than she was letting on, and his life outside the four walls of Judge Perry Nickels' courtroom was an unmitigated disaster, more or less.

He had on his favorite suit, the charcoal tropical wool with the white chalk stripe, still a bit threadbare, his baby blue button-down oxford pinpoint shirt, his red foulard tie with the black diamonds, and of course, his cordovan loafers with the tassels. They still needed polishing.

Burr loved Nickels' courtroom. The faded linoleum that smelled like Spic and Span and the varnished pews that smelled like Pledge. Even the stale air of the windowless courtroom.

But he was captain of his own ship. Not that he didn't expect some rough water. Burr loved all courtrooms, and he loved all trials. It was the one thing he knew how to do, even if this one didn't look too promising.

"Mr. Lafayette," Judge Nickels said again.

"Your Honor, I'd like to use one of my peremptory challenges."

Judge Nickels tapped his glasses on his desk, then looked at the would-be juror. "You are excused, Mr. Hagerty."

The gangly witness-not-to-be looked at up at the judge. "What does that mean?"

"It means you're not going to be on the jury."

"Why not?"

"Because you like WKHQ too much," Oswald said, still standing.

"That's enough, Mr. Oswald," Nickels said.

Burr looked at Oswald. "Good luck with your jury," Burr mouthed.

"Mr. Hagerty, the court thanks you for coming today, but you won't be needed for the trial."

"Why not?"

"Shoo." Nickels pointed to the door.

Hagerty started out. "I don't see why not. I really wanted to be on this jury. I really like that station."

"That's why," Burr said. But it wasn't.

"Bailiff, call the next prospective juror."

"Sarah Culver."

A heavyset woman in her thirties with short brown hair and glasses huffed her way to the witness stand. She rocked from side to side as she walked. She grabbed the railing on the witness stand and fell into the chair.

Oswald questioned her. She said she lived in East Jordan, worked as a secretary at the ironworks, and didn't listen to KHQ very often.

"I accept this witness," Oswald said.

Burr walked up to Ms. Culver. He tried to look at her hands, but she was sitting on them.

This is a problem.

"Ms. Culver, you said you listen to WKHQ sometimes. Is that right?"

She nodded.

"Do you like it?"

"I like country music."

"And you said you're a bookkeeper at the East Jordan Iron Works?"

She nodded again.

"Do you use a typewriter?"

"Mr. Lafayette, how could that possibly have anything to do with anything?" Judge Nickels said.

"I'm trying to get a sense of Ms. Culver's occupation."

Burr turned back to the potential juror. "Are you good at, you know, the typewriter?" Burr pecked a pretend typewriter with his fingers.

"That's not how you do it." She pulled her hands out from underneath her and air-typed with both hands.

She's not wearing a wedding ring.

Burr smiled at her. "Thank you so much," Burr said. "Your Honor, the defense accepts Ms. Culver as a potential juror."

Oswald hauled himself back to his feet. "Your Honor, the prosecution asks that this witness be excused."

"You just accepted her," Nickels said.

Oswald knows she's not wearing a wedding ring.

"The defense counsel is flirting with her."

"Nonsense," Nickels said. He turned to the pudgy typist. "You are impaneled."

"What?"

"You're on the jury."

"Good."

"Your Honor, the prosecution would like to use one of its peremptory challenges."

"For mercy's sake, we'll never get a jury. Will I ever be able to retire?" He looked down at Sarah Culver. "You are excused."

"What?"

"You're not on the jury."

"Oh." Sarah Culver gripped the railing and pulled herself to her feet. She shuffled out.

Damn it all.

* * *

Judge Nickels studied the piece of paper in front of him. He looked at Oswald, then at Burr. He picked up a pen, then made a show of making a checkmark on the piece of paper. He put the pen down and took off his glasses. He smiled at the prosecutor. "Mr. Oswald, you have now used the last of your peremptory challenges." He looked at Burr. "You, Mr. Lafayette, used your last one hours ago."

"I think I have one left, Your Honor."

"Nonsense." Nickels picked up his glasses and waved them at Burr, then at Oswald. "Listen to me, both of you. We are now going to pick ourselves a jury. Is that clear?"

I thought that's what we were doing.

"I've had enough of this folderol," Nickels said. "We've been fooling around all day. It's now three o'clock and we're going to pick ourselves a jury. Mr. Lafayette, you may voir dire, but I am going to limit the scope of your questions." He glared at Burr. "I am inclined to seat anyone who is breathing. Is that clear?"

They had been at it since ten that morning and had managed to impanel three jurors. Two women and one man. They needed nine more plus an alternate.

Burr knew exactly who he wanted on the jury. He had a pretty good idea who Oswald wanted, and he was fairly certain that Oswald knew who Burr wanted. They'd both used up their twelve peremptory challenges, disqualifying a prospective juror without giving a reason. They'd made it so difficult with voir dire that they'd gone through almost thirty prospective jurors before lunch and another twenty after lunch.

I think he means it this time.

Five more jurors and an hour later, Burr stood. "I object to this juror, Your Honor."

Oswald had finished questioning Lenora Franchi, a stay-at-home mother of five who hadn't missed many meals. Burr had asked her if she ever listened to WKHQ and, like virtually everyone else in the jury pool, she had. She had a wedding ring but no engagement ring.

"For the love of Mike. Why?"

"I think she has a predisposition against my client."

"Mr. Lafayette, she is obviously well qualified, and equally obvious, she is a woman whom you seem to prefer, for reasons of your own."

"Respectfully, Your Honor, I object."

"Mr. Oswald?"

"She's fine with me."

"Mrs. Franchi, you are hereby impaneled. Welcome to State of Michigan versus Fagan."

"What?"

"We're glad to have you."

"Thanks. Me, too."

The bailiff escorted her out of the courtroom. Nickels called for the next prospective juror.

Harold Stasen, a white-haired man with glasses and dressed in a sincere blue suit that actually fit quite well.

This could be trouble.

He sat in the witness stand and took off his glasses. The bailiff swore him in.

Oswald stood.

"Your Honor," Stasen said, "I don't believe I'm who you're looking for."

"Why ever not?"

"I can't spare the time away from work."

Nickels looked down at Stasen. "What is it that you do?"

"I pump out septic tanks, and I'm all backed up."

"Very funny, Mr. Stasen. You are hereby impaneled."

Burr stood. "I object, Your Honor."

Nickels pointed at Burr and curled his forefinger. "Up here, Mr. Lafayette." Then to Stasen, "You, out!"

Burr walked up to Judge Nickels.

"Closer," Nickels said.

Burr took another step.

"Closer. Close enough that you could put your chin on my desk."

"Your Honor ..."

Burr inched closer.

"Put your toes against my desk. That's it. Now lean toward me."

"Your Honor ..."

"Just do it."

Nickels leaned forward until he was nose-to-nose with Burr. "Mr. Lafayette, I am a simple, country judge. I don't have fancy suits or shoes with silly tassels, which, by the way, yours need polishing. I had hoped to never see you again, but this is my last trial. When it's over, I'm going to retire and go to Florida for the winter, where I can play golf every day."

Nickels sat back and smiled. Then he leaned in at Burr again. "But I can't go until this blasted trial is over and this blasted trial won't be over until it starts, and it can't start until we have a jury, which we don't. Is that clear?"

"Your Honor ..."

"I'm a simple, country judge. I already said that, but I've impaneled plenty of juries. Hundreds. So, I know a few things about jury selection. But for the life of me, I've never seen anything like this. *Never!*"

Burr took a step back.

"Step right back where you were," Nickels said. "This is how I see it. Your client is a woman, accused of murdering her husband. I'm sure Mr. Oswald is going to bring up why he believes she killed her husband. An affair being one of them.

"So, it stands to reason that your ideal juror would be a woman, preferably whose husband cheated on her and who's still mad as hell. You can't...."

"Your Honor ..."

"Let me finish. You can't ask that, but a divorced woman is the next best thing. That's why you asked if they had children and looked to see if they had a wedding ring. Every married woman I know never takes off her wedding ring. I've been married forty-two years and I've never seen the missus without it. Lovely woman." Nickels smiled at Burr. "And that's the same reason Oswald wants men. I don't think he cares if they're married. He just wants a man who wouldn't like the idea of being murdered by his wife. He might sympathize with Nick. Right so far?"

Burr started to say something, but Nickels waved him off.

"Which is why you didn't want Mrs. Franchi. She's a woman, but she's married. Which is why you looked to see if she had on a wedding ring. You could have asked, of course, but that would have made it too simple for our esteemed prosecutor to figure out. Oswald would rather have a married man, but he'll take a single man. It looks like he'll take a married woman, too. He's not as fussy as you are." Nickels looked at Oswald then back at Burr. "This is what I'm going to do."

"Your Honor," Oswald said, standing, "I feel I should be a part of your conference with Mr. Lafayette."

"I feel you should sit down and amuse yourself until I'm finished with Mr. Lafayette."

"Your Honor—"

Nickels pointed at the prosecutor's chair. "Sit down, Mr. Oswald." The judge curled his finger at Burr again. "I understand a bit about the ins and outs of jury selection. You're good at it. I'll give you that. But this is a small county. Very small. I don't know how many jurors we have left in the pool. It doesn't matter. I'm tired of this, and I'm sure our jurors, male or female, married or divorced, will give Mrs. Fagan a fair shake."

"Your Honor—"

"Quiet," Nickels said. We're going to have our little jury by 4:30 today, come hell or high water. Is that clear?"

"But—"

"But, if you don't cooperate, who knows how many men we might end up with. Or how many married women."

* * *

Burr held the cherry by the stem and dunked it in and out of his Manhattan. It was his first of the season, which officially began the Tuesday after Labor Day. The day he put away the Sauvignon Blanc and the day Jacob put his khaki suit in the back of his closet. Neither to come out again until Memorial Day weekend.

He sat on the front porch of Morning Glory and looked out at what was left of the Pine River. It had never been much of a river. Now it was a concrete channel dredged to twenty feet and straight as an arrow. The drawbridge and Round Lake were to his left and three blocks from where he'd somehow gotten out of a jam with the deputy. To his right, the breakwater and the sun setting on Lake Michigan, well south of west.

He'd asked Eve to rent them a house for the trial, and she'd found this white Victorian on the north side of the channel, two cottages from the beach. It was expensive, even for the off season. Burr had rented it for a month, but he didn't think they'd need it more than two weeks.

Jury selection hadn't gone exactly the way Burr had planned, but once he got in the courtroom, hardly anything ever did. The jury wasn't a disaster. It was better than some he'd had, and just because it was half men didn't mean they'd all think Molly murdered Nick. The women could go the wrong way, too. All in all, though, Burr would have rather had a jury full of divorced women whose husbands had cheated on them. Fair and impartial only went so far.

He dropped the cherry back in his drink and took his first sip. Two parts Maker's Mark, one part Martini & Rossi sweet vermouth, a dash of bitters, more than a splash of cherry juice and the two biggest maraschino cherries he could find. All in a rocks glass full of ice.

"Zeke, it tastes like dessert."

He pulled up the zipper on his Barbour jacket, waxed cotton that smelled like a camp tent, his second favorite coat, after his duck coat.

The sun sank into Lake Michigan. Burr felt the chill.

CHAPTER SIXTEEN

"All rise" the bailiff said. "The court of the Honorable Judge Perry C. Nickels is now in session."

They all stood. The jurors, the gallery, the court reporter, the deputy, the lawyers, and the star of the show, Molly Fagan.

Showtime.

Judge Nickels made his grand, if reluctant, entrance. He fussed with his robe, then sat.

"You may be seated," the bailiff said.

Nickels took off his glasses and looked out at the courtroom, then, "We are here in the matter of the People versus Molly Fagan." He looked at Molly, then at the prosecutor.

"Mr. Oswald, you may begin."

Oswald had on a black suit, white shirt and a blue and red striped tie. His chin hung over the front of his tie and his stomach hung over his belt.

The prosecutor put his hands on his table and pushed himself up. He walked to the jury.

"Ladies and gentlemen, I want to thank you in advance for taking the responsibility to perform your sacred duty as jurors."

Sacred?

"Trial by jury is one of the hallmarks of a free society and of our legal system, and anyone, no matter how guilty …" Oswald paused and pointed at Molly, "is entitled to be judged by their own peers."

Molly did as she was told and looked Oswald in the eye, not a defiant look but a sincere, "I-am-not-guilty" look.

So far, so good.

Oswald scowled at Molly, then turned back to the jury. "And this woman broke the holy bonds of matrimony." He paused again, then looked back at Molly. "By murdering her husband in the most horrific way."

Molly folded her hands and put them in the lap of her knee-length black dress. Gold earrings, her pink lipstick, a hint of mascara and no jewelry except for her wedding ring, which Burr had told her to make sure the jury could see. She put her hands on the defense table. The diamond in her engagement ring sparkled.

Well done.

Back to the jury. "But that wasn't enough. After Molly Fagan murdered her husband, she was bold. Very bold. She was so bold as to try and collect on his life insurance policy. After she murdered him."

The jury oohed and aahed.

Here we go.

Burr stood. "Your Honor, this was an accidental death. When someone dies accidentally, life insurance is almost always involved. That's what it's for."

"It's not your turn," Oswald said.

"Mr. Lafayette, you will have your chance to make your case. Please let Mr. Oswald make his."

"Respectfully, Your Honor, opposing counsel has a callous disregard for the facts."

"Sit down, Mr. Lafayette. And be quiet."

I think that got Oswald a bit off course.

The prosecutor cleared his throat. "As I was saying, the state is going to prove that Molly Fagan murdered her husband, that she committed first-de-gree murder and that, for committing that crime, she should be given the maximum punishment allowed by the laws of the people of the State of Michigan.

"Which is life in prison without the possibility of parole." Oswald hitched up his pants. "And what must be proved for you to make such a weighty decision? It's very simple. You must believe that the defendant ..." Oswald pointed at Molly again, "intended to kill her husband. That she, in fact, did kill her husband, and that she had a plan to kill her husband. That's what is required to find her guilty of first-degree murder. And that's exactly what I'm going to prove."

Oswald walked up to the railing of the jury box and put his hands on the railing. He looked at each of the jurors, one by one. "Would you like to know how she did it?" They all nodded. The Great Oz nodded back. "Nick Fagan was the owner of WKHQ. You all probably know about the radio station, and many of you probably listen to it."

More nodding.

"Nick not only ran the radio station, he was also the morning disc jockey. He was very talented. Good at everything he did. A very competent fellow.

"He worked very hard. He was very busy and didn't have much spare time. But there was one thing he loved to do." Oswald leaned in. "He loved to hunt for morels. Do you know what they are?"

They all nodded. "Of course you do. He loved to hunt for morels. He had a few favorite spots. Most of his favorite spots were under the ashes. Something about their roots."

They all nodded again. "On the day he was murdered …"

Burr stood. "Your Honor, I object. There's no proof that Mr. Fagan was murdered. And there won't be."

"Mr. Lafayette, this is an opening statement. Advocacy is allowed."

"Advocacy does not include lying, Your Honor."

"This is permissible puffery. Sit down and be quiet," Judge Nickels said.

Burr sat.

"Mr. Fagan was an expert morel hunter, and true to form, he found morels the day he was *murdered*." Oswald put some oomph in "murdered," then looked at Burr and sneered. "He took them to the Arboretum for dinner. He was friends with Cat Garrity, the chef, and she knew how to prepare veal morel just the way he liked it. Veal morel was Nick Fagan's favorite and her specialty."

Oswald leaned toward the jury again. "This is how the defendant poisoned him. Nick gave his wife the morels. She had them in a plastic bag in her purse. She gave them to the waitress who took them to the kitchen and gave them to Cat."

Oswald pointed at Molly then turned back to the jury. "Here's how she poisoned him. Do you know what she did?" Twelve heads shook 'no.' "She had poisonous mushrooms with her. She went to the kitchen and put the poisonous mushrooms in Nick's veal morel when she thought no one was looking." Oswald pretended to pour. He took a step back. "But someone saw her. The veal morel was served to Mr. Fagan only. The defendant, who also loved veal morel, made a point of not having any that night."

Burr stood.

"Sit down, Mr. Lafayette," Judge Nickels said.

"Your Honor—"

Nickels pointed at Burr's chair.

Burr sat. Ever so slowly.

Oswald is getting away with murder.

Oswald took a step back and put his hands in his pockets. "Mr. Fagan ate the poisoned veal morel. He became violently ill and was rushed to the hospital." Oswald looked down.

There's no way he can see his feet.

The jury leaned toward the prosecutor. He took a deep breath, then looked at the jury.

"Where he died a horrible death," he said in a voice that would wake the dead. "A horrible death." Oswald looked at Molly. She stared back at him. "It was a terrible thing to do and a horrible way to die."

They shook their heads as if one.

He's already got them trained.

"Nick Fagan was poisoned. He died of mushroom poisoning." Oswald cocked his head. "But how? Morels aren't poisonous. Even if they're not cooked properly, or if they're spoiled, morel mushrooms are not poisonous. Everyone knows that. You might get sick from bad ones, but you won't die.

"Nick Fagan didn't die from the morels he picked, but he did die from eating poisonous mushrooms. He died from eating another kind of mushroom, a highly poisonous mushroom that his wife, the defendant, put in his veal morel."

Oswald put his hands back in his pockets. "But you know what?"

A collective shake of the head, "no."

"Nick Fagan was a mushrooming pro. An expert. There's no way he would have ever confused morels with poisonous mushrooms." Oswald stopped again and looked at Molly again. "The only way poisonous mushrooms could have gotten into Nick Fagan's veal morel is if someone put them in there." Oswald pointed at Molly again. "She was seen doing it. The type of death cap mushrooms that killed Nick are only found in summer or fall. Nick was killed in May. So she must have collected them months and months before the murder. And that is the very definition of premeditation."

Burr started to stand, but Nickels shook his head at him.

"She was the one who had the poisonous mushrooms. She put them in

Nick's veal morel. There is a witness who saw her do it." Oswald smiled at the jury. "Yes, someone actually saw her put the poison in Nick's veal morel." He paused. "But that's not all. Why did she do it? Why would she do that? Why? I'll tell you why. She was furious with Nick. Incensed. Wild. She was jealous. She thought he was having an affair. She thought he was going to divorce her for someone else. She was sure he was carrying on. She was furious. She found out he had taken her off his life insurance and added this new person. That made things even worse. So, what did she do?"

Oswald walked to end of the jury box and back. "I'll tell you what she did. She poisoned her husband and got rid of the change of beneficiary form on Nick's life insurance policy. That way she would be rid of her husband and get the life insurance money.

"But it didn't work. Why?" Oswald paused again. "Because someone saw her put the poison in Nick's veal morel, and someone found the change of beneficiary form. It's really very simple. Molly Fagan poisoned her husband because she was jealous and because she wanted the life insurance money." Oswald pointed at Molly again. "This woman killed her husband. It's very simple. I'm going to prove it to you, and when I do, I ask you to find her guilty of first-degree murder." Oswald dropped his hand. He walked back to his table smiling at no one in particular.

Nickels granted them a ten-minute recess, then called them back to order.

"Mr. Lafayette, I assume you'd like to say something."

Burr stood. He started his ritual — his cuffs, his tie. Judge Nickels scowled at him. Burr didn't care. He walked to the far end of the jury box where he could see all the jurors, Oswald, Molly, and the gallery. He saw Julian Flintoff and Pearl Watson, the insurance creeps, sitting on the aisle in the way back of the courtroom.

I knew they'd be here.

Burr turned to the jury and smiled. "Ladies and gentlemen. My name is Burr Lafayette. I represent Molly Fagan, Nick Fagan's widow." He was careful not to say "defendant."

He looked over at Molly, who smiled weakly at him, as instructed.

He turned back to the jury. "There's a famous saying." Burr put his hands in his pockets. "You may have heard it. It goes something like this. No matter how much lipstick you put on a pig, it's still a pig." Burr looked at Oswald then started counting to himself.

One, two….

Oswald jumped to his feet. "I object, Your Honor. This is outrageous."

The gallery erupted. Nickels slammed his gavel, but the gallery kept on. The jury snickered.

"Shush," Nickels roared, but the gallery wouldn't be shushed. The judge hammered away with his gavel. Burr stood there with his hands in his pockets. The courtroom settled down.

Nickels waved his gavel at Burr. "Lafayette, I have never witnessed behavior like this. Not in forty years on the bench."

Come to Recorder's Court in Detroit for half an hour.

"Your Honor, this is my opening statement."

"You were insulting Mr. Oswald."

"I most certainly was not."

"He called me a pig with lipstick," Oswald said, whose face had turned a bright shade of barbecue.

The gallery erupted again.

Nickels pounded his gavel. "Mr. Lafayette, I am going to eject you from these proceedings."

Burr looked at Oswald.

He does look like a pig with lipstick.

Burr walked over to Nickels. "Your Honor, I most certainly did not call Mr. Oswald a pig with lipstick."

More snickering.

"Do not say that again. Now, get out."

"Your Honor, I think Mr. Oswald is being too sensitive. If you'll permit me to finish my opening statement, the context of my remark will become clear. When I'm finished, if you believe I insulted Mr. Oswald, I'll leave the courtroom and my able co-counsel can take my place."

Burr looked at Jacob, who was trying to sink under the defense table while twirling one of his curls.

"I object, Your Honor," Oswald said, still standing but not looking quite so much like a pig with lipstick.

"Sit down," Nickels said. "As to you, Lafayette, do not cross me again. Understood?"

Burr nodded yes but thought no.

Nickels leaned over his desk. "Mr. Lafayette, I hope this is my last trial, but I'm not going to fade away. We're going to have ourselves a merry little murder trial, then I'm going to glide out of here one last time." Nickels flattened his hand, palm down, and moved it up and down toward the door to his chambers.

Like a magic carpet.

"Is that clear?"

Burr nodded.

"Without any drama."

Burr nodded, but not too convincingly.

Drama is what a trial is all about.

"Mr. Lafayette, you may proceed. Sans drama."

"Thank you, Your Honor." Burr turned back to the jury. "Ladies and gentlemen, in my experience, and I would expect in your experience, things are often exactly what they appear to be. If the sidewalk is wet, it's probably because it's raining. It may be wet because the lawn is being watered, but it's probably because it's raining. Especially if there's thunder and lightning.

"And, in the tragic death of Nick Fagan, it appears that his death was accidental. And it was."

Burr leaned on the railing. "Why? Because people die of mushroom poisoning every year in Michigan. Right here in Charlevoix County. Because they pick the wrong mushrooms. They eat them and they die. Mr. Fagan picked some of the wrong mushrooms. They got cooked up in his veal morel. He ate them and died."

I know it wasn't an accident, but let's start here.

Burr turned and pointed at Oswald. "But he said someone saw Mrs. Fagan put the poisonous mushrooms in Mr. Fagan's veal morel in the kitchen of the Arboretum. That's what he said."

Burr looked back at the jury. "But how do we know what Mrs. Fagan put in the veal morel, or even if she put anything in it? She could have put spices in the veal morel. Nick Fagan was a very particular man, maybe even fussy. It's no stretch of the imagination to think that Nick could have given Molly his special spices and asked to put them in his veal morel. That makes perfect sense, doesn't it?"

The jury nodded.

"And if Molly wanted to murder Nick, why in the world would she do it where someone could see her? That just doesn't make any sense." He leaned back on the railing. "Does it?"

Most of the jury shook their head 'no.' Most of them, not all.

Burr took a step toward Oswald. "And that's why what looks like what happened is exactly what happened. It looks like an accident because it was an accident. Because no matter how much lipstick you put on a pig, it's still a pig." Burr nodded at Oswald.

Burr was sure he saw smoke coming out of Oswald's ears, but the prosecutor didn't move a muscle.

Burr walked to the other end of the jury box. "But just for a moment, let's suppose that Nick was poisoned. Horrible, but what if that's exactly what did happen?

"What if someone did poison Nick Fagan? Certainly not Molly, but what if someone else did? Nick Fagan was a very talented man. He was a hard worker. He was driven and ambitious. Very ambitious."

Burr looked down at his scuffed-up shoes, then back at the jury. "Nick had enemies. Many enemies. Nick played rough. He didn't care who was in his way. There's big money in radio stations. Big money. And Nick wanted it. He wouldn't let anyone get in his way. He had enemies, and one of them could have poisoned him."

I have no idea who.

Burr walked toward the defense table, then turned back to the jury. "Ladies and gentlemen, as I said, no matter how much lipstick you put on a pig...."

Burr smiled at Oswald, who didn't smile back. Burr looked at the jury. "The tragic death of Nick Fagan was an accident. Pure and simple, but ..." Burr looked down at his shoes again, then back at the jury. "But if Nick had enemies, and if he was murdered, it certainly wasn't by Molly."

Burr walked back to the defense table.

* * *

Nickels had had enough of them and adjourned for lunch at 11:30. Burr drove his merry band to the Gray Gables.

The dining room was mostly empty on Monday, but it would fill up this weekend when the tourists invaded for the fall colors.

Burr loved the Gray Gables. Appropriately named, it was a gray two-story with white trim on Belvedere, south of downtown; the dining room, long with dark paneling on one side and the bar on the other.

He was hungry. Arguing always made him hungry, and he'd be hungry as long as the trial lasted. He desperately wanted to start with their signature soup, the mushroom bisque, but decided on the navy bean.

Mushroom anything would be in poor taste.

He ordered the whitefish sandwich with fries, which he thought would go perfectly with a Labatt. He asked for a water instead.

* * *

"Call your first witness, Mr. Oswald."

The prosecutor stood. "The state calls Rory Nettles."

The thin man with the thinning hair walked to the witness stand. He was wearing the same blue suit he'd worn at the preliminary exam. He raised a bony hand, the bailiff swore him in, and the witness sat.

Oswald lumbered up to the witness. "Dr. Nettles. It is doctor, isn't it?"

Of course it is, but it's a nice start.

"Yes, I'm a physician."

"And you're the medical examiner for Charlevoix County. Is that right?"

"I am."

"Dr. Nettles, would you please tell us your educational background and your professional experience since you began practicing medicine?"

The medical examiner started with becoming an Eagle Scout.

"Your qualifications as a physician," Judge Nickels said.

Nettles looked like he was disappointed but skipped to medical qualifications.

"Dr. Nettles, did you examine Mr. Fagan's body after he died?"

"I did."

"And you did an autopsy?"

"I did."

"Why did you perform an autopsy?"

"I always do an autopsy if the death is suspicious."

Burr jumped up. "Objection, Your Honor. Calls for an opinion."

"Sustained," Nickels said.

One small victory.

Oswald wrinkled his nose. "Dr. Nettles, please tell us under what conditions you consider it necessary to perform an autopsy."

Nettles nodded at Oswald. "In general, I would perform an autopsy if the death occurred under unusual circumstances such as an accident, a drowning, a fall, or from unknown causes, as in this case."

"Was it clear to you, prior to your autopsy, how Mr. Fagan died?"

"I had my suspicions, which the autopsy confirmed."

"And what was the cause of Mr. Fagan's death?"

The coroner cleared his throat and boomed, "Mr. Fagan died from eating poisonous mushrooms."

"From eating poisonous mushrooms."

"That's correct."

Oswald hiked up his pants and turned to the jury. "Nick Fagan, the defendant's husband, died from eating poisonous mushrooms." He looked at each juror, one by one. They each nodded back at him. Oswald turned back to Nettles. "What exactly did you do to determine this?"

"I examined Mr. Fagan's blood and then his liver."

"And what did you find?"

"I found that Mr. Fagan's white blood cells had been destroyed, as had his liver."

"And this is what killed him?"

"It is."

"And is this what poisonous mushrooms do to a person?"

"Yes."

"Could this occur from any other cause?"

Nettles put his hands on the railing. His thin, bony fingers reached around the railing like snakes. "It's possible but highly unlikely. Mr. Fagan's internal organs had been destroyed."

The jury cringed.

This isn't good.

"And your opinion is that Mr. Fagan died from eating poisonous mushrooms?"

"Yes," Nettles said to the jury.

The jury shuddered.

Oswald and Nettles have been practicing.

"No further questions." Oswald nearly pranced back to his table.

Burr leaned in behind Molly toward Jacob. "Hand me the autopsy," he said, under his breath.

"Are you sure you want to do this?" Jacob said.

Burr nodded.

"I don't think it's a good idea."

Burr stood and walked over to Jacob. He opened his hand. Jacob handed Burr a file.

"Thank you."

Burr walked up to Judge Nickels. "Your Honor, I'd like to introduce Dr. Nettles' autopsy as Defense Exhibit One."

Oswald started to his feet and opened his mouth. He didn't say anything and sat back in his chair.

"Mr. Oswald?" Nickels said.

If he objects, it will destroy Nettles' testimony.

"No objection, Your Honor."

"Ms. Meecher, mark this as Defense Exhibit One."

The court reporter stamped the autopsy and handed it to Burr.

"Thank you." Burr flipped through the pages until he found what he was looking for. "Dr. Nettles, this is the written report of the autopsy you performed on Mr. Fagan. Is that right?"

"Yes."

"And this details the cause of Mr. Fagan's death?"

"Yes."

Burr turned toward the jury. "I'm surprised Mr. Oswald didn't introduce this into evidence."

Here goes.

"Dr. Nettles, please read this sentence. The one I've underlined." Burr handed the autopsy to Nettles.

"This isn't the cause ..."

"Read the sentence, Dr. Nettles. Read us what you wrote. Just this sentence."

Oswald stood. "I object, Your Honor."

He took the bait.

"What could you possibly object to? Your witness wrote this."

"Quiet," Nickels said. "Dr. Nettles, please read the sentence."

Nettles looked away, then started in a soft voice, "Mr. Fagan ..."

"Speak up, Dr. Nettles," Burr said. "For all the world to hear."

"You're on thin ice, Mr. Lafayette," Nickels said. He looked down at the coroner. "Please read whatever it is you've been asked to read."

"Mr. Fagan then suffered a cardiac arrest and died. He …"

"That's enough." Burr grabbed the autopsy. "Dr. Nettles, is a cardiac arrest a heart attack?"

"Yes." Nettles squirmed in his chair.

"So, Mr. Fagan died of a heart attack."

"Yes, but …"

Burr raised one hand, palm out to Nettles. He turned to the jury. "Mr. Fagan died of a heart attack. I have no further questions." Burr walked back to the defense table.

That should muddy the waters.

Oswald was on his feet before Burr could sit. "Redirect, Your Honor."

Burr popped up. "I object, Your Honor. The prosecutor had his turn."

"Lafayette has taken the autopsy out of context," Oswald said.

Burr glared at Oswald. "It's Mr. Lafayette," Burr looked at Nickels. "Your Honor, Dr. Nettles read from the autopsy word for word."

"It was taken out of context, Your Honor," Oswald said.

Burr walked toward the judge. "Your Honor, Mr. Oswald should have entered the autopsy as an exhibit. He didn't because he knew it would be damaging to his case. If anyone has taken anything out of context, it's him." Burr pointed at the Great Oz.

Nickels shook his head. "I am going to allow the redirect. You may proceed, Mr. Oswald."

"Your Honor—" Burr said.

Nickels slammed down his gavel. "Must you be so argumentative?"

"Your Honor—"

"You may proceed Mr. Oswald," Nickels said, then mumbled, "At this rate, I'll be dead before I can retire."

Oswald walked up to the coroner.

"Dr. Nettles, what did Mr. Fagan die of?"

"Mushroom poisoning."

Oswald looked at the jury. "Mushroom poisoning." He looked back at Nettles. "What role did the cardiac arrest have in Mr. Fagan's death?"

"The cardiac arrest was the result of the mushroom poisoning."

"Did the cardiac arrest cause Mr. Fagan's death?"

"Mr. Fagan's liver was destroyed from the mushroom poisoning. That is what killed him."

"Thank you, Dr. Nettles." To Judge Nickels, "I have no further questions."

"You may call your next witness."

Burr stood. "Your Honor, I have a few more questions."

"For heaven's sake, you had your turn."

"Your Honor, the prosecutor was allowed to redirect. I should have the same right."

"No."

"Your Honor, I only have two questions."

Nickels shook his head "no" but said "yes."

"Thank you, Your Honor." Burr walked back to Nettles, who wasn't at all happy to see him.

"Dr. Nettles, did Mr. Fagan have a heart attack?"

Nettles looked down at his bony hands, then over at Oswald.

"Dr. Nettles, I asked you the question, not Mr. Oswald."

The coroner nodded.

"Dr. Nettles, please answer the question. With your words."

"Yes."

"Thank you." Burr looked at the jury. "Mr. Fagan had a heart attack." He turned back to the coroner. "So, Mr. Fagan was alive, then he had a heart attack and died. Is that right?"

Nettles looked at Oswald again. Burr stepped to his right so Nettles couldn't see Oswald. The coroner looked at his hands again.

"I'll repeat the question," Burr said sweetly. "Mr. Fagan was alive, then he had a heart attack and died. Is that right?"

"Well, actually it was …"

Burr walked up to the witness box and put his hands on the rail and looked at Nettles. He moved a little to his right so Nettles couldn't see Oswald.

"Yes, or no?"

"Well …"

"Yes, or no?"

Nickels slumped in his chair.

"Yes," Nettles said.

"Mr. Fagan died of a heart attack." Burr looked at the jury. "I have no further questions."

Oswald jumped up, as well as a two-hundred-fifty-pound man could jump. He pointed at Burr. "Your Honor, the defense counsel is purposely twisting the facts. I must clear this up."

"Sit down, Mr. Oswald," Nickels said. "The members of the jury are not fools."

They're certainly not fools, but I hope they're confused.

Oswald started to sit.

"You might as well stay on your feet. Call your next witness."

CHAPTER SEVENTEEN

The prosecutor hitched up his pants. "The state calls Paula Caruso."

The short, plump woman with the big nose limped to the witness stand. She wore a belted gray dress.

She looks like a cloudy day.

Oswald helped her into the witness stand and held her arm as she sat.

The bailiff walked over to her. "Please stand."

She looked at him like he was crazy.

"Please stand," he said, again.

She grabbed onto the railing and tried to pull herself to her feet.

"You need not stand up, Dr. Caruso." Nickels looked at the bailiff. "Mr. Drum can swear her in while she's sitting." Nickels looked up at the ceiling. "I am surrounded by people who are rushing me to an untimely end," he said, mostly to himself.

"What did you say, Your Honor?" the bailiff said.

"Swear her in and be done with it."

The bailiff swore in the doctor with the limp.

"Dr. Caruso, you are indeed an expert in the field of mushrooms."

"Mushrooms and fungi," she said, emphasis on fungi.

"Of course, but today we're here to talk about mushrooms."

She nodded.

"Just to review, you were at the University of Michigan Biological Station at Douglas Lake for how long?"

"Twenty-five years."

"And where is that exactly?"

"It's on the south side of Douglas Lake, just northwest of Burt Lake."

"In the heart of morel country."

"It's about half a mile from the Douglas Lake Inn."

Oswald frowned. "In the heart of morel country," he said, again.

"It's more of a bar than an inn."

The gallery tittered.

Oswald ignored her. "Dr. Caruso, is the University of Michigan Biological Station in the heart of morel country?"

"Of course it is."

"And you're an expert on morels."

"I should say so."

"Dr. Caruso, the white morels, black morels and caps are edible, is that right?"

"Yes."

"But the false caps, the beefsteak morels, are poisonous. Is that also correct?"

"Yes."

"And do the beefsteak morels grow at the same time as the edible morels?"

"They do indeed."

"Thank you, Dr. Caruso. Is it easy to confuse the poisonous beefsteak morel with the edible morels?"

"No, they look entirely different."

"Could they be confused?"

"Not to the trained eye. Really not even to the untrained eye. Even the most novice mushroomer can tell them apart."

"Could you show us the difference?"

"I brought samples."

Of course you did.

Oswald walked back to his table. He reached underneath and picked up four sandwich-size plastic bags. He introduced them into evidence.

There's no way I can keep them from being admitted.

"Ms. Meecher, mark these as State's Exhibit One through Four."

Oswald handed the bags to Caruso. "Doctor, would you please tell us which morel is which and how to tell them apart?"

The professor took out the first mushroom. "This one is commonly called a cap. It has a very small top or cap. It's edible and couldn't possibly be confused with the other three."

Oswald took it from her and walked over to the jury with it. "Ladies and gentlemen, this is the cap. It has a stem and a very small head."

There were nods. A few of the jurors said "yes." One said, "I see."

Oswald put it back in the bag and set it on his table. He walked back to Caruso. "Please tell me about the other three."

She took out a mushroom. "This is commonly called a white morel. Because of its color. They come out before the blacks. The distinguishing feature of the white and the black is its cap." She held it up. "The cap looks like a hood over the stem. Like an umbrella. It hangs over the stem and is attached to the top of the stem." She turned it upside down. It was pitted underneath and hung over the stem like an umbrella. She repeated the demonstration with the black morel. Then she picked up the last bag and took out the beefsteak morel. "But this one, the beefsteak, it's also called a false morel or a false cap, is much different." She turned it upside down. "See here." She touched the underside of the cap. "The cap is attached to the stem. The cap doesn't hang or drape over the stem."

"I see," Oswald said. He showed all four to the jury. He picked out the beefsteak. "There's no mistaking a true morel for this one."

"No there isn't," one of the jurors said.

Oswald's got them eating out of his hand. So to speak.

The Great Oz walked up to the witness stand. "Dr. Caruso, do you think Mr. Fagan could have picked beefsteak morels by mistake and poisoned himself?"

"No," she said.

Burr jumped to his feet. "I object, Your Honor. Dr. Caruso can't possibly know what Mr. Fagan may have done."

"Sustained."

"Your Honor, I ask that the question and answer be stricken from the record," Burr said.

Nickels looked over at the jury. "Ladies and gentlemen, you will disregard Mr. Oswald's question and Dr. Caruso's answer." He glared at Oswald. "You know better than that."

"Yes, Your Honor. I apologize."

He's not a bit sorry.

"Dr. Caruso," Oswald said, "in your opinion would an experienced mushroomer mistake beefsteak morels for the edible mushrooms?"

"Absolutely not."

"Thank you, Dr. Caruso. You've testified that beefsteak morels are poisonous, but is eating them fatal?"

"No. They can make you very sick, but they're not usually fatal."

Here it comes.

"Is there a mushroom that grows in this area that is lethal?"

"Yes."

"And what would that be?"

"It's called an Amanita. We have four species in Michigan. They are all deadly."

"And when do they grow?"

"Summer and fall."

"I see." Oswald looked back at Burr. "Could Mr. Fagan have mistakenly picked Amanita mushrooms?"

"They grow later than the morels. There wouldn't have been any in May."

"Assuming that there happened to be one or two out, could they be mistaken for morels?"

"Absolutely not."

Oswald walked back to his table and reached under it for another bag. He introduced the Amanita into evidence, then showed it to the jury. It had a long white stem and a flat red top.

No one could mistake that for a morel.

Oswald strolled back to the witness stand. "Dr. Caruso, if Mr. Fagan ingested even one of these, would it be fatal?"

"Yes."

"But it's unlikely that Mr. Fagan, excuse me, *anyone*, would make that mistake?"

"Next to impossible."

"Thank you, Dr. Caruso," Oswald said. "So, in your opinion, an experienced mushroomer wouldn't mistake a false morel for an edible morel, and certainly wouldn't mistake an Amanita mushroom for an edible morel?"

"That's right."

"In your opinion how would an experienced mushroomer, like Mr. Fagan, die from mushroom poisoning?"

"Someone would have to put the Amanitas in his food."

"You mean intentionally poison him?"

"Yes."

Burr jumped up again.

"I withdraw the question." Oswald smiled at Burr. "No further questions."

Burr swept his hands through his hair, front to back. He looked at Jacob, who shook his head. Burr started to pick up his pencil but thought better of it.

"Should I excuse the witness, Mr. Lafayette?" Nickels said.

I have no idea where to start.

"Mr. Lafayette?"

Burr rummaged through the file in front of him.

"Mr. Lafayette, if you don't have any questions for the witness, I am going to excuse her." Judge Nickels turned to Dr. Caruso. "You may step down. Mr. Drum, please help Dr. Caruso back to her seat."

Burr stood, slowly. "Dr. Caruso, you testified that it is not difficult for an experienced mushroomer to tell the difference between a true morel and a false morel. Is that right?"

"Yes."

"But it does happen."

"Yes."

"Where do the true morels grow?"

"In mature forests. Generally, under the ashes."

"Under the ashes?"

"Under ash trees."

"I see," Burr said. "And do beefsteak morels grow in the same place as true morels?"

"Yes."

"At the same time of year?"

"Yes."

"Mushroomers do make mistakes, don't they? And pick the wrong mushrooms?"

"I suppose they do."

"Aren't there cases of beefsteak morel poisonings every year?"

"Yes, but …"

"Thank you, Dr. Caruso. You don't really have any firsthand knowledge about Mr. Fagan. Whether or not he was an experienced mushroomer. Do you?"

"I was told he was."

Oswald stood. "Objection, Your Honor. It has already been established that Mr. Fagan was an experienced mushroomer who wouldn't make that kind of mistake."

Now I've got him.

Burr pointed at Oswald but looked at Nickels. "Your Honor, this is hearsay. We have no testimony that establishes whether or not Mr. Fagan was an experienced mushroomer. For all we know, Mr. Fagan picked mushrooms at Glen's Market."

"You can't buy morels," Dr. Caruso said. "You can only forage for them."

Burr ignored her. "Your Honor, if the prosecutor wanted to establish that Mr. Fagan was an experienced mushroomer, he should have introduced testimony that established it. This is hearsay."

"Balderdash," Oswald said.

Nickels put his hands on his desk. "Mr. Oswald, I agree with Mr. Lafayette. There has been no evidence presented to support the fact that Mr. Fagan was an experienced mushroomer. Your objection is overruled."

Oswald sat.

"Thank you, Your Honor." Burr looked back at an unhappy Dr. Caruso. "So, Dr. Caruso, while it's possible for an experienced mushroomer to pick beefsteak morels, it's much more likely for an inexperienced mushroomer to pick beefsteaks. Is that correct?"

"Yes," she said, scowling.

"And you don't know whether Mr. Fagan was an experienced mushroomer or an inexperienced mushroomer, do you?"

"No," she said, still scowling.

"And people have died from eating beefsteak morels. Is that true?"

"Yes, but ..."

Burr put his hands in his pockets. "Yes or no?"

"Yes."

If looks could kill.

"So, it's possible that Mr. Fagan picked beefsteak mushrooms by mistake, ate them, and died. Is that possible?"

"Yes."

"I have no further questions." Burr walked back to the defense table and sat.

If the trial were over now, I'd win.

Jacob leaned over. "What about the Amanitas?"

"I have no idea."

Oswald popped up, as best he could. "Redirect, Your Honor."

Burr popped up. "Objection, Your Honor. The prosecutor has already questioned the witness."

"I need two minutes to clarify something," Oswald said.

Nickels looked at Burr. "You may proceed Mr. Oswald."

"Dr. Caruso, you said that it is possible to die from eating beefsteak morels. Is that right?"

"Yes."

"But Mr. Fagan didn't die from eating beefsteak morels. He died from eating Amanita mushrooms."

"That's right."

Nuts.

"Mr. Oswald, you may call your next witness."

Oswald put his hands on his table and pushed himself up.

Maybe I'm wearing him out.

"The state calls Christine Sawyer."

A perky brunette with chin-length auburn hair, a button nose, and a pale complexion walked down the aisle. She wore a blue blazer over a gray flannel skirt that did a poor job of hiding her legs.

She's quite good looking, but I don't think I'm going to like her.

The bailiff swore her in.

"Dr. Sawyer. It is doctor, isn't it?" Oswald said.

"Yes," she said, barely above a whisper.

"You're a medical doctor."

"Yes, I'm an MD with a specialty in pathology."

"From the University of Michigan?"

"That's right."

My fellow graduates will be the end of me.

"And you work at Henry Ford Hospital?"

"Yes."

Oswald went on and on with Dr. Sawyer's qualifications.

Finally, even Nickels had had enough. "Mr. Oswald, you have established that Dr. Sawyer is qualified. In fact, she's so qualified, I wonder why we need someone of her expertise at our little trial."

If you're on trial for murder, it's not a little trial.

"Dr. Sawyer, did you examine the contents of Mr. Fagan's stomach after he died?"

"I did."

"And what did you find?"

"I found that he had the toxins found in Amanita phalloides in his stomach. Those include amatoxins, phallotoxins, and virotoxins."

"What does that mean?"

"One of the toxins, alpha-Amanitin inhibits RNA polymerase II, causing protein deficit and ultimately cell death. The liver is the main target of the toxicity, but other organs are also affected, especially the kidneys and also the stomach."

This is why I hate science.

"And what does that mean?" Oswald said.

As if he didn't know.

Oswald fairly pranced back to his table. He picked up a file, brought it back with him and stood in front of Judge Nickels.

"Your Honor, I'd like to introduce Dr. Sawyer's pathology report that analyzes the contents of the stomach of the late Mr. Fagan."

Burr launched himself to his feet. "Objection, Your Honor. The defense was never provided a copy of this, this whatever-it-is."

Oswald hitched up his pants. "Your Honor, Dr. Sawyer was on the witness list provided to the defense."

Burr marched up to Nickels. "That doesn't matter. It has been clearly established in Brady vs. U.S. that the prosecution has a duty to provide the defense all evidence that may have a bearing on the case." Burr stared at Nickels, then glared at Oswald. "Prior to the trial," Burr said, now shouting.

"Brady doesn't apply here," Oswald said.

"It most certainly does, you pompous ass. That's the reason for the rule," Burr said, still shouting.

"Mr. Lafayette, do not raise your voice in my courtroom, and do not use that language."

Burr ignored the soon-to-be-retiring judge. "Your Honor, this evidence is inadmissible."

Nickels cringed. "What would you have me do?"

"You must not admit this into evidence."

"And if I do?"

"I'll move for a mistrial."

Oswald put his hands on Nickels' desk and leaned toward the judge. "Your Honor, if you grant a mistrial, we'll start over, from the beginning. Mr. Lafayette will have a copy of the report, but it won't change a thing."

"Your Honor," Burr said, not leaning in and not lowering his voice, "if the defense knew about this, prior to five minutes ago, we would have had the opportunity to find our own expert and analyze the evidence ourselves. If you admit this as evidence, we are taking the word of the prosecution's expert. You must not allow this into evidence. If you do, I will move for a mistrial."

"And I won't be retired," Nickels said, *mostly to himself.*

"Your Honor, the Brady rule is clear. Dr. Sawyer's report is not admissible."

Nickels put his head in his hands and shook it back and forth. He took off his glasses and cleaned them. He looked through them but didn't put them back on. He shook his head back and forth again, then put his glasses back on. He made a point of not looking at Burr. "I'm going to allow it into evidence."

"I move for a mistrial," Burr said.

"Denied." Nickels shooed Burr away with his hand. "Go back to your table and sit down, Mr. Lafayette."

Burr didn't budge.

"Go back to your table and sit down or you will be forcibly removed," Nickels smiled wickedly. "Nothing, not even a hole-in-one, would give me greater pleasure."

Burr walked back to the defense table as slowly as he could.

"What just happened?" Molly said.

We were euchred.

"It's just a minor problem with the evidence," he said.

Oswald introduced Dr. Sawyer's pathology report into evidence over another objection from Burr, also overruled. The prosecutor held the report in his hand, like a trophy, which it was.

"Dr. Sawyer, does this report contain the findings of your examination of the contents of the late Mr. Fagan's stomach?"

"It does."

"And what did you find?"

"Mr. Fagan's stomach contained partially digested food. Veal, rice, morel mushrooms. Various salad ingredients." She paused. "And Amanita phalloides mushrooms."

"You found Amanita mushrooms in Mr. Fagan's stomach?"

"Yes."

"In your opinion, what did Mr. Fagan die from?"

The perky doctor of pathology smoothed her skirt. "He died from ingesting Amanita mushrooms."

Damn it all.

"Were there any false morels, also called beefsteak morels, in his stomach?"

Dr. Sawyer folded her hands in her lap. "No."

"But I thought Mr. Fagan died of a heart attack." Oswald looked over his shoulder at Burr and smiled. Burr stuck out his tongue.

"The proximate cause of death was a heart attack brought on by ingesting the Amanita mushrooms," Dr. Sawyer said.

"Thank you, Dr. Sawyer." Oswald walked over to the end of the jury box and put a fat hand on the rail. "Ladies and gentlemen, let's put the fanciful and speculative theories of Mr. Lafayette to rest. Experienced mushroomer or not, Mr. Fagan did not die from eating beefsteak morels. He died from eating Amanita mushrooms, a deadly mushroom that is almost always fatal."

Oswald stood up straight and put both hands on the rail. "And as Dr. Caruso just testified, Amanita mushrooms don't grow when morels do. They grow later in the summer. Which means that someone must have picked the Amanita mushrooms prior to this May. They put the Amanitas in with Mr. Fagan's morels. And that means Mr. Fagan was poisoned intentionally."

Oswald pointed a fat finger at Molly. "By her."

Molly put her head in her hands and started to cry. Burr jumped up and tried to block the jury's view of his sobbing client.

I told her not to cry. Ever.

"Objection, Your Honor. There isn't an ounce of proof that my client killed her husband."

"That comes next," Oswald said.

"Do you have anything further, Mr. Oswald?"

"No, Your Honor." Oswald sat.

"Mr. Lafayette?" Nickels said.

Burr walked up to the perky witness.

I have no idea where to start. Again.

He put his hands in his pockets, walked in a circle and stopped in front of her. He looked down at his shoes, walked in a circle the other way around and ended up where he'd started.

"Mr. Lafayette, are you going to square dance or question the witness?"

Burr cleared his throat. "Dr. Sawyer, you testified that you examined the contents of Mr. Fagan's stomach. Is that right?"

"Yes."

"Did you examine Mr. Fagan's body?"

"No."

"I see." Burr rocked back and forth, heel to toe. "How did you examine the contents of Mr. Fagan's stomach?"

"The contents were frozen and sent to me by Dr. Nettles."

"So, you have no way of knowing if what you examined, in fact, came from Mr. Fagan's stomach?"

"Our policies are very strict."

"Do you know? Personally?"

The perky but pale doctor blushed. "No."

"For all you know, it could have been the contents of Santa Claus's stomach."

"I'm not going to answer that," she said, losing her blush.

"I asked you a question," Burr said.

Oswald sat up straight but didn't stand. "Asked and answered."

"Sustained. Get on with it, Mr. Lafayette," Nickels said.

I'm just getting warmed up.

"Dr. Sawyer, assuming that what you examined was indeed the contents of Mr. Fagan's stomach, do you have any idea how or when the mushrooms got in his stomach?"

"I assume he ate them."

"Dr. Sawyer …"

This time Oswald stood. "Your Honor, if counsel insists on prattling on about the evidentiary custody chain, I'm sure we can produce it."

It was Burr's turn to look over his shoulder at Oswald. "You do that."

Nickels slammed down his gavel. "Mr. Lafayette, if you have any questions of substance, ask them. If not, I am going to excuse the witness."

Burr ignored Nickels. "Dr. Sawyer, have you ever examined the contents of a stomach for Amanita mushrooms before?"

The good doctor curled her index finger toward Burr.

What's this about?

She curled her finger again. Burr took a step closer and leaned over the railing. She leaned toward him until they were nose-to-nose.

She spoke under her breath. "Mr. Lafayette, I have enough credentials to wallpaper your living room. I have examined so many stomachs, I could fill the gas tank of your car with their contents. Amanitas included." She wiped a stray hair out of her eyes. "And I have cancer. A nasty cancer. I may beat it. I may not. I am taking chemotherapy." She put her hand on her head. "This is a wig. I've lost all my hair. It's all I can do to testify. But if you think I'm going to put up with any more of your silly questions, you are grossly mistaken.

"The very next time you ask me a silly question, I am going to pull this wig off and tell everyone about my cancer. And that will ruin your credibility." She sat back. "Is that clear?" she said, for all to hear.

"I am so sorry," Burr said.

Nickels, who had been leaning in trying to hear what Dr. Sawyer had just said, spoke up. "Dr. Sawyer, you must speak up so we can all hear. I can't allow any of what you just said in the record unless you repeat yourself so we can all hear."

"I'll rephrase the question, Your Honor."

Burr smiled at the witness. "Dr. Sawyer, you said your examination of the contents of Mr. Fagan's stomach, if what you examined was actually from Mr. Fagan's stomach, revealed that it contained Amanita mushrooms. Is that correct?"

"Yes," she said, then mouthed, "you bastard."

"But even if that is true, you have no idea if someone poisoned Mr. Fagan, do you?"

"No." She put her hand on the top of her head.

"All you know is that Mr. Fagan had Amanita mushrooms in his stomach. You have no idea if anyone poisoned him. For all you know, Mr. Fagan may have put the Amanitas in with the morels himself. Isn't that right?"

The perky doctor gripped her wig.

"Go ahead. Pull it off," Burr said, *sotto voce*. He cleared his throat. "Do you know who put the Amanitas in Mr. Fagan's veal morel?"

"No."

He turned to Nickels. "I have no further questions, Your Honor." Burr turned on his heel and walked back to his chair.

Oswald struggled to his feet. "Redirect, Your Honor."

"I've had enough for one day. We are adjourned." Nickels slammed down his gavel.

* * *

Burr stood in the parking lot of the courthouse and watched Molly drive off in her Beamer.

"They won't let her have a car in prison," he said with no one around to hear. "At this rate, that's where she's headed."

He'd done his best to calm her down. Sawyer's report should never have been admitted. Oswald knew it. So did Nickels.

"He's not going to let anything get in the way of retiring. And golf."

The wind from the big lake blew in his face. A cold fall wind, colder than it should have been, even for late October. The daylight faded as he stood there. It wasn't six yet, but the days were short here. He felt his seasonal affective disorder coming on, a slow sadness brought on by the darkness.

"I'm going to have to find my lights."

* * *

"I have never seen you eat anything other than grilled cheese on white bread with the crusts cut off," Burr said.

"I saw him have oatmeal once," Eve said.

"All you ever have is a chicken Caesar." He paused. "With the dressing on the side."

"That's how I keep my girlish figure."

Jacob looked at Burr. "If you have one more whitefish sandwich, you're going to grow gills." He looked at his water. "I have tomato soup with my grilled cheese, but I'm sure this awful place doesn't have it."

After the mushroom disaster in Nickels' courtroom, Burr had offered to buy them dinner at the Villager.

They sat at a window booth, not that there was much to see. It was dark and Charlevoix was deserted. Other than a few locals and, now that the color was gone, even fewer tourists, there was no one around.

Burr finished his Labatt and ordered a second.

"Maybe you should stick with water," Eve said.

Burr desperately wanted a martini, but he needed to keep his wits about him, such as they were. It was all he could do to have a Labatt. Or three.

"It wouldn't be so bad if Oswald hadn't snookered us."

"It could be worse." Eve stirred her Bloody Mary again.

"How?"

"You didn't get thrown out."

"Jacob could take over."

Burr's partner shuddered. He picked up the menu. "Maybe they could make me a grilled cheese on white and cut the crusts off."

"You'd do at least as well as I did," Burr said.

Jacob cringed.

"Sawyer's report should never have been admitted," Burr said.

The waitress brought his second beer.

Burr looked out the window, then back at Eve and Jacob. "Our defense has pretty much gone out the window."

Eve took a bite of her pickle. Jacob swirled his water with his straw.

"If Nick died from eating Amanita mushrooms, it really couldn't have been an accident," Burr said.

"Because Amanitas don't grow at the same time as morels," Eve said.

"Bingo," Burr said. "So, someone, somehow, had some Amanita mushrooms and put them in Nick's bag of morels."

Jacob stopped stirring. "If they were out of season, the murderer must have somehow gotten them well in advance."

"That's what I'd call premeditation." Eve crunched her pickle.

"That's why I had to go see Nick's competition about the chain of evidence. And why I hoped Nick had gone to the station that day, but Melissa said he didn't." Burr finished his second beer.

"Now what?" Eve said.

"Oswald played it perfectly. He didn't let us know about Sawyer's report until it was too late to do anything about it. He took a chance that Nickels would let it in. It was a clear breach of the Brady rule. He counted on Nickels wanting to get this trial over with and retire. And it worked." Burr drank half his beer.

The waitress showed up with another beer.

There are miracles in the world.

"Are you ready to order?" she said.

"Could you please make me a grilled cheese on white but cut off ..."

Burr cut him off. He pulled three napkins from the dispenser and handed one to Jacob and one to Eve. He kept one for himself. "Here's what we're going to do. Jacob, I'll order for you. You order for Eve. Eve, you order for me. Anything from the menu. We eat what we're served."

"I won't do it," Jacob said.

"Have a little faith, Jacob," Eve said.

"I have all the faith in the world in Burr. That's why I'm not doing it."

Eve looked at her menu.

"Give us just a minute," Burr said to the waitress. Burr wrote something on his napkin and folded it in two.

"You didn't even look at the menu," Jacob said.

"I didn't need to."

Eve wrote down her choice for Burr. The waitress came back and took Burr and Eve's folded napkins. She looked at Burr. "So, you'd—"

"Surprise us."

"And you," she said, looking at Jacob. He studied the menu, scribbled on the napkin, then passed it to the waitress. She smiled and left.

"Now, what?" Jacob said.

"Now we really have to have a suspect or two. Someone who wanted Nick dead."

"Who would that be?" Eve said.

"Nick didn't have many friends, but I'm not sure anyone hated him enough to murder him."

"I can hardly wait to see what you ordered me," Eve said.

"I'm going to have water for my entrée," Jacob said.

"What we need are some suspects. We still need to find Alexandra McCall, and I don't think Molly is telling us all she knows."

The waitress arrived with their orders. She put a whitefish sandwich in front of Burr, a Caesar salad with grilled chicken, dressing on the side, for Eve, and a grilled cheese on white with the crusts cut off for Jacob. And a cup of tomato soup.

CHAPTER EIGHTEEN

"Mr. Oswald, you may call your next witness."

"Thank you, Your Honor." Oswald stood.

Please don't hitch up your pants.

Oswald hitched up his pants. "The state calls Jennifer Statler." Oswald smiled at the twenty-something, auburn-haired beauty as she walked toward him. She smiled back. The bailiff swore her in. Burr recognized her from somewhere.

She had shoulder-length hair, straight white teeth, and a crooked smile. She wore a black A-line dress, sensible pumps and a matching black purse she balanced in her lap. Burr thought she was quite pretty and probably young enough to be his daughter.

"Ms. Statler, you work as a waitress at the Arboretum."

That's how I know her.

"That was my summer job. I'm back in school now."

"Yes, but this past summer you worked at the Arboretum."

"Yes."

"Did you wait on Nick and Molly Fagan the Saturday night of Memorial Day weekend?"

"Yes."

"Do you remember what they ordered?"

"I do."

"Would you please tell us about it? What they ordered and when."

"Mrs. Fagan started off with a martini. She was very particular about it."

"Yes?"

"Bombay Sapphire gin. On the rocks. Very dry. Dirty with four olives."

It doesn't sound good. For once.

"Did you think that was unusual?"

"Not really. I had a lot of customers who were particular about their drinks. Especially martinis."

"Was there something special about this one?"

She scratched her nose. "Just that Mr. Lafayette always ordered exactly the same kind."

"Mr. Lafayette? The defense counsel?" Oz said. He looked back at Burr. "Yes."

Burr stood. "Your Honor, this is irrelevant and an unwarranted intrusion into my personal life. There is no point to this."

Oswald mouthed at Burr, "The point is you're a drunk." He turned to Judge Nickels. "The point is to show how well Ms. Statler remembers that tragic evening."

"Point taken. Get on with it, Mr. Oswald."

"Yes, Your Honor." Oswald flashed his cat-who-ate-the-canary smile. "Ms. Statler, did the Fagans order anything before their entrée?"

She nodded. "They both had the morel bisque."

"Was that on the menu?"

"Yes, we're known for it, but Mr. Fagan didn't think his was hot enough, so I took it back to the kitchen. Mrs. Fagan went to the bar and ordered another martini."

"Really." Oswald looked back at Molly then at the witness. "And what about the entrées?"

The witness looked at Molly. "Mrs. Fagan ordered the planked whitefish. Mr. Fagan asked for veal morel, but we were out of morels."

"I thought you said the Arboretum didn't have any morels."

"Cat, the chef, premade it and froze it."

"I see."

"What about the veal morel?"

"Mr. Fagan said he brought his own morels."

"Really," Oswald said again. "Was that allowed?"

The witness looked back at Molly. "They were regulars, so yes. Sometimes."

"Where were Mr. Fagan's mushrooms?"

"In Mrs. Fagan's purse."

"I see. And then what happened?"

"Mrs. Fagan got up and took them into the kitchen."

"Then what?"

"She gave them to Cat."

"Objection, Your Honor," Burr said. "The witness wasn't in the kitchen so she can't know what happened."

"Sustained." Nickels gave a world-weary look to the jury. "Disregard the last question and answer."

"What happened after Mrs. Fagan came back from the kitchen?"

The winsome Jennifer Statler sighed. "Mrs. Fagan ordered another martini. Then I brought the soup out. Mr. Fagan sent it back because he said it wasn't hot enough."

"And?"

"I took it back, put it in the microwave and brought it back out. Then the salads came. Mrs. Fagan ordered another martini."

"Her third?"

The witness nodded. Oswald looked over his shoulder at Molly. "My, my, my. And what was Mr. Fagan drinking?"

"He had a glass of wine before dinner."

"A glass?"

She nodded. "They had wine with dinner, but I don't think he had much of it."

"Did Mrs. Fagan go into to the kitchen again?"

The witness looked down, then back at Oswald. "After the salads came, I saw her go into the kitchen."

"Do you know why?"

"I think …"

"Objection," Burr said.

"I withdraw the question, Your Honor." Oswald paced back and forth in front of the witness stand.

Here it comes.

Oswald stopped next to the witness where he could see her and the jury. "When you brought out the entrées, did Mrs. Fagan have any of Mr. Fagan's veal morel?"

"Not that I could see."

"What did you think about that?"

"They each had their own bisque, but they had different salads, and they shared them. He had some of her whitefish."

Oswald looked at the jury. "Ladies and gentlemen, they ate off each other's plate except for the veal morel. The reason that Mrs. Fagan didn't have any of Mr. Fagan's veal morel is because she poisoned it when she went into the kitchen."

"Objection, Your Honor. This is pure speculation."

Nickels touched the tips of his fingers together. "Overruled. The prosecutor is allowed to state his theory."

Burr sat.

I knew I'd lose, but I had to do something.

"Your witness," Oswald said.

Burr walked up to the witness. "Ms. Statler, did you go into the kitchen when Mrs. Fagan was in there?"

"Well, I ..."

"Please answer the question."

"No."

"So, you really have no idea what went on in the kitchen, do you," Burr said, not asking.

"No."

"Did you watch the Fagans the entire time they were eating?"

"Well ..."

Burr took a step toward her.

"No," she said.

"So, you really have no idea whether or not Mrs. Fagan had any of Mr. Fagan's veal morel."

She stared at Burr. "I never saw her have any."

Burr tapped his foot. "Ms. Statler, how many tables did you have that night?"

She bit her cheek. "About four."

"About?"

"Four."

"That must have kept you busy."

She nodded.

"So, you'd spend about a quarter of your time with each table. Is that right?"

"I suppose."

"Plus, you'd be going back and forth to the bar and the kitchen."

The comely waitress bit her cheek again.

"So, really, you probably weren't watching the Fagans, say more than ten percent of your time."

Oswald stood. "Objection, Your Honor, this is all speculation."

Burr looked at Nickels. "Your Honor, the point is …" Then he looked at the jury. "With four tables on a busy Saturday night over Memorial Day weekend, Ms. Statler, no matter how gifted she is, does not have eyes in the back of her head."

He turned back to the cheek-chewing witness. "You really have very little idea what went on at that table and no idea what went on in the kitchen." Burr started to the defense table without waiting for an answer.

"Sustained," Nickels said about two minutes too late.

"I have no further questions." Burr said.

"Mr. Oswald, call your next witness."

Oswald put his hands on the table, made a face, and pushed himself up. "The state calls Cynthia Showalter."

The leggy blonde from the preliminary exam took the witness stand. She had sky-blue eyes and what was left of her tan. She had a dash of pink lipstick. That was it for makeup, but that was all she needed.

The bailiff swore her in.

"Ms. Showalter, you worked in the kitchen at the Arboretum on the night Mr. Fagan was poisoned. Is that right?"

Burr started to stand.

"I withdraw the question, Your Honor." Oswald smiled wickedly at Burr. *Well done. At my expense.*

"Ms. Showalter, you were working in the kitchen of the Arboretum on the Saturday night of Memorial Day weekend this past summer. Is that right?"

"Yes."

"And what did you do in the kitchen?"

"I was the salad girl."

"The salad girl?"

She brushed her hair off her forehead. "I made the salads."

Oswald nodded. "Of course. Ms. Showalter, did you see the defendant, Mrs. Fagan, come into the kitchen that night?"

"Yes."

"Please tell us about it."

"She came in twice. The first time she came in, she had a bag of morels."

"How do you know they were morels?"

"Mrs. Fagan handed them to Cat, the chef, and I heard her, Cat, say, 'These look like fresh morels.'"

Burr stood. "Objection, Your Honor. Hearsay. If Mr. Oswald wants to establish that the bag contained mushrooms, he needs to call someone who actually saw what was in the bag."

Nickels looked over his nose at Burr. "Must you always be so argumentative?" The judge looked at Oswald. "I am afraid Mr. Lafayette is right. His objection is sustained."

Oswald let his breath out. "Ms. Showalter, did you see Mrs. Fagan hand a bag full of something to the chef?"

"Yes."

"And what did the chef … Cat, I think you said her name is, do with what she said were mushrooms?"

"She put them on a cutting board and chopped them up. Then she made a sauce and sauteed the mushrooms. Then she …"

Oswald raised his hand and shushed her. "What did it look like to you that the chef was making?"

The leggy blonde rolled her eyes. "Veal morel."

"Thank you, Ms. Showalter." Oswald turned to the jury. "Ladies and gentlemen, the objection of Mr. Lafayette, notwithstanding, I think we have now established that the bag that Mrs. Fagan brought into the kitchen was indeed filled with mushrooms." Oswald looked over his shoulder at Burr then turned to the witness. "Did Mrs. Fagan come back into the kitchen?"

"Yes."

"Would you please tell us what you saw?"

"About fifteen minutes later, Mrs. Fagan came back into the kitchen. She looked around, then went over to where the veal morel was simmering. I saw her open up her hand. There was a baggie in it. She dumped the contents into the pot, stirred it and left."

"Did she know you saw her?"

"No."

"Did she say anything to anyone or go up to Cat and tell her what she was doing?"

"No."

"Did it look like she was sneaking?"

"Well …" Cindy Showalter licked her lips again. "It was really busy in the kitchen that night, so I don't think she thought anyone was paying much attention to her. I wouldn't say she was sneaking. She was just sort of acting like what she was doing was no big deal. Like she did this all the time."

Molly shook her head.

"Had Mrs. Fagan ever come into the kitchen before that fateful night?" Oswald practically spit out 'fateful.'

"Oh, yes. All the time."

"Really?"

"Is that unusual?"

The witness nodded. "Very, but it was an unusual situation."

Oswald stepped back. "How so?"

"We advertised on Mr. Fagan's radio station, so they were in all the time. It was mostly a trade. Food for ads. And he was so fussy. He was always sending things back. Mrs. Fagan was always coming in the kitchen. To smooth things over."

"So, you didn't think it was at all out of the ordinary?"

"No, I didn't."

"Thank you, Ms. Showalter."

Oswald turned to the jury. "Ladies and gentlemen, the witness has just testified that Mrs. Fagan went into the kitchen twice, once with a bag of morels, and then the second time, with another bag, which, I submit to you, were poisonous Amanita mushrooms. The kitchen staff was used to seeing her in the kitchen, so they didn't do anything about it."

Oswald, on cue, hitched up his pants.

"Mrs. Fagan went back to the kitchen and brazenly poisoned her husband's veal morel." The prosecutor pointed at Molly. "For all the world to see." He marched back to his table and fell into his chair.

Burr walked up to the witness. "Ms. Showalter, you referred to yourself as the salad girl at the Arboretum. Is that right?"

"Yes."

"Did you make very many salads on that Saturday night?"

"Yes. It was very busy, and it seemed like everyone wanted a salad."

"From my own personal experience at the Arboretum, you make a very good salad."

She blushed just a bit.

"About how many salads would you say you made that night?"

"I have no idea." She started counting on her fingers. "At least a hundred."

Burr smiled at her. "That's a lot of salads. So, you were busy with that?"

"Yes."

"Busy enough that you couldn't see everything that was happening in the kitchen. Could there have been other people who came into the kitchen that you didn't see?"

"Objection, Your Honor," Oswald said. "Speculation."

"Your Honor, if she was making a hundred salads, how could she possibly have seen everything that was going on in the kitchen?"

Nickels sighed. "Sustained. You need not answer the question, Ms. Showalter."

Let's try this.

"Ms. Showalter, do you use a knife to cut things up when you make salads?"

"Yes."

"Is it sharp?"

"Very." She beamed.

"So, when you're cutting things up for your salads, you have to concentrate on what you're doing?"

"Yes."

"And shut out the rest of the world?"

"Yes."

Burr looked back at Oswald.

"So, you wouldn't know what was going on around you while you were cutting and chopping."

"I guess not," she said.

"I guess not," Burr said. "Ms. Showalter, about how far away were you from Mrs. Fagan when she handed whatever was in the plastic bag to Cat."

"I'm not sure."

"About how far? An estimate will be fine."

She scrunched her nose, then, "I'm really not sure."

"Fifteen feet? Twenty feet?"

She scrunched her nose again. "Maybe fifteen feet."

"Fifteen feet." Burr rocked back and forth on his heels. "And the same distance when you say you saw Mrs. Fagan put something in the veal morel?"

"Yes."

"Were there people walking between you and Mrs. Fagan while all this was going on? Waiters? Cooks?"

"Yes."

"So, your view was at least partially blocked."

She wiggled in her chair. "Maybe a little."

"Maybe a little," Burr said. "Do you know what Mrs. Fagan might have put in the veal morel?"

"Well, do you?"

"No."

Burr turned to the jury.

"Ladies and gentlemen, what we have here is a witness who, because of her job, only looked in Mrs. Fagan's direction part of the time, and whose vision was partially blocked when she did look. And who, by her own admission, doesn't know what was in either plastic bag. For all she knows a dozen other people may have been waltzing in and out of the kitchen and pouring Rice Krispies into the pot." Burr hitched up his pants. "I have no further questions."

* * *

Nickels had had enough of them and adjourned for lunch.

Burr and his not so merry little band reprised lunch at the Grey Gables. Molly said she couldn't eat a thing, but Burr was starving. He ordered a bowl of navy bean soup, a cheeseburger and French fries. Eve had Scotchgarded his tie, but she sat next to him, at the ready with a napkin and a glass of water.

Jacob ordered his de rigueur grilled cheese. "I suppose Oswald will call chef what's-her-name this afternoon."

"Cat," Burr said. "Cat Garrity."

"What do you suppose Cat stands for?" Eve picked a crouton out of her Caesar.

"Catherine," Burr said.

"It stands for Cathedral," Eve said.

"Cathedral?"

"She was born in the Cathedral of the Most Blessed Sacrament in Detroit."

"I beg your pardon," Jacob said.

"Earlier than expected. It's on Woodward."

"How could you possibly know that?" Burr drowned a fry in his ketchup.

Eve dabbed at his tie. "That's what you pay me for." She speared a piece of chicken. "When you pay me."

"This has nothing to do with Oswald calling her as a witness," Jacob said.

Burr looked at Molly, who wasn't engaged in the origins of Cat's name. "I'd be surprised if he did call her to testify."

"Why?" Jacob said.

"She wouldn't admit to the possibility that the bag of morels may have had Amanitas in it." He dipped another fry. "Or that Molly might have had them in the second bag."

"I didn't," Molly said, close to tears.

"I know you didn't," Burr said.

But I'm not so sure.

"We've made it this far, but it may get ugly this afternoon," Burr said. He dipped a fry in his ketchup. The ketchup dripped on his tie. Eve rolled her eyes and dabbed it off.

CHAPTER NINETEEN

This is terrible.

The bailiff had called them to order, and Oswald had just called his first witness. He'd made a show of holding the swinging gate open for his witness, Kelly Fagan.

She raised her right hand and waited for the bailiff to swear her in. She had on a black dress, not a copy of Molly's but close, sensible pumps, and pearl earrings.

Her hair was black, like Molly's, a little shorter but pulled back like Molly's, and the same pink lipstick. She looked about ten years older, but the two of them could easily be mistaken for each other.

After Oswald made sure the jury got a good look at her, he nodded to the bailiff, and she was sworn in.

Oswald doesn't even have to ask her a question.

The prosecutor walked up to the former Mrs. Fagan, making sure to stand where the jury could see both of Nick's wives.

"Mrs. Fagan, would you please tell us your relationship to the deceased, Nick Fagan."

"We were married for seven years."

"And then what happened?"

"My husband had an affair with her." She pointed at Molly. "Then we got divorced."

Oswald put his hand on the railing and leaned toward her. "Mrs. Fagan, was the divorce your idea?"

"No. I wanted to work things out, but Nicky wouldn't hear of it."

"I'm sorry, Mrs. Fagan." Oswald patted the railing. "How did this all come about?"

"Nick was running a radio station in Detroit, a very popular station, and she …" This time she pointed at Molly. "She worked for him. They started carrying on, and then he divorced me."

"Did you know they were having an affair?"

"Not at first, but I found out."

"I'm so sorry." Oswald looked at the jury, then at Molly. The jury followed Oswald's eyes. "What did you do?"

I may regret this.

Burr pushed his chair back and stood, ever so slowly. "Your Honor, I object to this entire line of questioning. It has absolutely no bearing on Mr. Fagan's death and is totally irrelevant."

"Your Honor, it is totally relevant. It shows what kind of person the defendant is and what she is capable of."

"It does nothing of the sort."

Judge Nickels took off his glasses, looked through them and put them back on. "Mr. Oswald, I'm going to allow this, but you must connect the dots."

"Yes, Your Honor." Oswald winked at Burr.

Molly turned away. Burr leaned over to her. "I know this is terrible, but you absolutely have to keep your composure."

Oswald continued.

"Mrs. Fagan—"

"Objection, Your Honor," Burr said. "Mrs. Fagan is sitting next to me."

"Your Honor, it's customary to refer to a divorced woman as 'Mrs.'"

"Overruled. Mr. Lafayette, you are splitting hairs," Nickels said.

This is going to get worse.

"Mrs. Fagan," Oswald said with an emphasis on Mrs., "how exactly did all this come to pass. Your divorce, that is."

"As I said, she worked with my husband. Nicky worked so much that she probably saw him more than I did. So, she just seduced him. He was no match for her."

"So, she stole him away from you."

"That's right."

Burr stood, not so slowly this time. "Your Honor, respectfully, I haven't seen any dots connected yet."

"Your Honor, the point here is that the defendant stole Mrs. Fagan's husband. She began an adulterous affair and stole Mrs. Fagan's husband."

"It wasn't like that at all," Molly said under her breath.

"I know," Burr said.

"I have no further questions, Your Honor." Oswald sat down before Burr could say anything further.

I don't want to make things any worse than they already are.

"Mrs. Fagan, would you say that you had a happy marriage?"

"Yes."

"But you did get divorced."

"Only because of her."

"Did Mr. Fagan have any other affairs?"

"Not that I know of."

"Not that you know of." Burr put his hands in his pockets. "But he might have?"

"Objection, Your Honor. Asked and answered."

"Sustained."

"People get divorced all the time. And they don't murder one another, do they?"

"I suppose not."

"Mrs. Fagan, when Mr. Fagan divorced you, you didn't murder him."

"No, I didn't."

Oswald started to push himself to his feet.

"I withdraw the question, Your Honor. Nothing further." Burr walked back to the defense table.

Oswald stood. "The state calls Robert Davies."

Nick's old-money partner strode to the witness stand. He unbuttoned the jacket of his black suit with a wine-colored pinstripe. He wore a solid wine-colored tie to match and a starched white shirt and gold cufflinks.

The picture of arrogance.

The bailiff swore in Davies. Oswald made his way to the witness stand.

Compared to Davies, Oswald looks like he dressed at a thrift shop.

"Mr. Davies, you were one of Nick Fagan's partners at WKHQ. Is that right?"

"Yes."

"And can you tell me about your relationship with the deceased, how you knew him, what he did, and what you thought of him."

Davies ran a hand along the crease in his slacks. "Nick worked for me at a radio station I own in Detroit. Best manager I ever had. We were number one in just about every demo that mattered. When the opportunity to sign on WKHQ came along, I offered him a third interest to run it."

"And he accepted?"

"He jumped at the chance."

"And why is that?"

Davies looked at Oswald like he was his valet. "For one, WKHQ was and is a great opportunity. It's the best signal up here. There was a huge hole for a Top 40 radio station, and I gave him a piece of the deal."

Oswald nodded. "Anything else?"

"Well ..." Davies cleared his throat.

"Mr. Davies, was there any other reason you brought Mr. Fagan up here?"

"Well ..." Davies looked at Molly.

"Mr. Davies," Oswald said.

"Mr. Fagan was having a relationship with Mrs. Fagan."

"Molly Fagan?"

"Yes." Davies looked at Molly.

"Mr. Davies, please elaborate."

"Mr. Fagan was having a relationship with Molly Fagan. She wasn't Molly Fagan at the time. She worked in sales at my station. Mr. Fagan was married to the former Mrs. Fagan at the time. It caused a big problem at the station. A terrible scandal. So, I thought it would be best to get Mr. Fagan out of Detroit."

"And then what happened?"

"Well, I got the FCC license for KHQ. I moved him up here. He ended up divorcing and marrying Molly."

"Did Molly Fagan ever work at KHQ?"

"No."

"Did Mr. Fagan keep his hands to himself at KHQ?" Oswald looked at Molly and smiled. "So to speak."

"Not exactly."

"So, Mr. Fagan's philandering continued, even with his new wife?"

"Regrettably, it did."

"Did Mrs. Fagan, Molly Fagan, know this?"

"She found out."

"And what was her reaction?"

"She was furious."

"What did she do?"

Davies looked at Molly again.

"Mr. Davies."

"She came to the station on a number of occasions and caused terrible scenes."

"Was there anyone in particular he was … familiar with?"

"Alexandra McCall."

"Alexandra McCall," Oswald said. "So, Mr. Fagan carried on with Alexandra McCall. Mrs. Fagan found out, and she was jealous?"

"Yes."

"Jealous enough to kill him."

"Yes."

Burr jumped up. "Objection, Your Honor. Calls for an opinion."

"Sustained."

Oswald smiled at Burr and hitched up his pants.

I'm going to buy him a pair of suspenders.

"I have no further questions, Your Honor."

Burr walked up to the witness. "Mr. Davies, when a marriage doesn't work out, for whatever reason, and it comes time to end the marriage, there is generally a divorce. Is that right?"

"I suppose so."

"Mr. Fagan's first marriage ended in divorce. Is that right?"

Davies tapped his foot. "Yes."

"If the marriage of my client and Mr. Fagan were to end, it could end in divorce"

"Yes, but …"

"There would be no reason for it to end in murder." Burr tapped his own foot. "Not when it would be so easy to get a divorce."

"Objection, Your Honor," Oswald said. "Calls for speculation."

I made my point.

"I withdraw the question, Your Honor," Burr said. "Mr. Davies, would you say that Mr. Fagan was a competitive person?"

"I would."

"Very competitive?"

"Yes."

"So much so that he may have made enemies."

"Well …"

Burr walked back to his table, picked up a folder and returned to the witness stand. "Mr. Davies, I have a list here of the radio stations that WKHQ competes with. I interviewed many of the owners and managers. They all said that they hated Mr. Fagan. Does that surprise you?"

"Objection, Your Honor. No factual foundation for this has been established."

Nickels looked down his nose at Burr. "Mr. Lafayette, are you familiar with the rules of evidence?"

Burr nodded.

"Mr. Lafayette, you will abide by the rules of evidence. Is that clear?"

"Yes, Your Honor," Burr said as contritely as he could, although he wasn't a bit contrite.

"You may continue."

"Mr. Davies, would it be fair to say that Mr. Fagan had enemies?"

Davies took a deep breath. "I suppose so."

"Are you aware of any threats that had been made against Mr. Fagan?"

Davies didn't say anything.

Burr tapped the folder.

"Yes," Davies said.

"Thank you." Burr tapped the folder again. "Are you aware of any threats that were made on Mr. Fagan's life?"

"Yes."

Oswald started to stand.

I made my point.

"I have no further questions, Your Honor," Burr said.

Oswald called Melissa Warren, KHQ's business manager. She wore a blue jacket over a white blouse and a matching knee-length blue skirt.

The woman's version of a sincere blue suit.

The bailiff swore her in.

"Ms. Warren, you are the business manager at KHQ. Is that right?"

She straightened her skirt and put her hands in her lap. "It is."

"And where is your office?"

"It's across from Mr. Fagan's office." She paused. "Where his office was, I mean."

Oswald nodded. "Did Mrs. Fagan ever visit Mr. Fagan at the station?"

"Yes."

"Did you ever hear them arguing?"

"I did."

"Did you hear what they were arguing about?"

"Yes."

"Would you please tell us." Oswald stepped to the side so the prim business manager could tell the jury.

"They were arguing about Alexandra McCall."

"Alexandra McCall. The person who worked at the station?"

"Yes."

"What did Mrs. Fagan say?"

"She said, get rid of her now, and if you ever see her again, I'll kill you."

Burr winced.

Molly tugged at his sleeve. "I never said that."

Burr nodded at her.

One of them is lying. Maybe both.

Oswald turned back to the witness. "Ms. Warren, did Ms. McCall ever go into Mr. Fagan's office when he was in there?"

"Oh, yes."

"Did you ever see what went on? When they were together in his office?"

"I saw them kissing once."

"How did you see that?"

She smiled an I-didn't-mean-to-smile, smile.

"I knocked on the door and went in, like I always did. I didn't know she was in there."

"And?"

"They were kissing."

Oswald took three steps to the jury and raised his eyebrows. "Kissing?"

He sashayed back to the witness. "Did you see them together in his office any other time?"

"They were in there together many times, but there is one time that really stuck in my mind."

Oswald slid back in front of his witness. "What were they doing?"

Whatever it is, I don't want to know.

The prim business manager blushed, then looked at her feet. "I really don't want to say."

Oswald smiled kindly. "I'm sorry, Ms. Warren, but you're under oath, and we are here in the pursuit of justice."

Spare me.

She cleared her throat and spoke softly. "Mr. Fagan was sitting at his desk, turned sideways, and Ms. McCall, well, she was …"

"Yes?"

"She was on her knees. Between …"

Oswald raised his hand.

Damn it all.

Melissa Warren buried her head in her hands.

Oswald looked shocked.

He knew exactly what she was going to say.

The courtroom erupted.

Nickels turned red. He fumbled with his gavel, then beat it on his desk. "Quiet, quiet. We will have order."

The roar turned to a buzz. Nickels looked at his gavel but thought better of it. Oswald patted his witness on the shoulder and offered her his handkerchief. She wiped her eyes. Finally, the courtroom quieted. Oswald looked over at Burr and winked, making sure no one could see him.

"Your witness."

What could I possibly ask that won't make things worse?

Burr tapped his pencil.

Nickels rapped his gavel. "Do you have any questions for the witness, Mr. Lafayette?"

Molly's face was in her hands. She was crying softly. Burr put his hand on her shoulder. "We'll get through this." She didn't move. "You need to sit up. We can't let them get the best of us."

"Shall I excuse the witness, Mr. Lafayette?"

Burr stood. "Your Honor, the defense requests a thirty-minute recess."

Nickels tried to find his watch in the folds of his robe and finally gave up. "Bailiff, what time is it?"

The bailiff looked at the clock on the wall. "It's three o'clock, Your Honor."

"Mr. Lafayette, if you have any questions for Ms. Warren, ask them now."

Burr made a face.

"Do not make faces at me."

Burr ignored Nickels and walked up to the tattletale business manager.

I don't dare ask her anything about what went on in Nick's office. If anything ever did go on.

Burr put his hand on the railing. "Ms. Warren, as business manager, you are knowledgeable about the financial affairs of the radio station. Is that right?"

She folded her hands on her lap. "Yes," she said.

She's all put back together.

"And you must have known about the financial problems of the radio station."

"I'm not aware of any financial problems."

"Really? I thought it was common knowledge that KHQ was chronically late in paying its bills."

"Oh, no. That's not true."

Why would she lie about this? What else is she lying about?

"I see." Burr rocked back and forth, heel to toe.

"Ms. Warren, you also paid Mr. Fagan's personal bills, isn't that right?"

"No, not really."

"Not really." Burr rocked back and forth again. "What does 'not really' mean?"

"Objection, Your Honor," Oswald said.

"Watch your manners, Mr. Lafayette," Nickels said, scowling.

Burr nodded at the judge, insincerely.

"Ms. Warren, did you ever pay any of Mr. Fagan's personal bills?"

"Occasionally."

"And when you paid his bills, were they overdue?"

"I don't remember," she said, also insincerely.

Is she trying to protect Nick?

"Ms. Warren, isn't it true that Mr. Fagan had enemies, personally and professionally?"

"Oh, no," she said. "Everyone liked Nick."

Burr turned his back to her. On his way back to the defense table, he raised his hand and pooh-poohed her. "I have no further questions, Your Honor."

* * *

Burr turned the key in the lock and pulled the door open. He looked both ways. No one in sight. Then he stepped inside, shut the door and started up the stairs.

Nickels had adjourned them for the day after Melissa's disastrous testimony. Burr had taken them to dinner at the Argonne Supper Club, but no one ate much except Burr, who was always hungry, especially when things were going poorly, which they were in spades. Not to mention a powerful thirst. He had the house specialty, fried shrimp with cocktail sauce and fries. Sadly, they didn't serve Labatt. He limited himself to four Miller's.

"Nicky wasn't like that," she'd said.

Burr told her to forget about what the jury and the gallery thought of her and help him figure out how to get her acquitted.

The best Molly could do was to give him the key to the private entrance to Nick's office, and here he was at eight o'clock on a Wednesday night. A perfectly crisp and clear night in late October. Not a soul in sight.

He unlocked the door, climbed the stairs and walked into Nick's office. He stood in the dark, the only light in the room leaked in from the windows that faced the street. He looked over the buildings at Round Lake, a shiny, black sheet of glass. He had no idea what he was looking for or where to look for it.

KHQ played *Smooth Operator*.

Burr looked through the one-way glass at the offices. There was no one there. Why would there be? Just desks, chairs, and file cabinets.

The production studio, also dark, except for the stand-by lights on the tape machines, the cart machines, the turntables, and the other fancy electronics. He had no idea what they did.

A disc jockey sat in the on-air studio, facing a microphone, his back to Burr. He was thin with thinning hair, like Nettles, but he wore a T-shirt and jeans instead of a suit and tie. The studio was dark, except for the spotlights shining on the equipment. The jock spoke into the mic.

"That was Genesis. The Moody Blues' new one is up next."

Burr turned on the lights, sat at Nick's desk, and started going through the drawers. Pens, pencils, paper clips in the skinny middle drawer.

Then the files in the right drawer.

Your Wildest Dreams came on.

The one-way glass banged.

Burr jumped.

It banged again.

"What's going on? Who's in there?"

Burr opened the door to the studio.

The jock stood in the doorway. "What's going on? Who are you?" The jock had a clear, bass voice that sounded like it should have belonged to a fullback.

"I'm Molly Fagan's lawyer."

"I think I've seen you before."

"I thought this was a one-way glass."

"I saw the light coming under the door."

Burr's heart slowed down.

"Shit, my song's about to run out." The small man with the big voice ran back to the studio.

"Tommy Preston here with the top nine at nine. Starting at number nine is *Time After Time.*"

Burr sat back down at Nick's desk. He rifled through Nick's files. One after the other, nervous that Tommy would walk in any minute.

There's nothing here.

He finished looking through Nick's desk when Tommy made it to number three, but he stayed until he heard tonight's number one song, *Sweet Dreams* by the Eurythmics.

I love this song.

CHAPTER TWENTY

Burr licked the cream filling from his fingers. He'd driven to Johan's Bakery in Petoskey early this morning for a cream-filled long john with white frosting. They made the best he'd ever had, but it was all he could manage to keep the gooey white filling from dripping onto his tie. It actually turned out to be more than he could manage. There was a splotch on one of the red stripes on his repp tie. Eve, ever vigilant, quietly moved in and dabbed at the splotch.

"Will you ever learn?" she said.

Probably not.

"Thank God. Nickels is late," she said.

Burr had slept like a five-year-old on Christmas night, a five-year-old who believed in Santa Claus and who'd gotten everything he asked for. When he woke up though, it wasn't Christmas. He hadn't found anything at Nick's office, and more to the point, Oswald was thrashing him.

Molly looked like she'd been up all night. Jacob didn't look much better.

Fighting agrees with me.

Molly touched his hand. "It wasn't like how Oswald is telling it. Nicky wasn't like that."

In a gesture that reached the top-of-the-cliché pile, Burr patted her hand.

It just looks that way.

"I know," he said.

I may have had a client who didn't lie, but I don't remember when.

At last, Nickels made his grand entrance, as regal as he could make it when he was tangled up in his robe. "Mr. Oswald, you may call your next witness."

The Great Oz rose, ever so slowly, like bread dough rising in the oven. "The state calls Pearl Watson."

The diminutive Pearl Watson walked to the witness stand. She wore a gray suit, an ivory blouse with a Peter Pan collar, and two-inch black heels.

Burr didn't think she was an imposing presence, but she looked believable.

She'll be more believable than Flintoff.

The bailiff swore her in. She sat and Oswald walked up to her. He ran through her credentials and her employment at the Dearborn Life Insurance Company.

"Ms. Watson, did you work on Nick Fagan's case?"

"Yes," she said, with gravitas,

"How much was the policy for?"

"One million dollars."

Oswald looked at the jury. "A million dollars. That's a lot of money." He turned back to the witness. "Ms. Watson, when the policy was first issued, who was the beneficiary?"

"Molly Fagan."

"Molly Fagan," Oswald said. "And how long ago was that?"

"About five years ago."

"Five years," Oswald said.

We all know where this is going.

"Ms. Watson, did Mr. Fagan change the beneficiary?"

"Yes."

"And when was that?"

"He changed the beneficiary in May of this year."

"And who was the new beneficiary?"

A very pregnant pause from Pearl Watson, then, "The new beneficiary was Alexandra McCall."

"Alexandra McCall," Oswald said. "And what was the relationship between Nick Fagan and Alexandra McCall?"

"I believe they were lovers." Pearl Watson said, losing her pearl complexion.

The courtroom tittered.

Burr jumped up. "I object, Your Honor. This is outrageous. It's sheer speculation and totally unfounded."

"I will make my proofs." Oswald puffed himself up.

Nickels pointed his finger at the prosecutor. "Until you do, Ms. Watson's statement will not be allowed." He looked down over his reading glasses at the jury. "You will disregard Mr. Oswald's question and Ms. Watson's answer."

The jury nodded.

Too late.

Oswald cleared his throat. "Ms. Watson, you just said that Mr. Fagan changed the beneficiary of his life insurance policy to Alexandra McCall in May of this year, shortly before he was murdered. Is that right?"

"Yes."

Oswald smiled at Burr. "My, my, my." He waddled back to his table and picked up a single sheet of paper. He held it like it was the Bill of Rights. He walked back to Pearl Watson and showed her the paper. "Is this the form?"

She pursed her lips. "Yes."

"Your Honor, the state would like to introduce this change of beneficiary form into evidence."

"Your Honor," Burr said, still standing, "I am familiar with this piece of paper. The form requires the signature of a witness, and this form is not witnessed. It could have been signed by anyone. It has no probative value and cannot be introduced into evidence."

Oswald waved Burr off. "Your Honor, this form shows that Mr. Fagan was going to change his beneficiary. It shows his state of mind and what he intended to do. It so enraged the defendant that she murdered him."

"My client didn't even know that piece of paper existed."

I hope.

"Your Honor, the state isn't trying to use this form as a legally binding document. We are only using it to show Mr. Fagan's state of mind."

"There is no way of knowing who filled it out," Burr said.

Nickels blew all the air out of his lungs. He took a deep breath. "Mr. Oswald, I am going to allow this into evidence, but you are going to have to show why you believe that it was Mr. Fagan who filled out this form and signed it."

"Your Honor, how can you admit a form into evidence that is not legally binding?"

"It doesn't have to be legally binding to show state of mind," Oswald said.

"Hand me that form," Nickels said. Oswald passed it to Nickels. The judge studied it. Nickels looked down at the witness. "Ms. Watson, how and when did this come into your possession?"

"Mr. Davies gave it to me last June."

"Did he say how he got it?"

"He told me he found it in Mr. Fagan's papers."

"Objection, Your Honor," Burr said. "Hearsay."

"Quiet," Nickels said. "Did he say where he found it?"

"In Mr. Fagan's desk."

Molly said she never saw it.

Nickels put the form down in front of him. He twiddled his thumbs. Frontwards. Backwards. Then frontwards again. "In the interest of finding the truth, I am going to allow this into evidence. Ms. Meecher, admit this into evidence."

"I object, Your Honor," Burr said. "This was not provided to me before the trial."

"Did you or did you not see this at the preliminary examination?"

"According to Brady—"

"Overruled."

"I move for a mistrial."

"So noted. Again."

"I'd like a copy of that," Burr said.

Oswald nodded at the bailiff.

"Carry on, Mr. Oswald."

Oswald reached for the form. "May I, Your Honor?"

Nickels slid the form to Oswald.

Oswald picked up the piece of paper and walked over to the jury. "Ladies and gentlemen, this form names Alexandra McCall as the beneficiary of Nick Fagan's life insurance policy." Oswald looked over at Molly, who was holding her own. So far. He turned back to the jury.

"Do you know why this is important?" He showed it to the jury. "It's important because when Molly Fagan found out her husband was having an affair and was going to take her off his policy, she murdered him. Then she filed a claim with the old form. She murdered her husband because she was jealous and then tried to collect on his life insurance."

Oswald looked back at Molly. "But you made a mistake. You didn't know that Nick had already changed the policy. Did you?"

"It wasn't like that. I loved Nick."

Nickels banged his gavel. "Mrs. Fagan, you will not address this courtroom unless you are called as a witness."

Burr stood. "Your Honor, the prosecutor spoke to my client as if he expected an answer. Mr. Oswald provoked her. Intentionally."

"I most certainly did not," Oswald said. "Besides, she's guilty as sin."

Nickels rapped his gavel.

"I have no further questions, Your Honor." Oswald strutted to his chair as well as a large man could strut.

"Mr. Lafayette?" Nickels said.

Burr looked at Oswald's witness list. After Pearl Watson, the only witness left who could possibly make a difference would be the mysterious and missing Alexandra McCall.

She'll be the one who cooks our goose.

Burr stood. "Ms. Watson, isn't it true that Mrs. Fagan submitted a claim on her husband's life insurance policy in June of this year?"

"Yes."

"And, isn't it true that the Dearborn Life Insurance Company refused to pay the claim?"

Pearl Watson looked out into the gallery.

"Did the Dearborn Life Insurance Company refuse to pay the claim?" Burr said again.

She found who she was looking for. "Yes," she said.

"Ms. Watson, the coroner ruled that Mr. Fagan's death was accidental. The prosecutor, Mr. Oswald himself …" Burr swept his hand back at the prosecutor, "thought it was an accident. Yet your company refused to pay what was, and is, a perfectly legitimate claim. Why is that?"

Pearl Watson looked back in the gallery again.

Burr walked up to her and stood in her line of sight.

She tried to look around Burr, but he moved with her.

"Please answer the question," Burr said.

She leaned one way, then the other, and back again. Burr matched her every move.

"What are you doing, Mr. Lafayette?"

"Your Honor, the witness is trying to get her answers from someone in the gallery. I believe it's Julian Flintoff." Burr pointed at the steely general counsel of the Dearborn Life Insurance Company.

"I am not," Pearl Watson said.

"Then answer my question. Why didn't the Dearborn Life Insurance Company want to pay Mrs. Fagan's perfectly legitimate claim?"

"I object," Oswald said. "This case isn't about life insurance. It's about murder."

Burr put his hands in his pockets. "Your Honor, it is perfectly acceptable for the prosecutor to introduce a change of beneficiary form that is not legally binding, but when I try to find out more about the original policy, it isn't relevant. Why is that?"

Nickels took off his glasses and tapped them on his desk. "Regrettably, I agree with you, Mr. Lafayette." He looked down at the witness. "Ms. Watson, you will answer Mr. Lafayette's questions without any help from anyone in the gallery. Is that clear?"

She looked out at the gallery.

"Ms. Watson, turn toward me," Nickels said. "Answer Mr. Lafayette's questions while you look at me."

"Why did the Dearborn Life Insurance Company refuse to pay Mrs. Fagan's claim?" Burr said.

"We suspected fraud."

"On what grounds?"

"We found a change of beneficiary form that named Alexandra McCall as Mr. Fagan's new beneficiary."

"Was it legally binding?"

"Well ..."

"Was it or was it not legally binding?"

"No."

"No, what?"

"No, it wasn't legally binding."

"Thank you." Burr turned to the jury. "Ladies and gentlemen, the prosecutor would have you believe that this form shows that Mrs. Fagan murdered her husband. Nothing could be further from the truth. This isn't even a valid change of beneficiary form. It's smoke and mirrors." Burr rocked back and forth, heel to toe. "I ask you to disregard it." Burr looked back at Nickels. "I have no further questions."

"Mr. Oswald, you may call your next witness."

"The state calls Alexandra McCall." Oswald grinned at Burr.

Damn it all.

The mysterious, and up until now, the missing Alexandra McCall appeared from the back of the courtroom. Burr hadn't ever seen her, but he knew it was her. She was a vision of Molly five years ago and Kelly five years before that. She was taller than Molly and even better looking. Oswald had her dressed in black, just like Molly.

If Kelly Fagan had hurt him, Alexandra McCall was going to be much worse. It didn't matter what she said. All she had to do was sit on the witness stand and look like Nick's girlfriend.

Oswald stood at his table and let the jury take it all in. Molly cracked her knuckles. Burr leaned toward Molly. "Don't let her get to you. That's what Oswald wants. And don't crack your knuckles."

Molly looked at her hands.

Finally, Oswald walked up to the taller, younger version of Molly. "Ms. McCall, did you work at WKHQ?"

"Yes."

"How long did you work there?"

"From the time it signed on Nick until Nick died."

"How long was that?"

"Almost two years."

"Did you have a relationship with Mr. Fagan?"

She pulled down the hem of her dress and squeezed her knees together. "Yes."

"Were you lovers?"

She looked down at her lap. "Yes."

She's such an innocent.

"Did you love him?"

"Yes."

Are you going to cry now?

"Did he tell you he was going to divorce his wife, the defendant?" Oswald pointed at Molly.

"We were going to be married."

"Did Mrs. Fagan know about this?"

"Yes."

Oswald nodded. "What did she do?"

"She confronted me."

"She did?"

"Yes."

"What did she say?" Oswald took a step back.

"She said she'd kill Nick before she'd give him a divorce."

"She said she'd kill Nick?"

"Yes."

Oswald walked to the jury box. "Ladies and gentlemen, if there were any doubt in your mind that Molly Fagan killed her husband, it must surely be gone." Oswald looked at Burr. "Your witness."

Burr walked up to Nick's lover. "Ms. McCall, you just testified that you were having an adulterous relationship with Nick Fagan. Is that right?"

She sat back in her chair. "I wouldn't call it that."

"Really?" Burr put his hands in his pockets. "What would you call it?"

"We were in love." She stuck her chin out at him.

"You were trying to steal Mrs. Fagan's husband, weren't you?"

"Objection, Your Honor. Counsel is being argumentative."

"Your Honor, this woman tried to steal Mrs. Fagan's husband, and she's acting like she's Mother Teresa."

"Stop it, Mr. Lafayette," Nickels said.

Burr took a step toward the witness. "Ms. McCall, wouldn't it make sense that Mrs. Fagan would be angry with you for trying to steal her husband?"

"I don't know."

"You don't know? Are you kidding? You're an adulteress, and you don't know why Mrs. Fagan would be mad at you?"

"Stop it," Nickels said again.

Burr walked to the jury. "Ladies and gentlemen, I don't know how you feel about this, but I don't think you can believe anything Ms. McCall says." Burr looked back at her.

She didn't flinch.

She's a tough cookie.

Burr turned back to the jury. "Can you believe an adulteress? And, for that matter, people say things when they're mad. That doesn't mean they'd actually do anything," Burr said, careful not to mention threats and murder. "I have no further questions." He walked back to the defense table and sat.

The Great Oz stood and looked at the jury, "Ladies and gentlemen, the state has proved that Mr. Fagan died from eating poisonous Amanita mushrooms. We've also shown that there was no possible way that Mr. Fagan could have picked the poisonous mushrooms on the day he died because they were out of season." Oswald gave his signature hitch of his pants. "So, we know that he wasn't poisoned accidentally.

"We've also shown that Mr. Fagan was involved with another woman. He made her the beneficiary on his life insurance policy." Oswald pointed at Molly. "She found out all this and murdered her husband." Oswald looked back at the jury. "In fact, she was seen putting the poisonous mushrooms in Mr. Fagan's veal morel in the kitchen at the Arboretum.

"We have also proved that Mrs. Fagan was not only jealous, she was also greedy. She murdered her husband and then tried to collect on his life insurance."

Oswald pointed at Molly, then looked at the jury. "This woman is guilty of first-degree murder." Oswald turned to Nickels. "The prosecution rests."

"Mr. Lafayette, call your first witness." Nickels looked at his watch. "Never mind. We are adjourned for the day. Mr. Lafayette, your defense will begin Monday morning."

He slammed his gavel. "I have to lie down," he said on his way out.

Burr leaned over Molly. "Jacob, get a copy of that damned form and come with me."

* * *

Burr took Molly aside in the hall outside the courtroom. "I finally figured it out."

"Figured what out?"

"Your knuckles?"

She looked at her hands then put them behind her back. "My knuckles?"

"I thought it was just a tic. We all have tics." Burr ran his hands through his hair, front to back. "But it's more than that."

"I have no idea what you're talking about." She started down the hall. Burr put his hand on her shoulder and stopped her.

"I thought you did it when you were anxious. It made perfect sense." He looked at his hands then at Molly. "But there's more to it."

"I have no idea what you're talking about." She took his hand off her shoulder.

"You do it when you're anxious, but you really do it when you're anxious and lying."

"I've never lied to you."

"You knew all about Alexandra McCall."

Molly stepped toward Burr. "I most certainly did not."

"You're lying. You knew about her all along. I don't think you murdered Nick, but you've been lying to me. If it happens again, I'm going to withdraw as your lawyer."

"You wouldn't do that."

Burr rocked back and forth. "I may be entering the twilight of a mediocre career, but I'm not going to put up with lying." He turned on his heel and walked out.

* * *

Burr stirred the pot again. He sprinkled more cumin, then stirred again. He was still furious with Molly, but cooking helped calm him down.

She knew all about Alexandra McCall, but I'm not sure it really matters. Except to me.

"I'm going to faint if I don't eat something this very minute," Jacob said.

"Have another cracker."

Jacob has a way of bringing me back to Earth.

Burr stirred the pot again. He dipped his finger in the chili and licked it off. "It's almost ready."

"I hope Jacob didn't see that," Eve said.

"See what?" Jacob said.

Burr ladled his secret-recipe chili into three bowls and took them to the table. He opened another Labatt and sat down in front of the shredded cheddar, sour cream and saltines.

After Burr confronted Molly, he took a deep breath then followed her to her BMW. He opened the door and sat across from her in the passenger seat. It was cold, but the sun had heated up the leather seats. He'd cooled off a little and told her it wasn't as bad as it seemed, but he thought it was actually worse. Alexandra McCall had been the nail in Molly's coffin. If the trial had ended after Oswald presented his case, Molly would surely be convicted of first-degree murder, She didn't need to know that. Not now. What he needed Molly to do right now was nothing. He needed her to stay out of this while he figured it out. Whether or not she was lying.

He'd told her to go home and he'd take care of the rest. Which was why he was in the white cottage on the channel with Jacob, Eve, and his special chili.

"This is really quite good," Jacob said. "Much better than that miserable concoction at Beggars Banquet," Jacob said. "Not that I've ever had any. What did you put in it?"

Burr didn't say anything.

"It's the cumin," Eve said. "And the basil."

"That's not the secret ingredient."

"What is it?"

It's garlic, but I'll never tell.

Burr finished his beer, then studied the change of beneficiary form. "Eve, I think we need to get Harry up here. As soon as we can."

"We?"

"You," Burr said.

* * *

Burr lit another cigarette and watched the smoke drift over his shoulder. He and Zeke had been sitting on a log next to a muskrat house since three-thirty. The cattails behind them blew in the wind. The decoys swam in front of them, dancing in the wind and twisting and turning in the waves.

Burr had found this flooding east of Boyne City a week ago, but this was the first time he'd had a chance to hunt it. He knew he had no business hunting this afternoon, but it was Saturday, and he thought this was as good, or as bad, a time as any for a duck hunt.

"Zeke, old friend, maybe Victor is right about Freud." He blew smoke out of his lungs. "I would like to see Maggie. If she hasn't married that doctor."

The aging Lab stared at the decoys, then up at the sky. The sun ducked behind a cloud, and the pond was all in shadows. They hadn't seen anything flying yet, but there was still an hour left before sunset.

Burr kept his shotgun, waders, and a bag of decoys in the back of the Jeep this time of year. He thought Eve knew what he was up to this afternoon, but she hadn't said anything.

"There's something going on with the cast of characters at KHQ. I don't know what it is, and if I can't figure it out, I'm going to lose."

Zeke searched the sky. He looked hard to his right, then froze. Five mallards flew over the pond. Burr called them. They swung and started gliding back to the pond, looking down at the decoys. Burr leaned against the muskrat house and smelled the dying cattails.

The mallards, three hens and two drakes, circled the pond, lower now, once, twice, a third time. They set their wings, dropped their orange feet, and swung back and forth like falling maple leaves.

"I don't need to shoot, but I'll get one for you."

Burr shouldered his shotgun and killed a drake mallard.

Zeke fetched the duck. Burr picked up the decoys.

Zeke slept in the passenger seat, and the Jeep smelled like a wet dog. It had starting snowing on the way back to Charlevoix.

"It's early for snow, but not that early." Burr turned up the heat. "I've got to quit talking to myself when there's no one around." Burr looked over at Zeke. "You're here, but you're not listening. Again." Burr turned on the windshield wipers, but they didn't work right, just like they always didn't.

He dropped Zeke off at Morning Glory, then drove back to the radio station. KHQ played *In Too Deep*.

Burr turned the key in the lock, climbed the stairs to Nick's office and let himself in, just like last night. He looked into the studio. Tommy Preston sat in front of the microphone.

Burr sat at Nick's desk. KHQ played *Don't Know Much*. The refrigerator next to the bar hummed. "I know what I need and where to find it. For once."

"What did you say?"

Burr jumped.

"It's me," the disc jockey said. "I saw the light under the door again."

"I was talking to myself."

"When I do that, people think I'm crazy."

"Me too."

"My song's running out," Preston said again. He disappeared into the studio.

Burr opened the bottom right drawer. He took out a copy of a letter signed by Nick. He found a second letter and took that one out, too. "This should be all Harry needs. Maybe one more thing."

Burr rummaged through the drawer again. He found a four-column sheet of accounting paper. It was the aged receivables for KHQ's advertisers that had Nick's initials on it. "Harry will love this," he said out loud. "There I go again."

* * *

Burr celebrated the paper treasures he'd found in Nick's office with his signature martini at the bar at the Villager. "Now if I can just get Harry to show up." After two more martinis and a not-so-steady walk to the Jeep, the same sheriff pulled him over at the same place on Main Street. This time he wasn't so lucky.

Burr found himself alone in the drunk tank in the basement of the courthouse, one floor below Judge Nickels' courtroom.

"I have a trial in the morning," he'd said to the duty officer. "We can take care of this later."

"Now is a perfect time to take care of it," the duty officer had said, a jowly man who looked like he was counting the days to his pension.

"I'm Molly Fagan's lawyer. I have to be in court tomorrow."

"You do have to be in court tomorrow," the duty officer said. "Judge Striker will charge you in the morning."

They'd given him his phone call, but he had no idea what the number was at Morning Glory. He called Aunt Kitty who lectured him, then said she'd track down Eve.

He spent a fitful night on a mostly steel bunk next to a sink that dripped. He timed the drips, every three seconds, and finally fell asleep by counting them. It wasn't like counting his blessings.

CHAPTER TWENTY-ONE

The jailer brought Eve down to the drunk tank the next morning. She stood nose-to-nose with Burr, the steel bars in between them. "How could you?" she said.

"I didn't have that much to drink." Burr had a headache, but his head wasn't pounding. His mouth tasted like a garbage truck had spent the night in it.

"Just enough to get yourself arrested." She put her hands on her hips.

She's so mad she's not even tugging on her ear.

"The posse finally caught up with you."

Did they ever.

"How could you? Molly's on trial upstairs, and you're in here. You are such a fool."

"I'm sorry."

"Sorry isn't enough. Nickels made Jacob take your place, and all he's doing is blubbering. Just blubbering."

"I'm sorry," Burr said again.

"She had a chance with you defending her, but now she's as good as convicted," Eve said. "But she probably did do it." She stormed out.

* * *

Burr sat on his bunk counting the drips. "How could I have been so stupid?" He laid down on his bunk. "Damn it all."

"Who exactly are you talking to?" Judge Nickels stood in front of Burr's cell.

"This may be the stupidest thing I've ever done."

"Are you all right?"

"Damn it all," he said again.

"Come over here, Mr. Lafayette."

Burr sat up.

"Come over here, Mr. Lafayette."

Burr walked over to the steel bars, nose-to-nose with Nickels, just like he'd been with Eve.

"What were you doing over there?" Nickels said.

"When I talk to myself when Zeke is around, no one thinks I'm crazy."

Nickels looked at Burr's bunk then back at Burr. "In my entire time on the bench, I have never in my life had the misfortune to come across anyone like you."

"Yes, Your Honor."

"And all your partner can manage to do is blubber."

That's what Eve said.

"Mrs. Fagan is as good as convicted," Judge Nickels said.

Eve said that, too.

"This is what I'm going to do, and I'm sure I'll regret it." The judge shook his head. "You are going to be released in my custody for the sole purpose of defending Mrs. Fagan. When her trial is over, you will deal with the consequences of your actions. Between now and then, if I so much as see you sniff the cap of a bottle of gin, you will find yourself back here as a permanent resident. Is that clear?"

* * *

Burr stood in front of Robert Davies. He'd just started his defense, such as it was. Eve had come back to Burr's cell with a suit, shirt, tie, shoes, and a razor. He really needed a shower, not to mention a toothbrush. He thought he'd be all right as long as he didn't get too close to anyone. Mercifully, Nickels hadn't said anything about Burr's absence or the reason for it. Jacob refused to look at him.

Burr desperately needed Harry, but Eve, largely because of Burr's antics, hadn't been able to find him. Until she did, Burr was stalling, but he did have a few questions for Nick's patrician partner and his conflated sense of self-worth.

"Mr. Davies, according to Ms. Watson, you were the one who found the alleged change of beneficiary form naming Alexandra McCall as the new beneficiary. Is that right?"

"I object, Your Honor," Oswald said. "There's nothing alleged about it."

"Strike alleged," Nickels said to the court reporter. "Mr. Lafayette, you've just now gotten here. Do you have to be so argumentative so early in the day?"

"Mr. Davies, were you the one who found ..." Burr looked back at Oswald, "... the form?"

"Yes."

"And where did you find it?"

"In Mr. Fagan's desk."

"Where in his desk did you find it?"

"How could that possibly matter?" Oswald said.

Nickels rapped his gavel. "Please extend Mr. Lafayette the professional courtesy you would like extended to you."

Oswald looked at Burr. "If it was tit for tat, I'd be on my feet shouting."

Burr ignored him. "Mr. Davies, where did you find the form?"

"In the bottom right-hand drawer."

"And when did you find it?"

"I'm not sure exactly. A couple months after Nick died, I think."

Why didn't Molly find it?

Burr rocked back and forth. "What, may I ask, were you looking for?"

"We were having some problem collecting our receivables. I wanted to see if Nick had a receivables listing."

"Did you find it?"

"I did."

That's what I found.

"And what did you do with it?"

"I looked at it and left it there."

"Did anyone go through Mr. Fagan's desk before you did?"

"I have no idea."

"I have no further questions," Burr said.

"I have no questions," Oswald said.

Nickels smiled. "Will wonders never cease? Call your next witness."

Burr looked where Eve was supposed to be sitting. She wasn't there, which meant she still hadn't found Harry.

Nuts.

Burr had to get to the guts of his defense, that someone other than Molly put the Amanitas in the morels. It wasn't much of a defense, but it was all he had.

"The defense calls Earl Hickey."

Earl Hickey, more commonly known as Buck Houston, took the stand. The bailiff swore him in.

Burr walked up to the witness stand. Houston smelled like a full ashtray. Burr gagged and took a step back. He cleared his throat. "Mr. Hickey, you're commonly known as Buck Houston. Is that right?"

"That's right," he said in his clear baritone.

"And you're the general manager and one of the disc jockeys at WKLH in Gaylord. Is that right?"

"I'm also the owner," he said, still in his baritone and with a big smile.

"And you competed with Nick Fagan and WKHQ."

"That's right."

"And is it fair to say you were enemies?"

"I don't know if I'd go that far."

"Mr. Hickey, were you and your radio station at Car Wars at the Petoskey fairgrounds on Saturday, May 26, of this year?"

Hickey nodded.

"Let the record show that Mr. Hickey replied in the affirmative," Nickels said.

"And Mr. Fagan and WKHQ were also there. Is that right?"

Hickey nodded again.

"The court reporter can't record that you nodded. Mr. Hickey, please answer the question in words," Nickels said.

Hickey scowled then said, "Yes."

"And I think you told me earlier, that Mr. Fagan did the live broadcast for WKHQ from Car Wars. Is that right?"

Hickey started to nod but caught himself. "Yes," he said.

Here goes.

Burr stepped toward the chain-smoking disc jockey then stepped back. "Mr. Hickey, while you were at Car Wars, you would have had the opportunity to go to Mr. Fagan's car while he was broadcasting and put poison mushrooms in with the morels. Isn't that right?"

Oswald lurched to his feet. "I object your, Your Honor. There is no foundation for this. It's sheer speculation."

Burr turned to the judge. "Your Honor, the prosecution has made much of the fact that Mrs. Fagan went into the kitchen at the Arboretum and made unfounded claims that she put poisonous mushrooms in the veal morel." Burr glared at Oswald then turned back to Nickels. "I am merely pointing out that the custody of the morels, the chain of evidence, was not continuous. Mr. Hickey had an opportunity to put the poisonous mushrooms in the morels while Mr. Fagan was broadcasting."

"I most certainly did nothing of the kind." Hickey spit out the words. Burr took another step back.

Nickels tapped his gavel in the palm of his hand. "Mr. Lafayette, while anything is possible, unless you have some proof that Mr. Hickey did, in fact, break into Mr. Fagan's car, I am going to agree with Mr. Oswald that this is speculation."

Burr turned to the jury. "It could have happened this way."

"Stop it. Stop it right now," Nickels said. "I should have left you in the drunk tank," he said, mostly to himself.

"I beg your pardon," Oswald said.

"Nothing," Nickels said. He looked at the jury. "Ladies and gentlemen, you will disregard this line of questioning."

"I have no further questions," Burr said.

Nickels looked at Oswald who was still standing. "Mr. Oswald?"

Oswald turned to the jury. "Ladies and gentlemen, I hesitate to trouble you with this insulting line of questioning, but as a practical matter, everyone I know locks their car, and with Mr. Fagan's great interest in morels, I think it preposterous that he would leave his car unlocked." They nodded. Oswald turned to the witness. "Mr. Hickey, did you break into Mr. Fagan's car and put poisonous mushrooms in with the morels?"

"No."

"I have no further questions." Oswald sat.

"Mr. Lafayette, you may call your next witness." Nickels tapped his gavel again. "But you may not engage in this kind of frivolity."

"The defense calls Julie French." She was the general manager of the radio station in Petoskey. The woman who said she didn't hate Nick but did.

"Ms. French, were you at Car Wars on Saturday, May 26, of this year?"

"Stop it, Lafayette," Nickels said.

"Your Honor, the chain of evidence is critical to the defense. It is entirely possible that someone broke into Mr. Fagan's car and spiked the morels."

"If pigs could fly," Oswald said.

"With lipstick," Burr said.

"That's enough," Nickels said. "Mr. Lafayette, you are certainly entitled to your defense, but you must have some foundation for it. Failing that, this is speculation and will not be allowed."

"Your Honor, Sterling Mason, the owner of WMBN was also at Car Wars and also hated Mr. Fagan. And for that matter, Cat Garrity, the chef at the Arboretum also hated Mr. Fagan, and she had ample opportunity to spike the veal morel."

"Stop it, Mr. Lafayette. There will be no more of this."

Burr knew that none of Nick's competitors had murdered him or, for that matter, Cat. Oswald knew it. Nickels knew it. The jury knew it. Everyone in the gallery knew it. But it was all he had.

Where is Eve?

Burr walked up to Judge Nickels. "Your Honor, I'm trying to show a pattern. Nick Fagan, for all his talent, was a ruthless competitor. He had many enemies, any one of whom could have murdered him."

Oswald staggered to his feet. "Your Honor, if Mr. Lafayette has a few suspects, even one suspect, I think it's time he let the court know who they are."

Burr walked over to Oswald and stood nose-to-nose. "When you're the judge, you can make the rules. For now, sit down and shut up."

"What did you say?" Nickels said.

"We were exchanging pleasantries, Your Honor," Burr said.

Oswald started to say something.

"Call your next witness, Mr. Lafayette."

Burr was about to call Bill Gurney, the owner of the liquor store in Harbor Springs where Nick had the thousand-dollar balance, when Eve snuck in.

"Your Honor, may I have five minutes?"

"The hourglass of my life is running out while you dither."

"Did you find Harry?" Burr said.

She nodded.

"Where is he?"

"He's not coming."

"What do you mean he's not coming?"

"He said you haven't paid him for the last time."

"I paid him."

"No, you didn't."

"I paid him out of my own pocket. You have to pay me back."

"Of course."

"You don't have any money." Eve took off her coat and sat. "He'll be here tonight."

"You said he wasn't coming."

"Sometimes I like to see the panic in your eyes. It makes me feel like you're one of us."

* * *

Burr filled up the rest of his day questioning Nick's creditors. By the time he'd finished with the dry cleaner, Burr thought Nickels was capable of murder.

I'm sure he wishes he'd left me in the drunk tank.

After Nickels adjourned them for the day, Burr, Jacob and Eve adjourned to Morning Glory. The wind howled from the northwest, and the wind leaked through the windows. They could hear the waves breaking on the beach. Burr had a fire going in the fireplace, and they all had on their coats.

Burr didn't know if it was colder inside or outside, but with the cold shoulder he was getting from Jacob and Eve, he thought it was probably colder inside.

I deserve it.

Burr thought the wind would blow the ducks down from Canada. He wanted to be in a marsh with Zeke or at least have a martini and think about being in a marsh with Zeke, but this wasn't the time.

Harry walked into the living room at 7:30. He never knocked.

Harry wasn't quite fifty-five, but he looked like he was seventy-five. He was all of five-foot-six and built like a garbage can. Burr didn't know if Harry had retired from the state police or had been retired by the state police early — it depended on who you asked. Maybe because he smelled like Jim Beam. He had long, straggly blond hair; he'd grown it out when he left the state police. Burr thought it was Harry's protest against their brush-cut policy.

Harry had perfect vision, better than twenty-twenty, which was why he'd been such a great handwriting expert for the state police. Now he did it on his own. He and Burr had known each other a long time.

Harry sat down in front of the fire. Burr put the change of beneficiary form, the two letters Nick had signed, and the initialed accounts receivable listing in front of Harry. He went into the kitchen and came back with a glass of ice and a fifth of Jim Beam.

Harry filled his glass, drank half of it, studied the papers, then put them down.

"Well?" Burr said.

"Nothing from me until I get paid."

"You just got paid," Burr said.

"That was for last time."

"What if I don't like what you find?"

"My point exactly."

Burr poured himself some whiskey, thought better of it, and poured it back in the bottle. He got out the Lafayette and Wertheim checkbook.

"Your check's no good."

"How am I going to pay you?"

"I'll take Eve's check."

Burr looked at Eve.

Eve paid Harry, then wrote herself a check from Burr's checkbook. "I'll hold this until we get paid."

Harry drank whiskey and studied the signatures and the initials. Finally, he looked up. "You can't tell who's wearing a bathing suit until the tide goes out."

* * *

"Your Honor, this name was not on Mr. Lafayette's witness list. He cannot be allowed to testify."

Nickels ran his finger down Burr's witness list. "Quite right."

"Your Honor, Mr. Oswald's change of beneficiary form was not provided to me prior to the trial. It was sprung on me at the last minute. Mr. Nearly is necessary because of Mr. Oswald's surprise evidence."

"Mr. Lafayette, I will allow Mr. Nearly to testify, but you must show his relevance."

The bailiff swore in Harry Nearly. He wore a wrinkled suit that may have fit twenty pounds ago. Burr walked up to Nearly and took a step back. He still smelled like whiskey.

Burr ran through Nearly's qualifications, then walked back to his table and picked up his copy of the change of beneficiary form. "Mr. Nearly, have you examined this form?"

"I have."

Burr took a step back.

I hope Oswald doesn't get too close.

Burr held the form out to the handwriting expert, at arm's length. "Is this Mr. Fagan's signature?"

"No."

Burr made a show of looking incredulous. "You mean that the signature on the change of beneficiary form provided by the Dearborn Life Insurance Company is not Mr. Fagan's?"

"That's right."

"Are you saying that Mr. Fagan's signature was forged?"

"Yes, it's a forgery."

Oswald bolted to his feet.

That was impressive.

"I object, Your Honor. There is no foundation for this. No proof whatsoever."

Oswald walked right into it.

Burr walked back to his table and picked up the two letters and the ledger. He introduced them into evidence. Oswald swore under his breath.

"Mr. Nearly, in your analysis, you compared the signature on the change of beneficiary form to Mr. Fagan's signature on these two letters and his initials on the accounts receivable ledger. Is that right?"

"Yes."

"Did they match?"

"No, they did not."

"So, this is not Mr. Fagan's signature on the Dearborn Life Insurance Company's change of beneficiary form?"

"It is definitely not his signature."

"This is a forgery?"

"Yes."

Oswald stood again. "Your Honor, this has no bearing on Mrs. Fagan's guilt. Mrs. Fagan murdered her husband because she was jealous. This form is not determinative."

Burr took a step toward Oswald. "It was determinative when you wanted it to be."

"Your Honor," Oswald said, "it really doesn't matter whether or not this form was signed by Mr. Fagan or not. What matters is that Mrs. Fagan thought it was valid."

Burr took another step toward Oswald. "You've never shown that Mrs. Fagan even knew about this form."

Nickels shut his eyes and rubbed his temples. "This will be the end of me," He turned to the jury. "Ladies and gentlemen, you may use your own judgment in deciding whether or not this document is a forgery."

Burr turned to the jury. "The point is that this form is a forgery, but Mr. Oswald has presented it as a true document. What else has he told you that isn't true? What else has he cooked up?" Burr walked back to his table. "I have no further questions."

Oswald walked up to Nearly, then stepped back a-la Burr. "Mr. Nearly, you are a retired state police officer. Is that right?"

"Yes."

"Mr. Nearly, you were forced to retire from the state police because you had a drinking problem. Isn't that true?"

"I object, Your Honor," Burr said. "This is character assassination and has nothing to do with Mr. Nearly's qualifications."

"A drinking problem can affect's one capacity to do their job," Oswald said.

"You may question Mr. Nearly's qualifications, including the reason he retired, but you may not impugn his character."

"I have no further questions," Oswald said.

That hurt.

"The defense calls Julian Flintoff."

The general counsel for the Dearborn Life Insurance Company took the witness stand. The thin man with the pinched face wore a blue suit that didn't fit very well, a white shirt that didn't fit any better, and a solid red tie.

Flintoff dressed down for this.

The bailiff swore in the general counsel. Burr ran through what Flintoff did for the Dearborn Life Insurance Company.

"Mr. Flintoff, you and I have met before, haven't we?"

"I believe we have."

"We met when your company denied Mrs. Fagan's claim on her husband's life insurance policy."

"That's right."

"Mr. Flintoff, isn't it true that if someone murdered the insured, and the murderer was the beneficiary on the policy, that person could not collect on the policy."

"That is correct."

"So, in this case, if Mrs. Fagan were to be convicted of murdering her husband, she could not collect on his life insurance policy."

"That is correct."

"So, it would be in the interest of the Dearborn Life Insurance Company to have Mrs. Fagan convicted of murder?"

Flintoff cocked his head. "And why would that be?"

"So, you wouldn't have to pay the claim."

"I never thought of it that way."

"You never thought of having Mr. Fagan's signature forged so you could make Molly Fagan look guilty," Burr said, not asking.

"Objection, Your Honor, this is speculation and totally unfounded."

"Sustained."

"Mr. Flintoff, isn't it true that the Dearborn Life Insurance Company pays out fewer claims than any other life insurance company in Michigan?"

"I wouldn't know," Flintoff said, smiling.

This guy is unflappable.

Burr walked back to his table and picked up a file. "Mr. Flintoff, I have here the annual report of the Insurance Commissioner of the State of Michigan. It lists the Dearborn Life Insurance Company at the bottom of the list in terms of claims paid. Are you familiar with this report?"

Flintoff crossed his legs. "I don't think I've ever seen it."

"Let me show you." Burr opened the file.

"Your Honor," Oswald said, standing. "The state will stipulate to Mr. Lafayette's statement. Not that it matters in the least."

Damn it all.

"Isn't it true that you've done everything in your power, which is considerable, to prevent Mrs. Fagan from collecting on her husband's life insurance?"

"That's not true."

"And isn't it true that you are doing everything you can to assist Mr. Oswald in convicting Mrs. Fagan of murdering her husband so the Dearborn Life Insurance Company does not have to pay on Mr. Fagan's policy?"

"I am only interested in justice."

"Mr. Flintoff, are you a shareholder, a part owner, in the Dearborn Life Insurance Company?"

"Well ... I ..."

"Answer the question, Mr. Flintoff," Burr said.

"Yes."

"So, if this claim isn't paid, it helps you financially. Isn't that true?"

"The state requires insurance reserves, so technically ..."

Burr waved off his formerly cool-as-a-cucumber witness, now annoyed. "I have no further questions, Your Honor." Burr looked at the jury. "Other than to say that Oliver and Hardy here ..." Burr pointed at Oswald, then Flintoff "... are in cahoots."

"Strike that," Nickels said.

"Your Honor, I have just a few questions for Mr. Flintoff," Oswald said, standing. "Mr. Flintoff, where did you go to college?"

"The University of Detroit."

"And your law school?"

"Wayne State."

"How long have you practiced law in Michigan?"

"Thirty-seven years."

"Have you ever been disbarred?"

"No."

"Sanctioned?"

"No."

"You have been a pillar of justice in all respects."

Flintoff nodded.

"I have no further questions."

* * *

The four of them — Jacob, Eve, Harry, and Burr — sat at the kitchen table having Burr's leftover chili for dinner. Harry was chasing his chili with Jim Beam. Burr had a flank steak in the refrigerator, soaking in his secret marinade, but he didn't have the energy to grill it.

Jacob crushed a handful of saltines in his chili.

"Your chili ages well," Jacob said.

At least he's finally talking to me.

Burr fished a kidney bean out of his chili with a spoon and studied it. "I think he knew something was fishy, maybe not that it was a forgery." Burr dropped the kidney bean back in his chili.

"Don't play with your food," Eve said.

"There's something going on. I just don't know what it is," Burr said.

"We don't know if Oswald knew it was forged," Eve said.

Harry ate a spoonful of chili.

"You actually do eat," Eve said.

"Of course I eat." He took another swallow of his Jim Beam. Burr looked longingly at Harry's glass. "I'll tell you one thing that's going on," Harry said. Another spoonful and another swallow. "I don't understand why the radio station had trouble with their creditors."

"Why?" Burr said.

"Because almost all of the receivables in that ledger were under ninety days. You get into trouble when you can't collect your sales. Nick's station wasn't like that. They did a great job collecting."

Burr ran out of the room.

"Your chili is going to get cold," Eve said.

* * *

Burr went through Nick's desk again. He ransacked it this time. Nothing.

KHQ played *All I Need Is a Miracle*.

"Do I ever."

Burr looked across the room at the refrigerator next to the bar. "For as much time as I spend here, I should put a six pack of Labatt in there." He walked over and opened the refrigerator. It was empty except for two cans of Diet Coke. He walked behind the bar. Half a bottle of Bacardi. "Rum and Diet Coke. I suppose I could bring some Bombay over, too." He walked out to the bullpen and searched the sales desks. Also, nothing. Then he went into Melissa Warren's office. The bottom right double drawer of her desk was locked.

"There's nothing like a locked drawer."

He pulled on the drawer, but it wouldn't give. He pried at it with a pen. No luck. He straightened out a paper clip and picked it.

Here we go.

There was a knock on the door.

Damn it all.

He opened the door to the studio. Tommy walked in and looked over Burr's shoulder.

"Should you be doing that, Mr. Lafayette?"

"Of course I should."

"I don't think so."

"Why don't you go spin some records, and I'll take care of this."

"Melissa won't like it."

"Melissa doesn't need to know."

Tommy stood there with his hands in his pockets.

Burr ushered the would-be tattletale back to the studio. He searched the drawer he'd broken into. File after file after file. Nothing. Then, "Maybe this is what Harry meant."

* * *

Harvey Wall sat on the witness stand in a gray suit with a blue pinstripe, a white shirt, a club tie, and wingtips.

He doesn't look like a porn king.

"Mr. Wall, you are one of the owners of KHQ, along with Robert Davies and the late Mr. Fagan. Is that right?"

Wall folded his hands together on his lap. "I am."

"As an owner, you would be interested in the financial affairs of the station. Isn't that right?"

"Yes."

"And the station was and is very popular and does very well in terms of sales."

"Yes," he said, smiling.

"But the radio station has trouble paying its bills on a timely basis, something you yourself expressed frustration with."

"Damnedest thing." Wall banged on the railing.

Nickels looked down his nose at the witness. "Mr. Wall, you are in a court of law. Please conduct yourself accordingly."

"Sure," he said.

Burr walked back to his table, picked up a file and took it back to the witness stand. "Mr. Wall, this is an exhibit, an aged accounts receivable that was admitted into evidence yesterday. It shows the money the station's advertisers owed to the station." Burr handed it to Wall. "Are you familiar with this?"

Wall looked it over, then, "Yes."

"Don't you think it a bit odd that a station as successful as WKHQ would have no problem collecting its sales, yet still be unable to pay its bills?"

Wall didn't say anything.

Burr opened the file and took out another set of aged receivables. "Mr. Wall, this list of receivables is for exactly the same time period, but look at the ninety, one hundred twenty, and beyond columns. These columns are all full of numbers."

"I object, Your Honor. This has not been admitted into evidence," Oswald said.

"So moved," Burr said.

"Your Honor," Oswald said, "there is no way of knowing whether or not this is a forgery."

"That's something you'd know about," Burr said.

"Stop it, Mr. Lafayette."

"Your Honor, this is on the same paper as the one admitted yesterday. It was also found in Mr. Fagan's desk," Burr lied.

"That can't be," Oswald said.

"Were you snooping again?"

"Stop it," Nickels said. "I'm going to allow it. Ms. Meecher, mark this as Defense Exhibit Two."

"Thank you, Your Honor," Burr said. He turned back to the porn king shareholder. "Isn't it odd that there are two sets of receivables for the same time period?"

"I suppose."

"You suppose? It looks to me like someone was cooking the books. Is it possible that you were cooking the books and Nick found out? And then you murdered him. You're the master of not reporting income."

"That has nothing to do with it." Wall banged on the railing again.

"Aren't you being investigated by the IRS?"

"I'm not the one on trial here."

"I have no further questions," Burr said.

Oswald walked up to Wall and smiled. "Mr. Wall, were you involved in the day-to-day operations of the radio station?"

"No."

"Were you involved in collecting the station's accounts receivable?"

"No."

"I have no further questions."

"Mr. Lafayette, you may call your next witness."

I'm nowhere near reasonable doubt.

Burr tapped his pencil.

There's one more thing, but I'm not quite ready for it.

"Mr. Lafayette."

Burr stood. "Your Honor, I'd like to request an adjournment until tomorrow morning."

"You can't possibly be serious," Nickels said.

"Your Honor, this new evidence requires more investigation on my part."

"My stars." Nickels leaned back in his chair and shut his eyes.

Please, don't say anything about retiring.

Nickels looked at his hands. "I'm never going to be able to retire."

CHAPTER TWENTY-TWO

Burr sat in Nick's office for what he hoped would be the last time. It was dark inside, and darker outside. It was so foggy he couldn't see Round Lake.

"It's not a good time to be outside, even for a duck," Burr said out loud. He swiveled in Nick's chair and looked in the studio at Tommy. He was reading a comic book, his back to Burr. KHQ played *Throwing it All Away*.

"It must be a long song."

Burr walked over to the light switch and turned on the overhead lights. He sat back down in Nick's chair.

"If this doesn't work, I'm euchred."

Burr watched Tommy walk over to the window. He cupped his hands on it and peered in. There was a knock on the door.

"So far, so good."

Burr opened the door.

"Is that you, Mr. Lafayette?"

"In the flesh."

"You spend a lot of time here."

"So do you."

"I work here."

"Come in." Burr pointed at Nick's chair. "Sit right there."

"That's Mr. Fagan's chair."

"Sit down."

Tommy sat.

He looks nervous. Just the way I want him to be.

"Spin around a little. Live it up."

"Why would I do that?"

"Go ahead. Spin around."

Tommy swiveled back and forth, but he didn't turn all the way around. He started to get up.

"Sit down." Burr turned off the lights and sat in front of Tommy.

"What's going on?" Tommy said.

"What do you think is going on?"

"I don't know, but I don't like it." He started to get up again.

"Sit down," Burr said.

Tommy sat. "It's dark in here."

"That's what happens when the lights are off."

"I don't like this."

"Tommy, look out Nick's one-way window."

"Okay."

"What do you see?"

"I can see in the studio."

"Why can you see in the studio?"

"The lights are on in there?"

"Very good. The lights are on. Now, look at the bottom of the door to the studio." Burr pointed to the bottom of the door. "What do you see?"

"I don't know. Nothing, I guess."

"Very good again."

"I don't get it."

"Tommy, old friend, you said you knew someone was in Nick's office because you could see light under the door."

"That's right."

Burr pointed at the door. "There's no light coming under the door."

Tommy swiveled. "There is on the other side."

"Shall we go find out?"

The disc jockey squirmed in Nick's chair.

"Tommy, there's no light coming in under the door from either side. And you know it."

More swiveling. "Yes, there is."

"Don't lie to me." Burr turned on the lights. "When I was here last night, I was sitting here in the dark. There was no light coming underneath the door. There were lights on in the studio. I turned on the lights and you knocked. It made sense." Burr walked over to the one-way window. "You knew I was here, but you waited until the lights came on to knock. Why did you do that?"

"Because the light came under the door."

"Let's go find out."

Tommy gripped the arms on Nick's chair.

"Tommy, the one-way window isn't one way. Is it?"

"It's one way."

"Tommy."

"Yes, it is."

"Don't lie to me, Tommy." Burr walked over to the window and ran his hand along the glass. "Most of it's one way, but there's a little bit of it, somewhere, where someone inside the studio, someone like you, can see in here."

"No, there isn't." Tommy started to stand. "My song is going to run out."

"*Genesis* will understand." Burr pointed at Nick's chair. Tommy sat. "Are you the only one who knows about the special spot?"

"There's no special spot."

"What did you see, Tommy?"

"I didn't see anything."

"What did you do?"

"I didn't do anything. I swear I didn't." The music stopped, and there was dead air. Tommy ran back in the studio.

* * *

They were all in their places. Molly next to Burr, who was next to Jacob. Eve just over the railing, Harry Nearly next to her. Oswald across from Burr. Flintoff and the self-effacing Pearl Watson in the gallery along with the two suspect shareholders, Robert Davies and Harvey Wall, Melissa Warren sat next to them. The would-have-been next Mrs. Fagan, in a different black dress, sat by herself.

Burr had asked Molly to change her look today. She wore a burgundy dress and just a touch of lipstick. He hadn't said much to her since he'd confronted her so she couldn't be lying to him, and she wasn't cracking her knuckles.

And there, in the first row, for all to see, was Tommy Preston. All cleaned up but out of place and out of sorts in a baggy brown suit.

Donald Drum called them to order.

Nickels glided in. "Today we will have closing arguments."

"Your Honor, I have one more witness," Burr said.

"Will this never end?"

Oswald stood.

"Sit down, Mr. Oswald. Let's get this over with."

"Thank you, Your Honor." Burr turned to the gallery. "The defense calls Melissa Warren."

She looked surprised but made her way to the witness stand. She had on a cream suit with a taupe blouse and her sensible two-inch heels. Her blond hair framed her face nicely. Not much makeup, just lipstick and a touch of eye shadow.

She's all buttoned up.

She smoothed her skirt and sat. Judge Nickels reminded her she was still under oath.

It's all or nothing.

"Ms. Warren, earlier you testified that you walked into Mr. Fagan's office unannounced and saw Ms. McCall in a compromising position. Is that right?"

"Yes."

"Did anyone else see this?"

"We've already plowed this ground, Your Honor," Oswald said.

"Mr. Lafayette, this is a murder trial. We don't need to be titillated," Judge Nickels said.

"Your Honor, I am merely reviewing what has been previously testified."

"Well, don't."

"Ms. Warren, did anyone else see what you saw?"

"No."

"Are you sure?"

"I was the only one in the office. Except for Mr. Fagan and Ms. McCall." She tucked her hair behind her ears.

Aren't we confident.

"Ms. Warren, could anyone have seen into Mr. Fagan's office from the studio?"

"Oh, no." She smiled at Burr. "It's a one-way window."

"Of course it is." Burr put his hands in his pockets. "Ms. Warren, did you know that there's a spot on the one-way window that isn't one way?" Burr turned sideways and craned his neck. "If you stand just right, you can see from the studio into Mr. Fagan's office."

"That's not true."

"Oh, but it is."

"It's not true."

Oswald pushed himself to his feet. "Your Honor, there is no point in these two arguing."

"Quite right," Nickels said.

"I quite agree, Your Honor," Burr said.

"Tommy Preston, a disc jockey at WKHQ, is here with us today." Burr pointed at him. "He will testify that there is a spot where you can see into Mr. Fagan's office. And he did that very thing."

Melissa Warren scratched her nose, perfectly composed.

"Ms. Warren, did you know that Mr. Preston saw you in Mr. Fagan's office in the same compromising position that Ms. McCall was in?"

She sat up straight. "That is not true."

"Mr. Preston is here today. He'll testify that he saw you on your knees. More than once."

"You're lying," she said, not quite so composed.

"Your Honor, I'd like to dismiss Ms. Warren and call Mr. Preston. After he testifies, I will call her again."

"No, no, no," Nickels said. "Finish with Ms. Warren."

I knew you'd say that.

"Ms. Warren, I assure you what Mr. Preston will testify to. Perhaps we can avoid that."

The business manager blushed but didn't say anything.

Burr, hands in his pockets, rocked back and forth. "Alexandra McCall wasn't the only one in love with Nick Fagan. You were, too."

"I was not."

Molly buried her face in her hands.

"He let you think he loved you."

She shook her head.

Burr walked back to the evidence table and picked up a folder. He took out the two accounts receivable ledgers. "This is why he let you think he was in love with you. He wanted you to help him cook the books."

"That's not true."

"Oh, but it is. Nick wasn't stealing from the station and neither were you. That wasn't it at all." Burr turned to the jury. "Nick's ego was so big, WKHQ had to be the biggest, baddest radio station in northern Michigan, so he put every business he could on the air. Including businesses who couldn't or wouldn't pay. He put them on so he could show the world, especially Robert Davies and Harvey Wall, just how smart and how successful he was. But a lot them never paid. Nick didn't want to write them off, so he convinced you to doctor the books. It looked like everyone was paying, but they weren't. It was an illusion." Burr walked up to her. "I don't think you wanted to do it, but he said he loved you."

"That's not true," she said, but she looked a little nonplussed.

Oswald stood again. "Even if it is true, it doesn't mean anything."

Burr hitched up his pants and smiled at the portly prosecutor. "It means everything." He turned back to Melissa. "It was all going so well until Nick started carrying on with Alexandra McCall." Burr put his hands on the railing. "Isn't that true?"

"It's not true."

"You were jealous. Furious. You were beside yourself. If you couldn't have Nick, no one could. You knew Nick hunted morels. You picked Amanita mushrooms the summer before he died."

She looked at him, stone-faced.

"You hoped it would blow over with Ms. McCall. When it didn't, you bided your time and waited for just the right moment. Nick stopped at the station on his way home the day he died. You told me he didn't come in that day, but he did. He put the morels in the refrigerator in his office. You were there, and you put the Amanitas in with the morels. You made sure to take off their red caps so no one would notice. And you were sure no one would be the wiser."

"You're making all this up."

"I wish I were." Burr paced back and forth in front of her. "I don't know if you meant to kill him, but you did."

"It's not true."

"We're going to find traces of the Amanitas in Nick's refrigerator. That would do it."

She shook her head.

"Were you clever enough to disinfect the refrigerator?"

"None of this is true."

"Ms. Warren, we've established that Nick didn't sign the change of beneficiary form. It was forged. But by whom?" Burr looked at the jury, then back at Melissa. "You forged Nick's signature. You were the one who signed Nick's name. I'm sure Mr. Nearly can verify that it's your handwriting." Burr looked at Harry then back at Melissa. "Mrs. Fagan didn't find it when she went through his desk because it wasn't there. You forged his signature and put it in his drawer after she'd looked. You put it there so Robert Davies would find it and make things look worse for Mrs. Fagan."

"I most certainly did not."

Burr walked back to his table and picked up a single sheet of paper. "Should I read the letter that Nick wrote to you? The one where he tells you he loves you. That all he wanted you to do is help him a little bit longer."

Melissa put her hands on the railing and leaned forward. "It wasn't like that at all. We were in love. Nicky loved me. I know he did." She started rocking back and forth. "I didn't mean to kill him. I only wanted to scare him. I just wanted to make him sick. Then, when he got better, we'd finally be together."

* * *

Burr ordered his second tennis ball. Or was it his third?

Who's counting? He looked out the window. The last of the leaves were blowing off the trees, not red, yellow, and orange, but brown. The sky spit snow and the daylight was fading.

It's better to be inside today.

The four of them, Jacob, Eve, Molly, and Burr, sat at a window table at the Arboretum. It was 5:30 and already dark. Hoagy had left for Florida for the winter. KHQ played Kim Wilde's version of *You Keep Me Hangin' On* in the background. There were only two other tables taken.

Burr knew that Jacob and Eve were still furious with him. He was a bit surprised they were here. Not to mention Molly, but Burr had his own reasons for wanting her here.

I have some fences to mend.

Oswald's jaw had dropped when he'd heard what Melissa had said about poisoning Nick, but he did the best he could in his closing argument. Burr hammered on reasonable doubt in his own closing argument. With what Melissa Warren had just said, there was no possible way to believe beyond a reasonable doubt that Molly had killed her husband. He'd said it so many times that Nickels finally cut him off.

* * *

Two hours later, Molly had been acquitted, and here they were at the Arboretum.

"How did you figure it out?" Eve said.

Maybe she's not as mad as I thought. Winning always helps.

Burr chewed an ice cube. "It was the change of beneficiary form."

Eve fished the pickle out of her Bloody Mary.

Is that her second or third?

Burr chewed another ice cube.

Who's counting?

"I started to get suspicious when I found the two different accounts-receivable ageing reports for the same time period."

"You can't find anything," Eve said.

Burr ignored her. "It got me thinking about all the money problems Nick and the station had. They infuriated Harvey. Davies, too."

"I beg your pardon," Jacob said.

"I thought money must have something to do with it, then when I was sitting in Nick's office in the dark, and I couldn't see any light coming under the door to the studio, I started to wonder what was going on."

"It was a big jump," Eve said.

"It seemed like every time I went to Nick's office, the disc jockey knocked on the door. He said he could see light coming from underneath the door. It didn't seem quite right, and the last time I was there, I didn't turn the lights on. It didn't take too much to figure out it wasn't only a one-way window from Nick's office."

"I still think it was a big jump," Eve said.

"Not so big. Not after Tommy Preston told me what he saw."

"I can't believe you figured it out," Jacob said. He drank some of his ice water through his straw.

"It was the refrigerator that finally did it."

"Melissa was never going to confess." Burr drank some of his tennis ball. "Except for the letter."

"How did you find it?" Jacob said.

"I was sure there must have been a letter, but I wasn't able to find it."

"What do you mean?" Jacob said.

"That was a letter from Kelly about back alimony."

"What?" Jacob twirled one of his curls.

It's all over and he's still nervous.

"He was bluffing," Eve said.

"Bluffing?" Jacob said.

"You never had a letter?" Molly said.

"I knew she wouldn't want it introduced into evidence. That's the last thing she'd want."

"You never had a letter?" Molly said again. She looked at her wine but didn't take a sip.

"What will happen to Melissa?" She looked at her glass again and still didn't drink any.

That's a waste of a perfectly good Cabernet.

"That's up to Oswald. I don't know if what she said in court was enough to prosecute her. I really don't care what happens to her."

"Where's the justice in that?" Jacob asked.

"The justice is that Molly was acquitted," Burr said.

"You all must think I'm a fool," Molly said.

"No, no. Not at all," Eve said.

"He was so charming and so handsome. And he was good to me." She finally drank some of her wine. "But his ego got in the way."

"You weren't the only one he fooled," Eve said.

I never thought she killed Nick, but I'm pretty sure she was capable of it.

"I didn't want to believe what was going on. It was right in front of me, but I didn't want to see it."

I wonder if she's going to crack her knuckles.

"It was all an illusion," Eve said. "Just like a radio station."

I can't believe she said that.

"Now you can get the elevator fixed," Eve said.

"I like the stairs," Burr said.

Jacob looked at Burr. "And fix the roof."

"I'm going to buy you a bigger umbrella."

"I beg your pardon." Molly swirled the Cabernet but didn't drink any.

"Burr has a few problems with his building," Eve said.

Molly sipped her Cab.

Finally.

"I'll pay you as soon as I get the life insurance money," she said.

That's why I wanted you here.

Burr had caught up with Flintoff after the verdict about the life insurance proceeds. Flintoff said he'd have to wait for at least a month to get things sorted out. Burr told Flintoff he'd be at the Dearborn Life Insurance Company in the morning and wasn't leaving until he had a check.

Burr took a swallow of his tennis ball and wished Maggie were here.

Maybe she isn't too far along with that doctor.

The waitress came back. "Are you ready to order?"

"I think I'll start with the morel bisque," Burr said. "And a very dry, very dirty Bombay gin martini on the rocks. With four olives."

Jacob and Eve looked at him with daggers in their eyes.

"And your entrée?"

I don't think I'll have the veal morel.

THE END

Acknowledgements

To Ellen Jones for her copy editing, sage advice, encouragement, and deciphering the scratchings on the yellow pads that were the first draft.

To Mark Lewison for his copy editing, story editing, unflagging attention to detail … and especially his enthusiasm.

To Bruce Stickle, Ellen Jones, and Steve Spencer for reading the manuscript. They made many story suggestions and found countless factual, contextual, and typographical errors.

To Marilynn Smith for both her scientific expertise and practical knowledge of mycology.

To Trish Garber at WKHQ for allowing the radio station to be used in the book.

To John Wickham for his cover design.

To Mission Point Press for all their help in producing *Under The Ashes*. They have been absolutely spectacular: Sarah Meiers for interior design; Hart Cauchy for his insightful evaluation of the first draft of the manuscript; Tricia Frey for her great work with publicity and marketing; Heather Shaw for the production of *Under The Ashes;* Anne Stanton for her light but firm editing touch, for keeping me on schedule, and, most importantly, for her encouragement; and Doug Weaver for his help with the cover and for his steady hand.

Finally, thanks to my wife, Christi, for her unflagging support throughout the writing of *Under The Ashes*.

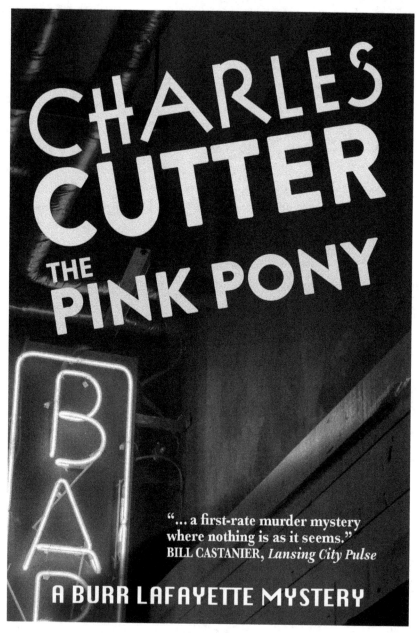

CHARLES CUTTER

THE PINK PONY

BAR

A BURR LAFAYETTE MYSTERY

"A smashing murder mystery featuring a quick-witted protagonist..." *Kirkus Reviews*

A BURR LAFAYETTE MYSTERY

"A smashing murder mystery featuring a quick-witted protagonist... Cutter's razor-sharp dialogue in the courtroom [is] truly unforgettable."

Kirkus Reviews

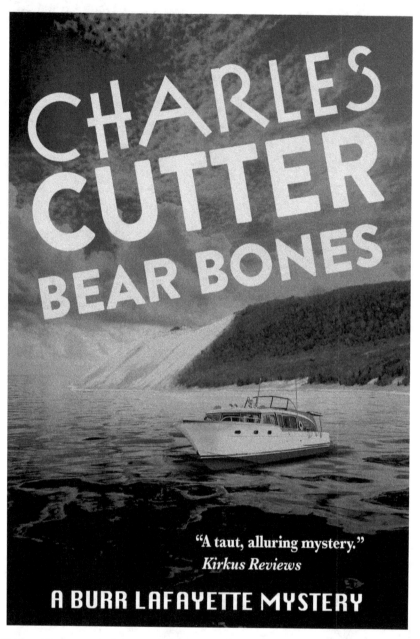

"A taut, alluring mystery."
Kirkus Reviews

A BURR LAFAYETTE MYSTERY

"Bear Bones and Burr Lafayette remind us of what we have and why we love where we are. Part mystery, part ode to the last best places, Cutter's prose captures the best of what is always slipping away. A page turner of a mystery."

Glen Young, *Bear River Literary*

CHARLES CUTTER

THE CROOKED ANGEL

"Another superb installment in this legal thriller series."
Kirkus Reviews

A BURR LAFAYETTE MYSTERY

Cutter's narrative maintains a relentless edge; numerous characters lie; and an unsettling ambiguity hangs over everything. Another superb, realistic installment of this Midwestern legal thriller series.

Kirkus Reviews

About the Author

Charles Cutter is the author of the highly acclaimed five-book Burr Lafayette legal thriller series. *The Pink Pony,* the first book in the series recently won First Prize in the Global Book Awards.

Cutter is a cum laude graduate of the University of Michigan Law School and a graduate with highest honors from Michigan State University. Before his writing career, he was in the media business and was a practicing attorney.

Cutter is active in conservation, most recently serving as chairman of the board for Pheasants Forever and Quail Forever, the largest upland conservation organization in the United States. He lives with his wife, two dogs and four cats in East Lansing. He has a leaky sailboat in Harbor Springs, and a leakier duck boat on Saginaw Bay.

Previous books in the Burr Lafayette series include *The Gray Drake, Bear Bones, The Pink Pony* and *The Crooked Angel.* They are available at Amazon and your local bookstore. Cutter has also written literary fiction, short stories and screenplays. He is currently at work on the next book in the Burr Lafayette series.

CPSIA information can be obtained
at www.ICGtesting.com
Printed in the USA
LVHW022137070423
743796LV00001B/71

9 781958 363638